Caribbean Stories

LAND OF THE *Fatherless*

FABIAN COMRIE

outskirtspress
DENVER, COLORADO

Caribbean Stories
Land of the Fatherless
All Rights Reserved.
Copyright © 2013 Fabian Comrie
v10.0

Cover Photo © 2013 JupiterImages Corporation. All rights reserved - used with permission.

Outskirts Press, Inc.
http://www.outskirtspress.com

ISBN: 978-1-4787-0622-9

Outskirts Press and the "OP" logo are trademarks belonging to Outskirts Press, Inc.

PRINTED IN THE UNITED STATES OF AMERICA

Acknowledgements

I am grateful to God for giving me the inspiration and all that I needed to write this book. I am also thankful to the following persons for their immense contributions: Monica Pucciarelli, Fran Gray-Friz, Dr. Eyton G. Mitchell, Jannette Mitchell, Clemis A. Moss, Carmen E. Boothe, Hazel Gardner, Robert Gardner, Kenneth A. Lazarus, Godfrey Comrie, Urgust L. Forbes, Kevin Forbes, Willow Fan, Holly Fan, Oscar Dominguez, Luis Dominguez, Clearence Wears, Gene Santiago, Edward Genevia, Manuel Garcia, Miriam Garcia, Vickie Marie Ignacio-Goh, Charimion Mercado, Josephine Maorallos-llagan, Rose McCoy, Krystle Guillermo, Tristie Yumul, Lisa Curtis, Gaylord M. Hill, Thomas Morring, Leon Jackson, Magdy Aziz, and Jose Marin of Progreso, Belize.

Contents

Land of the Fatherless

By Fabian Comrie

Early Jamaica

In 1494, Christopher Columbus and his crew landed in Jamaica. It was their second voyage to the Americas. Shortly after, Spain occupied the island and established a sugar industry through enforced slave labor. There was no gold to be found in Jamaica. The island was inhabited by Taino Indians. Due to the rigorous working conditions the Spanish enforced on them, their population diminished quickly. Indentured servants were acquired from the Middle East for their expertise in sugar production. The labor force was replenished with imported African slaves. The Jamaican sugar industry grew and became very profitable. Livestock, various ground provisions, fruits and vegetables were introduced to the island and cultivated widely. The Island's first infrastructure was created, and Spanish Town became the first capital city of Jamaica.

Compliance with slavery did not go well with some of the Africans. Many of them ran away and settled in the mountainous forest interior of the island. They were called Maroons. Some of the remaining Tainos joined the Maroons. The Maroons survived by farming, hunting wild pigs, and raiding sugarcane plantations and farms belonging to the Spanish. The plantation raids freed more slaves and hampered the Spanish progress.

In 1655, a British naval fleet commanded by Admiral William Penn and General Robert Venables, after a failed campaign to capture Hispaniola, set sail southwest to Jamaica. They took command of Jamaica and drove out most of the Spanish. Some of the Spanish escaped with the help of the Maroons. The British captured the island without much resistance. However, they might have been unaware that they had the Maroons to contend with.

The British established their government and secured themselves against a counter attack from the Spanish. The Spanish were not able to launch a counter attack because they lost majority of their naval fleet to the British, off the Canary Islands coast, in 1657.

During the seventeenth century, Spain had many cargo ships importing gold from Mexico, South and Central America. In 1658, the English government appointed a large company of men to serve a sinister cause. The British called them privateers. Later, they were called pirates and buccaneers. Most of them were desperate people, without hope, opportunities, friends, family, and country.

Port Royal, Jamaica became the base for the privateer. Their unscrupulous activities became legitimate under the auspices of the British government. They created turmoil and distributed agony as they robbed many ships belonging to Spain. The British and the privateers profited immensely. Approximately fifteen years later, Great Britain and Spain made an official agreement to disband the privateers. It was part of the declaration in the Treaty of Madrid known as the Godolphin Treaty of 1670. The government of Jamaica concealed the treaty from the privateers, and at that time, Henry Morgan, a privateer leader, took on several perilous endeavors and succeeded. The British government captured Henry Morgan, but he was vindicated because it was proven that he had no knowledge of the treaty. Because of his success, King Charles knighted him, and made him Lt. Governor of Jamaica. He remained in Jamaica, and in 1688, when he was fifty-three years old, he passed away.

The privateers who decided not to abide by the Treaty were no longer affiliated with the British government. The British government had abandoned the cause. The privateers were now called buccaneers and pirates. They were no longer welcomed in Jamaica, so they made their base in the Bahamas. Bounties were hired to capture and destroy them. Many pirates became infamous and rich. Many met a tragic fate.

Port Royal, in that era, became the richest city in the world. In

1692, it was devastated by an earthquake and most of the city submerged under the sea.

Jamaica, under British rule, continued investing and expanding the sugar industry with the implimentation of African slaves, resulting in an infringement upon the Maroon civilization. The Maroon raids increased, many slaves were freed, and war resulted. In the eastern Blue Mountains were the windward Maroons, and in the western Cockpit Mountains were the Leeward Maroons. Other pockets of Maroon communities existed throughout the Island, and these communities were united for the most part.

The Beginnings

James Gordon was born in Port Royal in 1677. His father was an indentured servant from the Middle East who was an expert in sugar manufacturing. He died shortly after James was born. James' mother was a Spanish woman who owned a brothel in Port Royal. By age fourteen, James had begun working on a cargo ship that sailed locally.

James knew a beautiful young woman named Hazel. They were not related, but their parents informed them that they were cousins. Hazel's father was a very successful retired pirate. He had made a fortune and invested it wisely. Hazel's mother had also made arrangements so that Hazel would get a proper education at a private school in England. Hazel left Jamaica when she was fourteen and returned when she was twenty. When she returned to the island, she was also married to a wealthy entrepreneur from Wales named John Crawford. Hazel was a woman of Spanish and British descent, but she inclined more towards the British because it placed her in a more favorable position with her husband's business connections. John Crawford and Hazel were beginning to establish a new sugarcane plantation in Easington, Jamaica.

In 1692, after a trip from Montego Bay, James returned home to Port Royal and discovered it had been devastated by an earthquake. His mother, Hazel's mother and father, and John Crawford died in that tragedy. Hazel escaped the tragedy because she was in Spanish Town managing one of John Crawford's affairs and spending time with her aunt, who died a month after.

The destruction of Port Royal brought about a turning point in their lives.

"I don't feel I can live here anymore," James said to Hazel, who was in tears, mourning her loss.

"What is it do you have in mind? Leave me alone and become a pirate," Hazel said.

"What else is there for me to do? I have never been to Spain or England. I also feel I would be a misfit in those places," James said.

"Who said anything about leaving Jamaica? Jamaica is my home too, and although I have lived in England for seven years, it's not the place I want to call home. My husband and my parents are gone, and I am grateful for what they have left me. You are foolish if you feel that you would be better off on your own. You're the only family I have left. Don't be stubborn. Stay with me. You won't regret it."

"I can take care of myself. I don't want to be a burden to you."

"If you work and pull your load, you will not encumber me, but if you are lazy, I will fire you. I feel your mother may have left some money for you also. I am aware of this because I made some transactions for her with the Bank of England. My mother even borrowed money from her once," Hazel said.

"Are you sure she left money for me?" James asked.

"Don't ask stupid questions. I am sure that I am doing exactly what she would want me to do for you, but if you go on your own, I will not help you. As a matter of fact, if you go on your own, don't call me friend or family. Just pretend you don't know me and I will pretend likewise!"

"You're serious," James said quietly.

"Of course, I meant what I said," Hazel replied.

"All right, I'll stay with you until I get things straightened out."

"I want this sugar estate to be successful, but I can't run it by myself. I am counting on you and Nev to help me."

"I know very little about farming," James said.

"It won't be easy," Hazel replied.

That day, they left the devastation in Port Royal and went to Easington, where Hazel's sugar plantation was located. Hazel's spouse and parents and James' mother's bodies were never recovered.

Hazel was greeted at the estate house entrance by two female servants.

"Where is Nev?" Hazel asked.

"He went over to the boiler room," one of the servants said.

"I need him," Hazel said.

"Yes ma'am," the servant replied.

Approximately thirty minutes later, a man riding a black horse approached the big yard of the plantation house.

"Who is that?" James said.

"It's Nev," Hazel replied.

Nev was a tall black man about six feet and muscular. He had a deep, soft voice. His lips were thick, his hair was very short, and although he had perfect teeth, he hardly ever smiled. He was wearing khaki pants and a shirt with short sleeves. He also wore a broad felt hat.

"You sent for me, Miss Hazel?" he said.

"Yes, I did."

"I'll be right back," Nev said, as he went to his horse.

"I have known Nev for more than three years. I trust him. My husband knew him for over ten years, and called him his best friend and the best business partner anyone could ever have. My husband taught him to read and do simple arithmetic. Nev taught himself more, much more. He has no credentials for his education, but I consider him to be highly educated. He continues to study as if he is not satisfied. It's not easy to find good, trustworthy friends with those who work with you. Give him your respect. Learn from him. He is not a slave, so don't make demands of him. He bought his freedom from my husband several years ago. He could have left. For him and his family to have stayed is a blessing," Hazel said.

Learning the Essentials

James, Hazel, and Nev sat on the porch outside the kitchen. Nev gave Hazel a report of what was needed to be done and how much progress the plantation was making. Hazel knew the welfare of the slaves was very important, so she implemented rules to prevent uprisings and ward off confrontations in order to maintain a peaceful coexistence.

Hazel made sure the slaves would get Saturdays and Sundays off; the women and children would not harvest sugarcane. Periods of rest were integrated into the working day, especially when it was very hot. Hazel was against beating or humiliating slaves. In any disputes or conflicts, a thorough investigation was conducted before any judgment was considered. The women's priorities were to take care of their home while the men worked. These were some of Hazel's fundamental rules.

"Nev, this is my cousin, James. His mother also died in the earthquake," Hazel said.

"It's good to meet you, sir," Nev said.

"It's good to meet you too, sir," James replied.

"We are making three boiler rooms on the southeast side near the sea. Later, I will show them to you, and then I will show you the rest of the estate," Nev said.

Approximately fifteen minutes later, the men left together, riding horses, for a general tour of the estate.

"If you don't mind my asking, how old are you?" James asked.

"I am twenty-four, and you are seventeen," Nev answered.

"Yes, you are right. Where are your parents?"

"They are dead."

"Do you have a family or relatives?"

"The woman with the broad straw hat that stood next to Hazel is my wife, and we have two boys," Nev answered.

"Where are you from?"

"I was born in the Blue Mountains," Nev replied. "Don't ask many questions. Just observe and learn."

"I feel like I have known you for a long time," James said.

"Thank you, it's a good sign. I feel the same way too. Are you ready to manage a plantation of this magnitude?"

"Yes, I am."

"It won't be long before you will be a major decision maker. Hazel and I, the slaves, the animals, and even the sugarcane fields welcome you as our partner, but you are not quite ready to make any major decisions as yet. Don't be disappointed. When the time comes, and that time will come soon, you will be ready. I will teach you everything to the best of my knowledge, and support you to the best of my abilities," Nev said.

"Why did you stay after you purchased your freedom, may I ask?" James said.

"John and Hazel are like family to me. One of their dreams is to have a successful sugar plantation. One of my dreams is to see Hazel succeed. John is gone, but Hazel is still here. She is not only my boss. She is also my friend. If Hazel succeeds, everyone will benefit; so will you."

James felt Nev was truly committed to see the business prosper. "Nev, I will do my best too. I will not leave."

Nev laughed. "I'll show you the three boiler rooms. These are places where safety is priority. This is where the sugarcane is processed. No one shall work here more than ten hours a day or five days a week. This prevents accidents and burnouts. The boiler rooms should be off limits to children. I have no problems with the women who want to work here. The boiler rooms operate seven days a week during the harvest."

After an extensive overview of the new boiler rooms, they rode through the cane fields.

"Maintenance of the sugarcane field is important. The fields should be well irrigated but not too saturated. The land must rest at least every seven years in order to replenish its nutrients. Planting peanuts can replenish the soil. Lightning also helps replenish the soil, but we have no control over lightning. Resting the land is the best option. Most of the women here prefer to stay home and work in their personal gardens that provide most of the food for their family. If the women work the fields, they will have no time for their family. The women are the motivating force behind the men. Happy women make happy homes. Happy homes make a peaceful community and a successful plantation. Unhappy men will rebel, and they will burn this place in the blink of an eye. Have you ever seen a plantation burn, sir?"

"No," James said.

"Let's go meet the servants. Preservation of morale is essential for the slaves," Nev said.

"I understand."

"There was a slave girl that belonged to a plantation near Morant Bay. She fell in love with a young man from another nearby estate. They visited each other secretly, and their love for each other grew. The girl's master was informed about the relationship and forbid her from seeing the man. The master, shortly after, sold the girl to another master who took her overseas. We don't know what happened to the girl. The young man ran away and joined the Maroons. He led many raids on the plantation where the girl once lived. The young man eventually killed the girl's former master."

"That's a sad story."

"Deprive a person of their dreams, and they will become a nightmare. Remember, the fellowship of an organization is important at all times. In times of crisis and in times of peace, good leadership is not without good fellowship," Nev stated.

The slave quarters were on the northwest side of the plantation near the estate house. By this time, it was getting dark. It was approximately 8:00.

As they rode into the small town, they met many slaves who greeted them cheerfully and went their way.

It was summer. In the summers, the field workers usually started working early and stopped before the middle of the day, then started working again before the sun set. This prevented most heat injuries.

Nev continued to lecture James as they rode together.

"Do not show preferential treatment or give rewards to a particular few that you consider loyal. It is not necessary. It will cause segregation and portray that you desire unlimited control over your servants. There are strengths and weaknesses in every worker. Give aid to them when they need it the most. Encourage them whenever you can. Time off from work, freedom to express and celebrate will keep morale high. These men know they are slaves, but if you disrespect and mistreat them, they will plot perils for you and cheer on your torment and suffering. They may not be in Africa, but the African culture is the only thing they brought to Jamaica with them, and it is very powerful. They will come to you with many sophisticated problems. Be reasonable with your resolutions and judgments. Don't discount their beliefs. They believe spirits exist, and at times, they will employ them to perform deeds of good and sinister intentions. Do you believe in spirits, James?"

"Yes, I do."

"Why is that?"

"I have seen many ghost ships at sea; even ghost canoes with Taino Indians," James replied.

Nev laughed out loud, but in an instant, he became serious again. "Let's meet some of the people in the village," he said.

Friday Evenings

The slave quarters were organized like a small village. There were small two-room houses with kitchens on the outside. There were four small houses on approximately an acre parcel of land, and at the extreme rear of the parcels were the latrines. The population was approximately 237: about 105 men, 95 women, and the rest children. In the middle of the town, there was a seven-acre field for activities and recreational occasions.

"Nev, what are you doing here so late, looking for girls?" an elderly woman said, carrying a bunch of green bananas.

"My friend is here looking for girls, but not me," Nev replied.

"And who him?" the woman asked with a heavy accent.

"Miss Hazel's brother."

"Come over mi yard, mek mi gi him some banana porridge."

"Yes, Miss Janna," Nev replied.

The men dismounted their horses and followed the woman into her yard, where there was a group of about seven men, ten women, and many children.

"Evening, ladies and gentlemen," James said.

"There are no gentlemen here. These men are far from being gentle, including you and Nev," one of the women said. She was approximately twenty-two years old, about five feet five inches, with a dark complexion and a face that was pleasant and calm. She was beautiful.

"Meet my wife, Yanera," Nev said.

"Nice to meet you," James said to Yanera.

"Yanera has a special gift of seeing the unseen and interpreting dreams," Nev said.

Yanera was the village medicine woman, midwife, and Nev's significant other. She was following in her family's tradition, and slowly replacing her grandmother as one of the community leaders. Her grandmother was one of the women among the group conversing with someone else.

Some of the other women were peeling and quartering the green bananas. There was a big clay pot on a wood fire with water, and a jug of goat's milk was next to the fireside. A clay basin with mixed grated bananas and nutmeg was also near the fire. The women mixed the grated bananas with the milk and nutmeg, then poured it into the pot of boiling water with a small amount of sugar. Then they pulled apart the firewood from under the pot to reduce the flames and the heat.

"The bickle will be ready soon," one of the women said. She stirred the porridge slowly.

"What are they cooking?" James said to Nev quietly.

"Banana porridge," Nev replied. "Every Friday night, the people come together to socialize and drink porridge. Porridge can be made from corn, banana, cassava, rice, oats, or wheat."

One woman offered some porridge to James. She poured it in a coconut shell container. James accepted it with hesitation.

"It's hot, let it cool," the woman said, smiling.

James smelled the porridge, tilted and blew inside the container, and tasted the porridge.

"How is it?" Nev said.

"It's very hot, but it smells good. I'll let it cool for a while," James replied.

They served the porridge in coconut shells for everyone. The cooks continued making more porridge. The people talked of a hurricane because it was hurricane season. They talked of building stalls for a small market where they could sell some of their farm produce. They wanted to get it done before the end of the year. They talked of many other important things. At the same time, two men sitting next to the fire continuously played a low, soft-toned rhythm on bongo drums. The music was very relaxing. James finished his porridge and looked off in a yonder gaze, like he was daydreaming.

"Do you want some more?" Yanera asked.

"Yes, thank you," James replied.

This time he had no reservations.

"So you like it?" Yanera asked.

"It's delicious," James answered.

James and Nev socialized with the servants for approximately three hours; then the people randomly began to retire.

"It's getting late, and I am tired," Yanera said as she gathered the empty coconut shells. "When the food is done, it's time to leave."

"Well, this was good, until next time," Nev said.

Nev and James bade farewell to the slaves and left for the plantation house. When they arrived, Hazel was on the third-floor balcony looking out over the estate.

"You're still up," James said.

"Just not tired as yet," Hazel replied.

"She never sleeps until she knows everyone is safe," Nev said.

"Yanera!" Hazel called out.

"Yes, ma'am."

"I have been waiting for you."

"Is there something wrong, Miss Hazel?" Yanera asked.

"No, just glad you're back," Hazel said.

Even though Hazel confirmed nothing was wrong, Yanera sensed that she wanted to speak to her privately. "I will be with you shortly, ma'am," she said.

Mysteries and Fortunes

Two weeks later, they convened for a meeting. It was around 6:00 p.m. and they sat around the big kitchen table discussing what they had to do to make the plantation successful. Yanera wanted a school for the children. Nev wanted to open a marketplace where the slaves could trade their excess vegetables and ground provisions. Nev also wanted to train more men to work in the new boiler houses and make them as safe as possible. Hazel wanted to staff the plantation house adequately and run the plantation more efficiently.

A week later, they convened in the kitchen again.

"I feel comfortable here. I want to make my home here," James said.

"I have good news for you too," Hazel said. "I made some enquires about your mother's finances with the Bank of England. She managed to accumulate a fortune over the years. She named you as her only beneficiary. Her bank account is yours to claim as soon as you can. The bank would not disclose the exact amount to me, but I would imagine that it was over 30,000 pounds."

The news was pleasing to James. The meeting ended on a good note.

Nev and James retired to sleep, but Hazel and Yanera stayed up talking about many things.

Yanera said to her, "I know you are expecting, ma'am."

"I have been waiting for you to tell me," Hazel said.

"Some things are better left unsaid. Some revelation takes on a process, and some information is so sensitive. I have to be careful. Limit your sugar consumption and stay active during your pregnancy; this will help you deliver a healthy baby," Yanera said.

"Is it a boy or girl?" Hazel asked.

"It is a girl, ma'am."

"I have no doubts in what you know, but tell me, how do you get your information?"

"I receive it in many ways, through dreams, feeling, and the voice from within. A person communicates in different ways, with their tongue and their body. The words they say may not be what their body conveys. The body has a true language, and it never lies. Take, for example, James and Nev. They hardly ever smile, but their eyes tell you when they are in a good mood, and it's like they are smiling," Yanera said.

"What are your feelings about James?" Hazel asked.

"James may seem naïve and inexperienced, but he is a blessing in disguise. He is trustworthy, strong, and devoted. He is a refuge in times of trouble. We can count on him. He will have to take the lead soon. Nev, on the other hand, is not suited to be our leader. He would be resented by the rest of the plantations owners. They would do whatever it takes to suppress us because Nev is black. You would also face similar circumstances because you're a woman," Yanera said.

"I agree with you," Hazel said.

"I am thankful to you for saying you don't have any doubts in my abilities, because I am doubtful at times. There are many things to learn, but James is suitable and ready to be in charge with our support," Yanera stated.

They stayed up late and talked. Yanera and Hazel were the best of friends. Yanera and her grandmother had psychic abilities. They were the ones the slaves sought whenever they had complex issues. The responsibility was a burden to her sometimes. For this reason, Yanera wanted to start a school and train some assistants because she felt most of the problems were a matter of common sense. A basic education was necessary for the people, but it was unusual to conduct a school on a plantation in that era.

The next two weeks, James learned he had inherited 50,000 pounds. He decided to stay and become a shared owner of the estate with Hazel. He offered Hazel 20,000 pounds, and she accepted his offer. Over the following months, he built two log facilities near the plantation house. One served as a school, and the other was a community center and library. Two months later, he built a clinic. Then he designated another area and made stalls for a marketplace. He bought more cattle, horses, goats, and donkeys.

Rayne

Seven months after, Hazel gave birth to a baby girl and named her Rayne. She was born on a rainy day. She smiled a lot and Hazel was very happy. "God has given me a child from my late husband," she said, and she grieved no more about him.

At that time, the estate cultivated mostly sugarcane. It took two years from the time the cane was planted until it was fully ready to be processed into sugar. James and Nev decided that they would use some of the land to plant grass because the livestock was increasing. Raising cattle was also profitable.

The small marketplace that James had built was busy. The boiler houses were in operation around the clock. James Gordon and Hazel became famous on the island as their estate became one of the most successful plantations in Jamaica. For seven years in a row, the sugarcane fields yielded greatly, and sugar production was continuous. Some of the other plantations nearby and throughout the Island were having setbacks due to loss of labor, runaway slaves, and raids. Some plantations suffered complete loss from arson and major larceny.

There was news of a revolt in St. Ann, where an estate house was burnt and the supervisors were murdered. However, the Easington estate suffered no raid from the Maroons because James and Nev traded with them and sometimes gave them gifts of livestock and sugar.

In 1726, the governor of Jamaica, Lord John Ashcroft, invited James and Hazel to attend the yearly Governor's Christmas Ball at the governor's mansion in Spanish Town, Jamaica. James was impressed, but for Hazel, it was not a big deal.

"I will not be able to attend the Governor's Ball. I attended one in the past, and I was disappointed. Everyone was bragging about how successful they were. I didn't feel I belonged there. I am certain that you and Nev will have a good time," Hazel said to James.

"Nev shares the same feelings, but he expressed it with different words," James replied.

"What did he say?"

"Rats don't picnic with cats, he said." James laughed.

"Where is Rayne?" Hazel asked.

"She is with Yanera at the school."

"Did you know that she will be ten years old next month?"

"I know, and that's amazing. All the children here are thriving well, and I am getting old. The school has been so beneficial to them."

"I would like for Rayne to start attending school in England, before she is fourteen years. I don't want her to fall behind in her education," Hazel said.

"She will be all right. She is smarter than me at anytime," James replied.

The Aristocrats

It was December 17, 1726, a week before Christmas, on a Friday morning. James and Nev got ready and left for the Governor's Ball in Spanish Town. Spanish Town was approximately twenty miles away. They wanted to get there before sunset.

"You don't have to come," James said to Nev.

"I know you can take care of yourself, and I will not be able to enter the ballroom. This is just courtesy. Keep up, we got a lot of ground to cover," Nev said.

"I hope it doesn't rain tonight," James replied.

The men arrived just before sunset. Their horses were valeted.

"I am a little sweaty for this occasion," James said.

"Don't worry. You look marvelous," Nev replied.

"James!" a chubby Englishman called out.

"Rammy!" James answered.

"Look at you, a big-shot now," Rammy said.

"No, sir, you're the bigger shot," James replied.

"It's good to see you. You have grown into a fine lad. Your mother would be very proud of you."

"It's good to see you too, Rammy."

"You both look wonderful," Rammy stated.

Only Rammy and James entered the ball. Rammy was an ex-pirate who became a legitimate businessman. He was a breeder of cattle and the owner of two large stores that sold everything from buttons to rifles. Rammy was discontented with the British government because they did not acknowledge his marriage with an African woman with whom he had fathered five children. Rammy was five feet five, stout, loud, and humorous. He spoke the genuine truth in a raw manner, and it rubbed some people the wrong way sometimes. Nevertheless, he was a good friend of Hazel, Nev, and James.

"How is your family?" James said.

"They are well; the children are healthy as ever. Their mother is more bossy than any British administration," Rammy replied.

"That is good," James said.

"My wife wants to import some of the vegetables and fruit seeds from Africa. She believes they would thrive here," Rammy said.

"I have a marketplace for the slaves to trade on the plantation, and so far, it is doing well," James said.

"My wife heard of your trading market. Now I am being pressured to open one."

"Believe me, Rammy. The marketplace is packed on Fridays and Saturdays. Many of the customers are aristocrats too. I always go there on Friday evenings to get a bowl of porridge. It's the best."

"What kind of porridge do you get?" Rammy asked.

"Mostly banana, corn, and rice," James replied.

"You should try the arrowroot porridge, it's the best ever," Rammy said.

"This way please," one of the butlers said as he directed the guests into the ballroom.

Many of the guests were plantation owners. Most of the plantation owners were also members of the Jamaican Parliament. James and Rammy were not politicians. They were the exceptions. The men introduced themselves to some of the guests as they walked around the large ballroom. The ballroom and dining area were elaborate and set in accordance to the celebration. The dining area had the best food and the finest liquor.

James overheard some women gossiping quietly about them.

"That fat man has taken a slave woman for a wife," one woman said.

"In this day and age, that is so rude," another woman said.

"I beg to differ," an old lady dressed in purple said. "What's improper is when the married plantation owners impregnate the slave girls, disregard their children, and call them bastards. Then their wives refuse to accept the true affiliation between their children and their husbands' children. What right do we have to entitle a child at birth as illegitimate while we are covered in iniquity? What that man has done is set a high moral standard that Englishmen should adopt when they find a slave girl suitable to be their sweethearts. That man has taken his girlfriend, who was a slave, and elevated her. Love has no boundaries among race or culture, but prejudice does." The old lady turned away from the rest of the ladies whom she had addressed. She seemed displeased with their company. She was approximately four feet eight inches, very pretty, and eighty years old.

The rest of the women were silent after she spoke.

"Miss Rose," Rammy said to the old lady. "You look splendid tonight."

"How are you, Miss Rose?" James said.

"I am well, thank you," Miss Rose replied. "James, I would like you to meet my granddaughter from England who recently arrived on the Island. I don't know where she is now, but later, she will come around."

"I am looking forward to seeing her."

Suddenly, a butler approached James and told him that the governor would like to see him in his office. James followed the butler upstairs to a balcony that overlooked the Kings House property and the House of Commons. There were two large chairs, and a fireplace made of thick stones. On the fireplace was a pot of coffee. The governor was standing on the balcony, overlooking the property.

"Good evening, Governor Ashcroft," James said.

"Call me John, Mr. Gordon," the governor said.

"You can call me James also, Governor."

"Make yourself comfortable and have some coffee," the governor said.

"The coffee smells great."

"It tastes good too."

The governor and James were silent for a moment. Then the governor began to speak.

"Being a planter should not be a prerequisite to vote or be a politician. Although I hold the position of acting governor, I am a businessman first. The previous governor was the owner of several plantations, but he lost them all. His policies almost led the country into a revolution. His plantations were burnt, and his slaves ran away. There are others now who manage their estates without buying more slaves. They never have to deal with revolts. They make enormous profits, and their slaves are contented and healthy.

"I commend you, James, for the splendid work you are doing. You have been in the business for a little over ten years, and you've been very successful. It will be very hard, hard as hell, for the older planters to follow a younger man's example because you have set a remarkable one. Age and experience may not be relative to wisdom, but being stubborn seems to get concentrated for the arrogant as they get older."

"The credit is not all mine. Without Hazel, Nev, and Yanera, I would be lost. They taught me management skills and many other things. The workers are not only my slaves, but they are my friends. I incorporate their ideas and skills into the business also. The marketplace and butcher shops were their idea. Improvement for the slaves has resulted in my success. Labor is never forced on the children, and everyone has weekends off. We try not to abuse the land or the people," James said.

"Most the plantation owners in Jamaica are incapable of innovating and thinking progressively. Asking them to treat their slaves with dignity is beyond them, but I will demand of them to notice what you have done, and hope that your success will inspire them to evaluate their ways and make changes that are conducive to progress. We definitely need to mandate and provide guidelines of how a plantation should operate and conduct relations with slaves. The slave revolts are originating from abuse; not to mention the raids from the Maroons in the interior of the country who claim that we have invaded their land and undermined their sovereignty. There is a lot of work to be done. I will need your alliance to make this country better. Thank you for your time. Until next time," the governor stated.

Love at a Glance

The governor was worried.

"Let's go downstairs, James," he said.

The men left the balcony and joined the crowd. James saw Rose, who was with her granddaughter Ann. Ann was tall. She was the tallest woman in the room, and she stood out elegantly. Her hair was dark. She had a beautiful face and piercing blue eyes. She looked confident, but at the same time, she was humble. James stared at her in admiration. When she saw him looking at her, she smiled, and then he approached her.

"Miss Ann, would you like to dance?" James asked.

"Mr. Gordon, I don't know how to dance," she said.

"You know my name?"

"My grandmother told me so much about you. I feel I know you already," Ann replied.

"Well, I hope that I have met some of your expectations."

"From appearance you're a fine man, Mr. Gordon. You have passed all that I expected and more."

"Are you looking for a man to marry?" James said to her quietly.

Ann laughed. "You're very direct. Don't expect too much. I am only here for five months, and I have mentioned to my grandmother more than enough times that I have a promising husband waiting for me when I return to England."

"I am sorry. I am happy that you are about to become a wife," James said.

"Thank you," she replied.

"Don't forget to invite me to the wedding. I want to see the very lucky man." James felt disappointed that Ann was engaged. He liked her very much, and he was very attracted to her. "I have never been to England, but hopefully, one day," he said to Ann.

They talked for a while and shared a drink or two. Later that evening, James met Rose again.

"Miss Rose, I have been looking for you," James said.

"And may I ask why?" Miss Rose asked.

"I wanted to dance with you before I leave."

Then Rose approached him closely and said quietly, "You left Ann alone."

"She said she was engaged, Miss Rose, and I feel I should leave her alone."

Rose smiled. "Oh my son, you have no idea," she whispered to him.

"What do you mean?"

"Can't you tell when a woman admires you? My Ann is not looking for a gentleman to pamper her. She's not looking for a pirate either. I am not a matchmaker, but I know when a hunch is good. I know my girl. Be courageous and don't give up so easily. I see the way you look at her, and the way she behaves around you. If that isn't chemistry, I am not eighty years old. Be brave and take that woman like an eagle takes a snake for a meal, but if you hurt her, I'll kill you myself, for she is my granddaughter."

Rose said this quietly, and it resonated into James' awareness. He was convinced and confident that his pursuit of the beautiful Ann Morgan should commence.

The big hall was filled with guests. There was an area for dancing and an area for dining. The dining area had many tables that easily fit four to six adults. In one corner, the food was laid out on several large tables. There were servers who helped maintained an order to the lavish feast. The music was provided by two pianos and a violin. The musicians played continuously.

It was approximately 9:45 p.m. when Rammy met with James again and told him that he would be leaving soon.

"Don't leave me here alone. We can travel on our way home to-gether," James said.

"Why don't you stay at my place until tomorrow?" Rammy asked.

"That will work with me too," James said.

"I have to be in Constant Spring tomorrow," Rammy replied.

"I will be back shortly. Don't leave without me." James said.

James looked around and went over to where Ann and Rose were.

"It would not be proper for me not to invite you for a weekend at my estate since you are here on vacation," James said to Rose and Ann.

Ann looked at her grandmother, but Rose did not hesitate to reply.

"Send a buggy to get us as soon as you can. We will stay with you for the rest of the week. I am so grateful. I don't want to stay in Spanish Town anymore," Rose said.

Ann had no choice but to go along with her grandmother.

"I will send an escort for you tomorrow," James said.

Rose lived on a sugar plantation in the parish of St. Catherine.

James, Rammy, and Nev left shortly after to Rammy's farm, ap-proximately five miles from Kings House, Spanish Town.

The next day was Saturday and the men rose early and left. They rode together and talked.

"Sugar is profitable now, but its production requires very hard work. I prefer investing in livestock," Rammy said.

"Sugarcane farming is good business now," James said.

"Yes, it is for now, but ten years down the road, the land will be drained of its nutrients, and it will not be able to yield anything," Rammy said.

"After several years, we have to plow the land and rest it for a year. Remember, we also have the cattle and coffee. This is our tenth year. In four years, we will rest the cane fields again," Nev said.

"We had no choice but to diversify," James said.

"Like those Bradfords, after they got rich, they left. They were some wicked bombo rass," Rammy said.

Everyone laughed.

Shortly after, the men arrived at a crossroad. Nev and James rode on to Eastington. Rammy went to his home in Constant Spring.

James and Nev arrived home in the afternoon.

The New Arrivals

In the evening, a man and two women with a donkey came to the plantation house. The man was a tall British migrant. The women were of dark complexion. Everyone thought the women were his slaves, but the man declared boldly that the older woman was his wife, and the younger woman was his daughter. He said his name was Albert Johnson. He stated that he worked on a plantation in St. Catherine where the slaves revolted and killed the overseers. The owners were absent. They lived in England. He also stated that he and his family were spared because the slaves said he treated them fairly. Hazel agreed to permit Albert and his family to stay for a week until they were well rested and fit to travel again.

"What is your wife's name?" Hazel asked Albert.

"Her name is Manwa, and my daughter's name is Myka."

Myka was approximately sixteen, and when James saw her for the first time, he was in awe because she was good-looking. She was a woman with thick, long black hair. She was tall. Her smile was captivating. In James' eyes, she was perfect. James did not gaze at her too long because he did not want her or anyone to notice him, but at the same time, he could not keep his eyes off her. He was glad that Hazel offered them a place to stay.

James requested to have Myka stay at the estate house as added help. He convinced Hazel that she would be a good companion for Rayne.

"She can still stay in the quarters with her family and work here," Hazel said.

"It would be easier if she stays in the house," James replied.

"What about Albert and Manwa? Do they want their daughter to stay in the plantation house?" Hazel said.

"We'll see what we can do. He came here because he heard of us from the other slaves at the plantations from where he came. We've never had a revolt, and the Maroons never raid this place."

"Knock on wood. Make him an offer he will not easily walk away from. You obviously like his daughter. She and Rayne have quickly become friends. I feel they will be an asset to the estate, but talk to Nev and see how he feels about it."

"I'll wait until the end of the week before I make any decisions. Why did you say I like their daughter?" James asked.

"The way you look at her. You look at Myka as if she walks on water," Hazel replied.

The next day, Myka moved into the estate house. Albert was given a horse and a place to stay. He rode and worked with James and Nev. The men went to the Yallas River one day to see if they could construct a bridge across the river.

"We tried to build a bridge here a few years ago, but the heavy rains came and the river rose and swept it away. There is just no way around it," James said.

"How deep is the river?" Albert asked.

"It's about fifteen feet in the middle," Nev answered.

"A ferry would be a good option, but the river current is too swift. A permanent bridge would have to be very strong," James said.

"I have an idea, but I have never put it into practical use. Nothing fancy, but I feel it will work," Albert said.

Albert began to explain his idea in detail, and after James and Nev understood the idea, they were convinced it would work. The main suggestion Albert made was to construct the bridge when the river is lowest.

At the end of the week, the men went to the marketplace. This was one of the places where some of the slaves usually convened on Friday evenings. They were cooking corn and arrowroot porridge this time. They had music, a moderate soft rhythm played on goatskin drums by a man and a woman. Even though the music was soft, it was audible from afar. The women shared the porridge in coconut shells.

"This is good," Albert said.

"Miss Yanera, I haven't seen you in a long time," James said.

"You spend most of your time with Nev. You know where I am," she said.

"How are the school and the clinic coming along?"

I have read the Bible, *Don Quixote*, and now I am reading *The Merchant of Venice* to the children, but we need a lot more books, newspapers, and books of different subjects," Yanera answered.

"I will see what I can do," James said.

"This porridge is good," Nev said.

Quietly James asked Yanera, "Tell me your feelings about Albert."

"He is purposeful, dedicated, and compassionate. That's all I can tell you of him," she said.

"He is like me."

"Not at all, sir."

"How am I different?"

"You have a stronger appetite, you are much stronger, and what motivates you is different from what motivates him. You are not easily satisfied, but you like simplicity. You will change as you get older," Yanera said.

"I must be more like Nev then," James answered.

"Nev is hard to read, maybe because we are very close, but between you and him, there isn't much difference," Yanera said.

"Talking about me again," Nev said to Yanera and James.

"I was curious about Albert and whether to hire him permanently," James said.

"We could use some extra help. If you intend to expand, we will definitely need him. Albert is knowledgeable," Nev said.

Albert was enjoying himself. It seemed like he was right at home as he sat and conversed with some of the slaves.

"This is what life is all about, good people, good times, and good food," Yanera said.

In another hour, the gathering began to dissipate. Albert, Nev, James, and Yanera went home.

That night, Nev and James stayed up late since it was Friday. They sat on the third-floor balcony of the estate house overlooking the plantation.

"I know God has been good to us over the years, but I feel we can get better. I am still not satisfied," James said to Nev.

"Many plantation owners are moving back to England fearing a revolution like the one in Hispaniola," Nev said.

"I was born in Jamaica, my father is Jewish, and my mother is a mixture of many nations. I am Jamaican. This is my home, and I want to live here in peace."

"I agree, this is my home too, and I have no intentions of going to Africa to live. I feel it's a good idea to expand and improve."

"We will definitely need Albert with us."

"Absolutely."

"We will have to create a position for him," James added.

"I noticed his daughter, Myka, has captured your attention," Nev said.

"She is something else, but how did you know I am attracted to her?"

"You're always asking and looking for her. Even though you do not speak to her much, you seem to like her around. The servants say that she is in your favor. That means you are looking out for her. Your behavior towards her may be subtle, but it's genuine and obvious."

"I feel good whenever I see her."

"She is very pretty."

"Miss Rose and Ann will be here tomorrow," James said.

"Sir, be careful of these women and how you relate to them. At first, everything seems well, but if you disappoint them, they may become hostile towards you. It may not be possible to share the kind of love you have for these women. Lust can get you in for trouble quick, but despite it all, they are remarkable women, and you should consider yourself lucky with the choices at hand," Nev said.

"You have always given me good advice, but I will go about this one with caution."

"Believe me, sir, relating to women is where I am weakest," Nev replied.

Torrential Downpour

James and Nev retired for the night shortly after. At approximately 6:00 p.m. the next day, Rose and Ann arrived at the plantation house. They were welcomed by the staff.

On the morning of the following day, Saturday, January 1727, the weather took an unusual turn for the worse. A dangerous storm threatened. It was unexpected at this time of year. A dark, heavy cloud stretched forth from beyond the horizon of the sea and over the island. The characteristics of this cloud were atypical. As it spreads swiftly across the sky, it diminished the daylight. The sea was also rough and troubled. The wind gradually increased and became violent.

Everyone was in a rush preparing for the impending bad weather. They were not panicked, but they were busy.

"Nev!" James called out. Nev did not answer. "Looks like it's going to rain heavy," James said to Albert.

"Let's get some help and secure the animals in the stables!" Albert replied.

"Yes sir!" the servants replied.

"Where is Nev?" James asked out loud.

"Nev went to secure the boiler rooms, and also to warn the workers in the fields of the dangerous winds that threaten," one servant answered.

"Why is everyone so uptight about a shower of rain?" Ann said.

"This is not just rain, ma'am. There is a powerful thunderstorm that is forthcoming. It's unusual at this time of year, but it's what the weather indicates," Myka replied.

A few hours later, the cloud completely covered the sky as far as the eye could see. The winds picked up, and it started raining. Nev returned and said the plantation was in good order, and the slaves were prepared for the bad weather.

"Albert has not returned yet," James said to Hazel and Yanera.

"He will find his way back if he is okay," Hazel said.

"Yanera, do you know exactly where he went? I know he had to secure the animals in the barns," James stated.

"I don't know where he is, but you can ask my grandmother," Yanera replied.

Approximately two more hours passed, and Albert was still missing.

"Where is Albert? The weather is getting worse. It's going to get much darker soon," Hazel said.

"I am not able to pinpoint exactly where he is right now," Yanera said.

"I will go and search for him," James said.

"I will go with you, sir," Nev replied.

"My grandmother might be able to help you," Yanera said.

The men left on horseback. They rode through the slave quarters and inquired about Albert, but no one knew where he was. They went to the boiler houses, all three of them, and still there were no signs of Albert. Then they went to Yanera's grandmother, a psychic, and she directed them towards the Yallas River. She said Albert would need their help soon. The men went and searched the woods near the Yallas River. They found some tracks that led them alongside the river, and to their surprise, they saw Albert coming up a slope out of the small valley nearby. He was leading a donkey and a goat. James and Nev rushed to meet him.

"We have been looking for you," James said.

"This goat has given birth to three kids. I knew she was missing when I secured the other animals in the stables. All the goats returned except her. She would not have left her kids behind because she knows that they would not be able to withstand the weather conditions out in the open, so she secured them as best as possible near the place she gave birth. The goats were feeding in this area yesterday, so I figured she would still be here," Albert replied.

"Where are the kids?" Nev asked.

"They are in the hamper," Albert replied.

"Give the goat to me, and ride with Mr. Gordon," Nev said. "It's going to rain harder soon."

The men headed for the plantation house. Nev led the donkey with the hamper while riding his horse. Albert and James rode the other horse and the goat followed. Everyone was glad when they arrived home at the plantation house. They secured the animals in one of the stables, and shortly after, the wind and rain intensified. Inside the plantation house, the three men and the women sat at the large kitchen table and talked of many things. They shared many jokes and stories. In the evening, it became darker earlier than usual, and it made the time seem later than it was. Rose and Ann were happy to be with them.

"Mr. Gordon," Albert whispered.

"Yes sir," James said.

"I appreciate you letting my family and I stay here, and for coming to my rescue today. Next week, I'll try and find employment in Spanish Town or Kingston."

"Albert, if you and your family leave here, you would break many hearts. The position of chief overseer is yours for the taking. I hope you have no objections. The estate belongs to Hazel, myself, and Nev. If you accept the job, we will look after you and your family, and give you a wage that is more than anyone else will offer. If you stay with us for more than seven years, you will become a vested partner."

"Sir, I am grateful. You have given me a lot already. I accept the work gladly. My family and I feel this place is good for us."

"Thank you for saving our goats. It is that attention and concern that makes me want you to stay," James said.

"I like this place too, and I know the people here care about my family and me," Albert replied.

At that moment, Ann, Hazel, Nev, Myka, Rose, Manwa, Yanera, Albert, and James came together to share the moment and celebrate because Albert and his family were staying permanently. They celebrated long into the night as the rain continued to pour heavily. The raindrops splattered loudly as they fell. A drop of rain was approximately a liter of water. Outside was soaked. The ground had small waterways, like little streams and miniature rivers. The water utilized these pathways and flooded some areas in the sugarcane fields. James and everyone continued to delight themselves with conversation while drinking coffee, ginger beer, wine, and eating sweet potato pudding and boiled chicken.

A little before midnight, everyone scattered to their beds. James went upstairs to his balcony room on the third floor. He was tired and tipsy, but at that moment, Ann tiptoed her way to James's quarters, which was an open room. James was resting, slightly asleep, when he felt someone gently touched him. He was suddenly awoken.

"Ann," he said.

"Don't speak so loud," she whispered. She lay beside him and placed her head on his chest. "The night is cooler than usual. I am afraid, lonely, and cold. Your body is warm. Since I've been in Jamaica, I have been longing for someone like you to make me feel safe and warm. Tonight you won't have to imagine making love to me, but do as you have imagined. Love me for real. Do to me whatever you desire. Make me feel good."

James was uncomfortable at first, but his sexual appetite arose. Ann sensed that James could not resist her or restrain his passion. Whatever she was doing felt good. He reacted instinctively. The falling rain smothered the noise of their passionate lovemaking.

"Don't make so much noise or everyone will hear," James said.

"Let them hear, I want them to hear. I don't care," Ann replied loudly. She took charge of the moment and nothing else mattered.

About 5:30 a.m., Ann went back to her room and slipped into the bed with her grandmother, trying her best not to wake her, but Rose turned to her and said, "I told you he was wild." Ann did not respond.

Grandmother Knows Best

In the morning, the rain ceased and the men went out over the estate to assess the damages. They returned and reported no loss of life to human or livestock, but there were extensive floodings and damages to the roads and sugarcane fields. Rose and Ann did not leave as planned because of the devastation brought about by the storm.

The next Friday, six days after the storm, they stayed up late at the estate house again. Rose was complaining that she felt like she was suffocating and she could not breathe with minimal activity. However, it did not affect her upbeat personality. She seemed very happy. She was also more talkative than usual. She was telling jokes and stories of her life's adventures.

As for James and Ann, their attraction for each other grew, but it was still a secret to everyone else because Ann was engaged to a man in England. After 8:00 that night, Rose said she was tired and was going to sleep.

"Are you feeling better, Miss Rose?" Yanera asked.

"I feel much better, my child. I just need to sleep with an extra pillow or two because when I lay flat, my chest feels heavy, and my legs are very swollen," she said.

"Tomorrow we'll take you to Kingston to see a doctor," Hazel said.

"I am eighty years old. Don't worry too much about me. My time is winding down, and I have lived a wonderful life. I will see everyone in the morning. By then, I should feel better," she said, and then she went to bed.

Ann went to bed with her, but when her grandmother fell asleep, she slipped away and spent the night with James.

The next day, they went about their usual activities. At 9:00 a.m., Yanera inquired about Rose. Ann replied, she was still sleeping.

"She was not feeling well yesterday, so it would be normal for her to be tired now," Hazel said.

"My grandmother is all right, but I will check on her," Ann said.

Yanera drew closer to Nev and whispered to him, "I know something is wrong."

Ann went to the bedroom where Rose was, and suddenly she screamed out, loudly.

Everyone proceeded to the room. "She is not responding!" Ann said.

Albert placed the back of his hand on her cheeks and felt for a pulse on the side of her neck. "She is gone," he said.

At this moment, Ann began to weep and Myka held her closely. The men left the room.

"I will get a box and take the body to the dead house in Kingston," Nev said.

The next day, Nev took the body to the morgue.

Some of the slaves cried and many of them comforted Ann.

"How did Yanera know something was wrong with my grandmother?" Ann asked James.

"I don't know," James replied.

Later that week, Ann went to see Yanera.

"Miss Ann, I am honored that you have come to see me, but you could have sent for me," Yanera said.

Ann entered the small house as Yanera welcomed her in. They sat at the small kitchen table. Yanera offered her a cup of ginger tea, a piece of roast yam, and some callaloo.

"I want to thank you personally for everything you did for my grandmother since you have been here," Ann said. "She loved me very much. I did not do enough for her when she was alive. I noticed you and her became very close in a short time."

"You were blessed to have a grandmother like her, and I was blessed too for knowing her. You and your grandmother shared a lot in common. She knew this. You did a lot for her, so don't worry. It always seems like we haven't done enough for our loved ones when they pass," Yanera said.

"Some of the servants say that you can see into the spirit world. Is this true?" Ann asked.

"My dear, common sense is what I use. If Miss Rose gets up every day at 6:00 a.m., and one day she is sleeping until close to midday, automatically this small thing would alert your senses."

"You're right."

"Someone is coming," Yanera said.

However, no one was in sight. They continued talking and eating. Five minutes later, a man was seen coming in the distance down the road. When the man was in the yard, Yanera told him to come inside and sit around the table. The man was apprehensive to say what his visit was about, but Yanera assured him that it was okay to state what he wanted with Ann present.

The man's name was Macky.

"Ma'am, I tell you that my farm cannot yield any food because the bad-minded people put black magic on me. Nothing develops properly or produces what I planted. I need you to get this curse off me, Miss Yanny," he said.

"Mr. Macky, if you follow my instructions, your field will produce food. However, you have to start over again. Don't worry about this year's crop. Only a few weeks left in the reaping season anyway. Listen good, Macky. Whenever your neighbors and the people that live near you start to prepare their fields for planting, then you should also prepare your field. Whenever they plant, you plant. Whenever they weed out the shrubs and mulch, you do likewise, and reap only when they reap. Follow their actions to the minute. Be kind to them, and do not let them know that you know about the curse. Make no quarrels or mention to anyone that I advised you, and please, don't ever talk about the curse anymore. Remember also to boil the water you and your family drink. That's all I have to say, Mr. Macky. Go now in peace," Yanera said.

"Thank you, Miss Yanny," Macky said. He left the way he came.

Meanwhile Ann was observing.

"Macky claims to be a farmer, but he plants his crops out of seasons and reaps too early. He hardly ever take care of his fields, yet he blames his neighbors for cursing him," Yanera explained.

"I see what you mean," Ann said.

"If I don't help him, he will go somewhere else and get bad counseling, and then he shall be truly bewitched," Yanera said.

"I see clearly where intelligence and common sense can emulate magic, but still I don't know how you could tell that there was a visitor coming."

"I saw the dog stand up, wag its tail, then he looked at me. That's a sure sign that someone is coming."

Ann smiled as she looked at Yanera.

"When do you plan to bury Miss Rose?" Yanera asked.

"I will take the body to Manchester, England. She spent the last fifteen years here in Jamaica, but she wanted to be interred in England."

"The morning she passed, I felt someone touched me here in my kitchen. It felt like her. I didn't see anyone. That is why I went to the plantation house and enquired about her."

"She came to say good-bye."

"You understand more than you know, Miss Ann."

The women talked for more than an hour before leaving for the plantation house.

Over the following two days, Ann made preparations to leave for England. James paid for her passage and escorted her to the harbor three days later.

"When will you return to Jamaica?" he asked.

"Soon as possible. Rose had a lot of land in the interior of the Island, but it is no place for sugarcane. My uncle will become the owner, but he has always wanted to return to England. He lives in St.

Elizabeth. I know my grandmother had deeded me in her will, but I will see to that matter when I get back to England," Ann said.

"Are you still planning on getting married?"

"I can't give you a definite answer. I love my fiancé, and he is a good man. You're a good man too. I love you very much, but it is more complicated than it seems. It's not easy for me. You will have to give me some time and space to think this over," Ann said.

"So you will leave me in Jamaica empty and broken-hearted?"

"You can't give up so quickly. The moment you give up, the moment after is when what you hope for comes through. The thing I admire about you is that, in all your success, you are humble and naïve, which makes you a remarkable person. Our relationship may take a different path from what you expect. Life is life, and the life I planned is not always the one I live for the most part. Follow your heart and be true to yourself and everyone. Sometimes the right decision does not makes us happy immediately, but it places us on the right path to be truly contented." Ann's eyes were filled with tears when she said this.

James knew what she said was true. "I don't understand why things went the way it did. Where did I go wrong?" James asked.

"One day you will understand. I hope that day comes soon."

"You may never return. I will always love you too," James said.

"All aboard!" one of the ship's sailors said.

James and Ann hugged each other and kissed. Immediately after, she boarded the ship. The ship was estimated to arrive in England eight weeks after it departed Jamaica.

James went home after and went to work as usual. He gave the order for Albert to construct a bridge across the Yallas River. During this time, a regiment of 5,000 British soldiers and hundreds of trained military dogs arrived on the island. Trackers were brought in from Central America. The British government was about to wage war on the Maroons because of the recent raids on some of the plantations.

Era of Changes

"**B**efore we start the bridge, we have to wait until the water level gets low," Albert said, "but it's not too soon to start planning and gathering the materials."

"Let me know what you need, and I will start getting them," James said.

Over the next few months, Albert gathered stones and logs of all sizes. He had his crew cut and shape the stones according to his specifications. He made two dams that rerouted the water flow. No one really knew what he was doing, but they followed his instructions diligently. Albert was focused and meticulous. Five months later, when the weather was dry, Albert started constructing the bridge.

James had not heard from Ann since she left, but he received a letter from her uncle, who wanted to sell some land in eastern St. Elizabeth. Most of the land had never been used for farming. It was not suitable for sugarcane production either because it was mountainous and far from the sea. James called a meeting to discuss the matter.

The meeting was on a Saturday evening. James decided to stop working early because he did not feel well. He went to his quarters to think and rest. Myka was in the room at that time cleaning. She wanted to leave and allow James to rest, but James insisted that she continued working while he relax and meditate. He watched Myka work, cleaning his furniture and folding his clothes. Her beautiful figure was pleasant to look at. Myka could feel his eyes scanning her, but she paid no attention to him as she worked. It was not unusual for James to look at her for a long time, and it was known to most of the women on the estate that James flirted with his eyes, but he would never use words.

"Is everything all right, sir?" Myka asked.

James hesitated for a while; then he answered that he had a slight headache.

"You have been getting up early and working long and hard without resting," Myka said.

"I feel very tired too," James replied.

"You might be exhausted, sir."

"Exhausted, what do you mean?"

"It's a combination of being very tired and dehydrated. That may be the reason for having a headache, sir."

"You're very observant," James said. "Do you like living here?"

"Yes, I do very much, and I like the school and the children too," she answered. "The school has given me the opportunity to teach and learn. It hasn't been easy, but I must learn as much as I can."

"Rayne has been requesting more reading materials, but she will have to wait," James said.

"She has taught me most of what I know. Soon she will be as educated as Miss Hazel and Yanera," Myka said.

James smiled. "Rayne will be going to boarding school in England when she is fourteen years old."

"That is three years from now."

"Girls become women much faster than boys become men."

"Why is that, sir?"

"I wish I knew, but you are a prime example."

"When I finish putting away these clothes, I'll make you some mint tea and give you a head and back massage. It will make you feel much better," Myka added.

"Thank you very much. I am looking forward to it," James said.

Later in the evening, after dinner, James held a meeting in the big kitchen of the estate house. He and Albert went over the plans for the bridge.

"It's going to be a flat bridge, and the material we'll be using can be acquired on the island," Albert said.

"Was it necessary to make two dams?" Nev asked.

"The riverbed must be completely diverted in order to set the columns firmly. The two dams will redirect the water completely. I will need to make a longer and wider bridge than usual to compensate for the swell of the river in the rainy seasons," Albert answered.

"We will support you as best as we can. Let us know what you need," Hazel said.

"The coffee trees on the hillside are thriving. There is not much we can do about the downed sugarcane from the recent storm. The minor damages to the slave quarters and boiler rooms have been repaired," Nev added.

"I am seriously considering purchasing some more land in the interior of the island. Rose's brother, Lord Mans, has invited me to see the property in St. Elizabeth. I want to visit him next week. I would like Nev to accompany me. Our good friend Rammy might accompany us too, but I will need to get in touch with him first," James said.

The meeting continued on as they drank peppermint tea that Myka made. After a few hours, everyone went to their quarters. James retired for the night as everyone else. He sat in a large rocking chair on the third-floor balcony, looking out over the estate. He could not sleep. He went downstairs to the kitchen to get a cup of mint tea. Myka was sitting at the large kitchen table reading a book.

"What is it you're reading?" James said.

"*Don Quixote*," Myka replied.

"I started reading that book, but I got bored and stopped."

"Yet you have read *The Alchemist* more than once."

"I don't understand that book either, but one day I might. It is very interesting."

"Does your head still hurt?"

"Not as much as this morning," James replied. "Come with me upstairs, I have something to show you."

They went upstairs to James' quarters. He took a map of Jamaica out of a book and showed Myka the parish of St. Elizabeth, the place where he planned to buy some land. They were sitting comfortably.

"You smell good," James said. "What perfume are you wearing?"

"It's not perfume, it's the mint leaves that I use in my bath," Myka replied.

James began to touch Myka on her shoulders. Then he ran his hands through her hair and down her back.

"Your hair is nice," he said.

"You like it?"

"I like everything about you. You are a beautiful woman."

"You like Ann too."

James was silent for a minute.

"I want to stay here with you for a while. It's nice up here," Myka said.

"Your parents may not approve of you spending time with me, especially your father," James said.

"I am almost nineteen years old. Why do I still need approval from my father? If I wanted to stay for all night, it's my decision."

"You have a valid argument, your majesty."

"Tell me what these signs and symbols on the map mean, sir?"

"Absolutely. It's easy to learn," James said.

They fell asleep eventually, and when morning came, Myka was awake and working in the kitchen.

That day, James thought about her often while he worked. In the evening, he went to the kitchen after everyone had eaten. He knew Myka would be there. Myka also looked forward to seeing James because she thought about him during the day too. James waited as he slowly ate his dinner; then Myka walked in.

"Evening, sir," she said.

"How are you?" James said as he looked at her briefly.

Myka looked at him and asked, "You're not hungry?"

"I haven't eaten much all day either," James replied.

"Are you feeling better?"

"I feel much better."

Myka started to clean the dishes as James looked out the window and wandered in his thoughts.

"Do you like music?" James asked her.

"Yes," Myka said. "Do you like dancing, sir?"

"I like to read, dance, and sing," James replied.

"I like listening to good music and reading, but please don't sing at this time or you might disturb those who sleep," Myka said.

"I know you like love stories."

"Only the ones with good endings."

"Love seems to come easy for a beautiful woman, but for a man like me, love is hard to find. And if I find a little, it's usually for a moment, then it goes."

"Is that speculation or fact, sir?"

"For me it's a fact, and for others it's not a fact." James laughed.

Myka smiled while she looked at James and said, "My love is not little, nor will it go away. It's enduring and growing continually every day, like a spark of fire that has found its way in a dry, endless sugarcane field. My love is strong and burning away furiously. This fire is not intended to destroy, but to fulfill and make way for rejuvenation. My love will not burn you or anyone else, sir."

"Let's go upstairs. The moon is full and the view from the balcony is spectacular," James said.

Myka followed James upstairs. They talked of many things as they took in the view. James could not stop touching her. Myka welcomed his gesture of affection. An hour later, Myka went to sleep. James was alone and very lonely.

The next day, James got a message from Rammy stating that he would accompany him on the journey to St. Elizabeth.

Later that day, James rode with Nev, overseeing the estate. The two men rode slowly alongside each other on the dirt roads among the sugarcane fields.

"You have something on your mind, sir?" Nev asked.

"Yes," James said.

"What is it, sir?"

"It's about Myka," James replied. "I can't stop thinking about her."

"Why is that?"

"Myka is here and she is not committed to a man. Ann is engaged to another man, and she will forget about me soon. Myka is single and ready."

Nev brought his horse to a halt.

"When I first met Yanera, she was very young. I flirted with her and she was friendly, but when I told her I loved her, she became angry and withdrew from me. I had no explanation for the way she reacted. I told her the truth, and I did not know what to do, but I never stopped caring about her, in spite of her resistance. I became consistent with my kindness towards her. I was not overbearing or jealous. Her welfare had become my concern.

"Myka will not be easy. I would pursue her if I wasn't married or I did not know better. Yet, the worries Yanera imputed to me when we first met wore me out. Next time, try and figure out your issues of courting without me. It's easier for me to study the universe than deal with a woman's personality. I am glad we'll be going to St. Elizabeth soon," Nev said.

"I don't understand."

"Women focus on things men take for granted sometimes. For instance, when a man says 'I love you' to a woman, and it's the truth, she usually knows it, but if it's a lie, she knows it too. However the case, whether it is true or false, you're still in for a lot of trouble. This is my opinion. You are a lucky man, James. Good-bye. I will see you later," Nev said, and then he rode off swiftly.

Nev gave James the impression that he didn't want to talk about the matter too much, and James was slightly embarrassed.

In the evening, James sat on the third-floor balcony looking out over most of the plantation and the ocean in the far distance. He thought about Ann and realized that he might never see her again. Suddenly, Myka came running up the stairs. She was returning a book that she had borrowed. She was surprised when she ran into James. He grabbed her and held her close and firm. She resisted for a second, and then she relaxed.

"Don't let me go," she said quietly to James.

He started kissing her all over, ravishingly, and she quickly became equally aggressive. It seemed that they had seriously anticipated this moment—a moment that instantly submerged both of them into a magical lovemaking frenzy that went on for hours. Their passion for each other was strong, so strong that their satisfaction was only achieved through a sensual romantic escapade that lasted until morning.

In the morning, James left Myka in his room asleep. He was in the kitchen relaxing when Nev alerted him of a visitor.

"Rammy will be here shortly. He is down the road on his way here," Nev said.

Myka arose from her sleep shortly after. "I have to go and help prepare breakfast," she whispered to herself as she got dressed in a hurry.

James went outside to meet Rammy as he entered the estate house yard.

"Rammy, welcome to my humble home," James said.

"There is nothing humbling about this place except those goat kids eating the grass over there," Rammy said.

"Well then, welcome to our beautiful, elaborate palace," James said.

Everyone laughed and Nev smiled.

"Mr. Rammy!" Hazel called out when she saw Rammy in the front yard standing with his horse. She ran from inside the house and embraced him.

"Look at you! You look just like your mother," Rammy said.

They convened, approximately two hours later, in the large kitchen.

Myka and her mother had finished preparing the breakfast.

The day passed peacefully, and they came together in the evening again, for dinner.

"The bridge is in progress. Another two weeks before we begin the platform. The pillars are strong and ready," Albert said.

"The coffee trees are okay. Next year, the first crop should be ready," Nev said.

"If you guys are planning to become absentee owners, then you're in for a disappointment in the long run," Rammy said.

"This is our home. We were all born here except Albert. Where else should we go," James said.

"All right then, this property in St. Elizabeth will be gone soon if we don't move fast and buy it. It will be in the hands of a politician who will post no trespassing signs all over it, then sell it to foreign investors at a very inflated price," Rammy said.

"They will buy it only to resell it for a profit?" Hazel asked.

"Most definitely," Rammy replied.

"Let's go see the property and purchase it," James said.

"When are you planning to leave?" Yanera asked.

"We should leave next week, the latest," Rammy said.

"The sugarcane business has been profitable so far, but it's time to expand. This land that we desire is far and remote, but it is valuable. It is a wonderful opportunity," Nev said.

"Myself, Nev, and Rammy will go to St. Elizabeth. Hazel, Yanera, and Albert will remain here and manage the estate until we return," James said.

"How long are you planning on staying there?" Hazel asked.

"Two to three weeks," James replied.

A New Frontier

Rammy stayed at the estate for the rest of the time until they were ready to leave. He entertained everyone with stories of his seafaring days as a pirate until it was late. Rammy was an impressive storyteller. He told stories of sea monsters, ghosts, beautiful women, and of escaping perilous circumstances.

They planned to start the journey to St. Elizabeth on the following Monday.

James was looking forward to the trip. His thoughts were preoccupied with purchasing the new property. Myka, on the other hand, felt resented and alienated because James had been spending a lot of time with Rammy and Nev. He never invited her to his room again. The Saturday night before they went on the journey, James was up late. He was upstairs on the third-floor balcony overlooking the estate as usual, thinking and mumbling to himself.

Myka made a cup of mint tea, sweetened with honey, and brought it to him.

"Thank you," he said, and then he tasted it. "It has a lighter taste than usual."

"It's sweetened with honey, not sugar," Myka replied.

"Honey, ah."

"Yes," Myka answered.

When she answered, James looked out into the horizon and mumbled, "Honey would be a good substitute for sugar."

Myka drew close to him and held his right hand, at the same time looking at him as if she wanted to tell him something. James turned and looked at her momentarily, but pulled away. Her garment was exceptionally revealing. Myka was longing for some affection, but James did not realize it.

"I have to write this down," he said.

"Write what down?"

"Bee farm for making honey."

Myka felt James was not attracted to her anymore. He was not receptive to her feelings. She felt her love for him had only resulted in a one-night stand. "Good night, sir," she said, and left slightly angry and very heartbroken.

Early the next day, James, Rammy, and Nev left for St. Elizabeth. They took a boat from the Kingston Harbor. The harbor was busy. The men helped to secure their three horses on the boat.

"Let's hope the weather stays calm. We should be in for a good journey along the south coast of Jamaica," the boat's captain said.

Within one hour, the boat set sail out of the harbor. The journey was 75 miles west, and it was expected to arrive the next day. In the morning, the boat docked in Black River, St. Elizabeth. The captain of the boat requested 25 shillings more.

"What you need twenty-five shillings for?" Rammy asked loudly.

"Expenses, for water and feeding the three greedy horses," the captain replied.

Rammy paid the captain the 25 shillings. "Our horses might be greedy, but they are far from being lazy like the crew on this boat," he said. "The place we are going is located in the mountains. It will take another two days of traveling to get there," he said to the others.

The men walked through the town of Black River in single file, leading their horses; rendering warm greetings as they journeyed, portraying themselves as friendly because they were strangers. The northerly path they journeyed gradually inclined and became more winding. Their ascent into the interior of the Island had begun.

They mounted the horses and rode at a steady pace for approximately three hours until they came upon a steeper upgrade they called Spur Tree. They dismounted their horses and continued to move on up the mountainside on foot.

"How long we have left to go?" James said.

"Another day or two," Nev said.

"When shall we rest?" James asked.

"We'll rest when it gets dark," Rammy replied.

"Can you keep up?" James said, looking at Rammy.

Rammy did not answer. They walked for four more hours, occasionally stopping to drink water and rest.

"Seven more miles, sir, then we will be on top of the hill, where the terrain will level off," Nev said.

"That's the best thing I have heard all day," James said.

"You look weary and dizzy, James. You think you can make it before it gets dark?" Rammy asked, but James did not reply.

They continued the journey until it was about 6:00 p.m.; then they came to the top of Spur Tree hill, where they rested. They were now heading on a northern trail that was fairly level. The northern trail was a grassy landscape with patches of forest and meadows.

"We know where we came from, and we can see where we are going," Nev said.

The men found a small clearing about half a furlong off the trail among some trees. They secured the horses and set up camp.

"Look at that, miles and miles of virgin land with forests, rolling hills, and savannahs, good for raising cattle," Rammy said.

They made a small fire and some tea, and roasted sweet potatoes for dinner. The night came quickly. There was a new moon and the stars were visible. The forest was filled with the sounds of wildlife, and the conversations of the men were amplified. The mosquitoes were out in large numbers, but the smoke kept most of them away.

"The fire attracts the insects, but the smoke drives them away," James said.

"We only need the smoke to ward off the insects, and a little heat to keep us warm," Nev replied.

"Smoke without fire, and fire without heat; if you see any one of these elements without the other, then you have encountered a powerful spirit," Rammy said. "They say Jamaica is populated with all manner of spirits," he added.

Neither James nor Nev replied. Rammy liked to talk about spirits. His stories seemed realistic, but for the most part, they were not true. In Jamaica, at that time, talking about spirits, especially in the wilderness, was tantamount to summoning one. James and Nev were not going to take part in a conversation that was potentially dangerous.

"I will read a passage from the Bible before we rest so angels may watch over us tonight," James said.

"A fallen angel can take on the appearance of a beautiful woman. I know of an incident that took place in Tortuga. Did anyone know that there are vampires in Tortuga?" Rammy asked. No one responded. "I will tell the story another time."

"Don't forget to cover your face when you sleep or the mosquitoes will feast on it," Nev said.

The men lay on thick mats and used their saddles as pillows. The horses were secured nearby.

Red Berry

In the morning, Nev was the first to rise. He made lemon grass tea sweetened with sugar for everyone.

"The mosquitoes didn't eat my face, but they ate my arms," James said.

"The place looks different from yesterday," Rammy said.

"Why is that?" James asked.

"I have lost my sense of direction," Rammy replied.

"We are not lost. I left markers to keep us oriented, and I have been charting our approximate location on a map," Nev said. "We'll be going northeast and it's this way."

They left on their horses and followed a path that led them into a very large cornfield. As far as they could see, there were cornstalks on either side of the trail. Thousands of parakeets flew away as they rode past. In the distance, the village was visible, and behind the village were some mountain ranges. The mountain ranges were covered in a forest, for the most part.

"This is it. This is Redberry!" Rammy said out loud.

After they passed through the cornfields, they came upon a large area with young coconut trees. There were five men, three women, and four donkeys.

"Good day, ladies, and good day, gentlemen," Rammy said.

They returned the salutations.

"We are looking for Lord Manville," James said.

"Mr. Gordon," one of the women said.

"Yes, I am James Gordon."

"Lord Mans has been expecting you for over a week now. Sammy, you and Bevis take these men to see Lord Mans," the woman said.

Suddenly, the women surrounded them. The women drew their pistols.

"We don't mean any harm, Mr. Gordon, but we have to make a search for weapons before you enter our village," one of the women said.

They searched them and found no weapons.

"Not even a pistol?" one of the women asked.

"There is no need for one," James said.

They were allowed to continue the journey into the village escorted by Sammy and Bevis. The men rode into the village, but then they were taken outside the village into an orange tree grove. At the end of the grove on a small hill was a large two-story log house. The men dismounted the horses and started walking. It was midday. The sky was blue with small patches of white clouds. The temperature was cool. The air was fresh with a light fruity aroma.

"You can't see the sea coast from here, but the mountain view is just as spectacular," Rammy said.

They were greeted by a short black man at the entrance of the house. His name was Lazarus. He was about sixty years old and looked physically fit. He took the horses from the men and led them in the back of the yard.

"It's about time you men arrived. I have been expecting you." A tall white man with curly hair, approximately seventy years old, stood on the upstairs porch that surrounded the second floor. He was standing with his hands resting on the rails and looking down at them.

"Mans! Are you able to see us without glasses?" Rammy said.

"Rammy, I can hardly see you, but I can smell and hear you from a mile away," Lord Mans replied.

"If you smell anything good, it's me, and if you smell anything bad, it's these men with me," Rammy replied.

"All of you come up here, anyway. Laz has some good food ready for us," Lord Mans said.

Lord Mans and Rammy knew each other from past times. They were glad to see each other again. The men sat together and had lunch. They had fried fish, callaloo, rice and peas, and avocadoes.

"Where did you get the fish?" James asked.

"We raised them right here in Redberry. We have several artificial ponds for raising fish that can survive in fresh water. The idea to raise fish came from the slaves and servants," Lord Mans said.

"Looks like it is going to be hard to part from this place," Rammy said.

"I would like to see Redberry progress without the turmoil that faces the rest of the nation. That's why I was happy when Rammy mentioned to me that he was a close friend of yours. I never had an upheaval here. The people here treat me well. If I sell this place to a tyrant, the people here will revolt. Your record speaks for itself, Mr. Gordon."

"I will be lucky if I purchase this place. It is pristine," James said.

In the evening, dark clouds overcast the village, and multiple lightning flashed and streaked through the sky, with thunder balls blasting loud like explosions. A thunderstorm was inevitable, and the village was settled in to weather the storm.

"Don't be afraid. This place is known for its thunderstorms and lightning extravaganzas. The slaves say that lightning makes the soil fertile, and it is as necessary as the rain," Lord Mans said to James and company.

"That's what Nev told me a long time ago," James replied.

The men made themselves comfortable. Lazarus prepared their beds and showed them where they should stay for the night. They planned to explore the land in the next two days before they would negotiate a sale price. The rest of the evening they talked and entertained themselves with potato pudding, rum, and coffee. As the rain came down swiftly, the men settled in comfortably.

"Tell me, Laz. What you roast the fish with?" Rammy asked.

"Pimento, onions, salt and pepper. The proper portion is the key to the recipe. A touch too much of salt can spoil everything, but it's the pimento wood that gives the roast fish that special flavor. Even when I roast pork, I use the pimento wood. It gives the meat a flavor that is appealing. There is an abundance of pimentos, eucalyptus, cedar, blue mahoe, and a limited amount of mahogany in the mountains."

"I have several maps of the area. Tomorrow, Lazarus will be your guide and take you wherever you want to go," Lord Mans said.

"How big is the land?" James asked.

"Two hundred thousand acres," Lord Mans replied.

"That is a lot of territory to cover," James said.

"Do not rush to explore the place, Mr. Gordon," Lord Mansville stated.

The next day was Friday. The men got ready and left to see the property. It was approximately 9:30 a.m. when they left. Lazarus led the way and Nev stayed in the rear. The men explored the northern half of the property. They ascended the ridges in the north, and from there they could see the entire property.

"I never thought that the interior of the Island was so diverse with wildlife. Fellows, I aim to harness the honey from the bees, let the cattle and the horses run free," James said.

"If you plan to raise pigs, please don't let them roam free. The wild pigs will become possessed with devils and turn into monsters, monsters that will ruin the agriculture day and night. They go through a transformation just as a grasshopper transforms into a locust. No, you don't want pigs to roam free," Lazarus said.

"Is there a river on the property?" James asked.

"No sir, but the aquifer is not very deep. It is easy to dig a well. It would be wise to build a few reservoirs to provide water in times of drought," Lazarus replied.

The men rode all over the north side and spoke of many things, until late in the afternoon.

"We will return home now before it gets dark. It may rain also," Lazarus said.

The men returned to Lord Mansville's home just before dark. Dinner was ready. They ate and talked about what they saw during the day. They concluded that the land had great potential.

"I hope you don't intend to destroy the property by establishing a sugar plantation; if so, may lightning rain down and burn it," Lord Mans said.

"I will make a pledge not to produce sugar on this property," James said.

"In that case, the price of the property has just been reduced by five percent."

Everyone laughed, except Lord Mans.

The next day, the men explored the southern side of the property. It was just as impressive as the north side; however, their tour was interrupted by a brief shower of rain, so they returned to the house. On Thursday, the men decided to stay within the vicinity of Redberry.

"Today, the sky is blue and there is not a single cloud in sight. The air is fresh and clean," Nev said.

"Is this a sign that it will not rain today?" Rammy asked.

"I don't know," Lord Mans replied.

In the evening, the men met to talk about the sale price. They sat together at the dining table, and Lord Mans presented his terms.

"I would like to keep this house with seven acres surrounding it. I will return to England, but I want my house kept so that if and when I or any member of my family visits Jamaica, they will have a place to stay. Rose was my sister, and Ann sent a letter to me, telling me about how well you treated her and her grandmother. This house will be kept for Ann with the seven acres and also another one hundred acres on the southwest corner for her.

"The inhabitants of the village are not all slaves. Some of them have bought their freedom, and some of them are indentured servants.

Treat them well and allow the indentured servants to complete their terms. The village belongs to all of them. Without them, I would not have survived or succeeded. I might have the title to this land, but the people that live here belong here. They have the right to be here. One might choose to purchase this land, but in truth, the land chooses its custodian and owns him or her for a time," Lord Mans said. Then he paused for a moment.

"My price is eighty thousand pounds," Lord Mans said.

"The price is very high," James said as he squeezed his chin with his thumb and index finger.

"How much do you feel it's worth?" Lord Mans said.

"Sixty thousand pounds."

"Seventy thousand pounds and you get to keep the house."

"Seventy thousand pounds and everything belongs to me. You and any members of your family are free to stay here as my guest when they visit," James said.

"Done deal, that's it," Lord Mans said.

The men arranged to make the title and monetary transfer the following week in Spanish Town. Further purchase agreements were made without conflicts. The following day, Sunday, they left Redberry and headed home. They went home the same way they came, but they stopped in Old Harbor and rode to Spanish Town. In Spanish Town, James made some monetary transactions with the Bank of England and the local land authority. From there, they went to Rammy's home in Constant Spring, where they spent the night. The next day, James and Nev rode home to Easington.

The Blue Mountain Maroons

When they arrived home, they were greeted by Hazel and Yanera with some bad news. Myka was missing. She had been gone a day already.

"Where has she gone? What happened, and why did she leave? Is there a possibility she might be in danger?" James asked Hazel, Albert, and Yanera.

"I don't feel she is in danger," Yanera said.

"She took her donkey and left to be with her aunt," Albert said.

"Where does her aunt live?" James asked.

"She lives in the Blue Mountain Ranges. She is my wife's younger sister. She is the Queen of the Maroons. Her name is Nanya. If Myka is with her, she is safe, but she will be in danger if the British soldiers and their dogs attack."

"I will go and get her," James said. At the same time, Manwa, the mother of Myka, spoke. "Myka left on her own free will. I tried my best to stop her, but she was too adamant."

James was silent, but he was obviously in a state of fear.

"She is a woman now, and as much as we wanted to restrain her, I knew it wouldn't be right," Albert said.

"You're both right, she is not my slave. I might be overreacting, but Myka, your daughter, is the woman I want to be my wife. I must go and find her and know why she left," James said.

Albert and Manwa were very surprised.

Shortly after, everyone returned to their usual duties.

"I don't know how to tell you, but Myka belongs here with us, sir. She left because she feels you don't love her, but I know she loves you and you love her too," Yanera said.

"I want her to be here also," James said.

"Nev knows the Blue Mountains like the palms of his hands. He is willing to go with you. The sooner you leave to get her, the better it will be," Yanera said.

James went to see Nev a few minutes later.

"Nev, we have to go and get Myka," James said.

"I have been ready and waiting for you to say when, sir," Nev said.

"Early morning, before sunrise. I know I will not sleep tonight, but I have to be patient. The horses need the rest too," James said.

"Myka can be miserable sometimes, even though she is very pretty, but I must say, I want her back as bad as you," Nev said.

James and Nev arose early the next day. They took their horses and headed into the Blue Mountains. They followed a trail that led them to the Rio Grande River. Then they followed a path that inclined diagonally. The hillsides were covered in a forest that was fertile and steep. It was a place where tributaries flow abundantly, and where many birds and all the wildlife on the Island flourished.

In the evening, the men arrived at a place called Cedar Valley, where two large rivers merge, the Negro River and the Yallas River.

"We will rest here for the night, sir," Nev said.

"If it wasn't for the moonlight, this place would be very dark. How far do we have left to go?" James asked.

"At least one more day; we shouldn't rush. This journey will test our endurance. Remember to cover your face when you sleep and listen well."

The men rested well and in the morning, James arose first and made a fire and some peppermint tea. They also had a piece of cornmeal cake which they brought with them. Shortly after, the men resumed their journey on foot and the horses followed. It was too perilous to ride the horses on the steep terrain. The men ascended into the Blue Mountains at a steady pace. By afternoon, they were high enough to see the ocean and small harbor towns of Morant Bay and Kingston, but they still had a long way to go to the summit.

"The Maroons probably know we are here, but it's a sign of respect to announce our presence, and let them know we come in peace," Nev said. He'd brought a conch shell horn with him to make the signals. He blew it five times. It was loud and echoed all over the mountain forest. "The Maroons will not attack us if we are not a threat."

"I know we are not alone because I have been hearing a knocking in the forest," James replied.

"That is the sound of the woodpecker bird. They make their nest by pecking out holes high in tree trunks. The Blue Mountains are the home of many birds found nowhere else on the Island, but the woodpecker is everywhere in Jamaica," Nev said.

"I have noticed more chicken hawks than usual too," James said.

"Oh, if you see any bird eggs on the ground, do not touch them. It will bring bad luck, and when you see the small red-winged parrot, it's an indicator that the elevation is over fifty-five hundred feet."

The men were now traveling on a direct path to the summit called the Ladder of Jacob. It was one of the steepest climbs of the journey. They were above the forest and looking down at its canopy. The air was thin and cool. Half an hour later, they reached the summit and rested on the plateau. The view was spectacular. They could see the sea coast to the east, north, and south, and patches of clouds beneath them. The place was rugged, but peaceful and beautiful.

"We will rest in this area, sir. Night will come soon," Nev said.

"When will we go to the Maroon village?" James asked.

"Don't worry, they will approach us soon." Nev blew the conch shell three more times, and then they prepared themselves to rest.

Night came. The moon was full and the stars were on display.

"The heavens seem very close here," Nev said.

"I hope Myka is okay," James replied.

"Myka is *copacetic* right now. It's not necessary to cover your face. It's too cold for the mosquitoes, and the air is thin. They will not come here."

"I have always admired the way you and Yanera relate, Nev. You seem to understand each other, and you spend the right amount of time together."

"The truth is, I don't understand her, but love allows me to cope with the misunderstandings. We've been together for a long time, and she knows me very well. She is able to encourage and motivate me, although sometimes she puts me down too. Our relationship is not all a bed of roses. We have to weed out some thorns occasionally, and although you don't see us talking too much, she has found ways to communicate to me without speaking."

"You're a lucky man."

"You're luckier," Nev replied.

The men talked and James made a fire and some fever grass tea. Nev had one more cornmeal cake left.

"I feel Myka wanted to find out if I loved her," James said.

"Just like the wind blows and the trees grow, love comes and goes. Love is painful without trust. You are a man of good intentions, and Myka is very beautiful and lucky just like you. I feel you're making the right decision. Drink more fever grass tea, man, and listen to the songs of nature around you."

"I will agree with you. She is amazingly beautiful, but then you say you don't understand Yanera, who is your wife. How can you understand Myka?"

The night became exceptionally cooler, but the mats and blankets and the small fire provided just enough heat and light. They were comfortable and they slept well.

In the morning, when they woke, they were surprised to notice they had company. They were in the company of seven Maroons. The Maroons maintained the fire and prepared more tea.

"We heard your signals, and we have been watching you since yesterday," one of them said.

The men introduced themselves. The Maroon squad leader name

was Cojohn. They were armed with rifles. The sandals they wore were made of goatskin, and short pants allowed them to be flexible.

"We are looking for a young woman who came here two to three days ago," Nev said.

"A woman with long, curly black hair with a stubborn, ugly donkey that only listens to her?" Cojohn asked.

"Yes," James said.

"Is this woman one of your slaves?"

"No, she is not a slave."

"Has she stolen something valuable from you?"

"No, she has taken nothing of value from me."

"Don't tell me that your heart isn't valuable."

The men laughed, but James remained neutral.

"Your heart is with her. We will take you to see her when night comes," Cojohn said.

"How do you know about our situation?" James asked.

"She has stated that she has given her love to a man with a hard heart, but by the looks of things, you don't seem that way because you would not be here."

They gathered their belongings and started walking. The Maroons were not hostile to them, and James felt at ease. The men walked approximately four miles heading north into more mountain ranges and plateaus. The place was rugged. The Maroons spoke in another language that James could not understand, but they also could speak English. Their language contained English, Spanish, and the languages of Western Africa.

James moved close to Nev and asked him quietly what the Maroons were talking and laughing about.

"They say that most of the plantation owners call the Africans savages. Yet they have many children with the African women. In your case, they say Myka's love has subdued you; her love is the master, and you have become her servant. Pay no attention to their statements because they are only intended to make them laugh and not to provoke you," Nev replied.

The Maroons sounded a horn, and told James and Nev to wait at the present location for another party who would escort them into the village. Cojohn and his men were on guard duty. They had left their area of surveillance.

James and Nev waited for approximately ten minutes. A party of ten more Maroons came upon them from all directions. Six of them were women. One of the women was the leader.

"My name is Joanya," she said. "I know your visit is peaceful, but we are required to conduct a search."

James and Nev were checked for weapons, and then they were blindfolded. They were led for another hour on their horses. They heard water falling and the children playing. It felt as if they were inside a forest. It was another twenty minutes before their blindfolds were removed. Nev and James were brought before a council of seven. There were three men and four women. They were dressed in purple, white, and blue. Their shoes were made of leather and goatskin.

"It's good to see you again. Nev," the woman who sat in the middle said.

"It's good to see you too, Nanya."

"And how are you, Mr. Gordon?" Nanya said.

"I am well."

"I know you are here for Myka and you want to take her back with you. No one has ever returned to their master after coming here, and no plantation master has ever come here to claim their slave. These circumstances are unusual, but love works in mysterous ways for the benefit of us all. We cannot decide whether Myka should return or stay. The decision is hers. Since you did not come to take her by force, we will not intervene. You are welcome to stay here and persuade her to return with you peacefully. Be understanding and be patient with her, Mr. Gordon. You will need some time. She is also expecting."

"I was unaware she was expecting," James replied.

"Are you not happy she is with child, Mr. Gordon?"

"I am happy, but this is new information for me."

"Enjoy yourself here, Mr. Gordon. I have nothing more to say," Nanya said.

James did not see Myka in the village, but he was informed that she would be there by early afternoon. James was anxious, but hardly showed it.

In the early afternoon, he saw a woman at a far distance with a donkey. He could not clearly recognize her, but he felt it was Myka. All the women dressed similarly, but when she got closer, he knew it was not her. He went to meet her anyway.

"Masser, my cousin is washing at the river. She will return shortly," she said when James approached her.

James waited and then he saw Myka and approached her.

"Myka, how are you?" he asked.

Myka was coming from the stream where the women washed and dried their clothes. The hamper on the donkey was filled with laundered clothes.

"I have come to ask you to return home with me," James said.

"My home is here now," Myka replied.

At the same time, James tried to touch her, but she pulled away.

"Don't touch me," she said as she walked away leading her donkey.

Moments later, James and Nev were together.

"Myka saw me and didn't say a word to me," Nev said.

"Don't worry. She is going to see us often for a few more days. It's our perseverance against her resistance," James said. "Tell me, Nev."

"What is it?"

"It feels like I have shit in my pants, and everybody knows it, except me," James said.

"If we join the elderly men and have some of their food, we might hear some good words and fill our stomach," Nev answered.

They joined the crowd of men, women, and children around a campfire playing drums, dancing, and singing. Some of the elders told stories of wars and ghosts until it was very late. Then the villagers slowly retired for the night. Nev and James slept under a small bungalow with open sides. It was made of small wooden posts, with a roof covered by coconut leaves. It was enough shelter if it rained.

The Exodus

In the morning, they arose to the smell of coffee roasting and the sound of roosters crowing. A boy, approximately twelve years old, came to where James and Nev were sleeping. He told them that Nanya, the village leader, requested their presence. The men went to see her immediately.

Nanya was awaiting them.

"Mr. Gordon, I was alerted of the news that there are British soldiers setting up garrisons in three areas of the lower Blue Mountains. A buildup of this multitude is an indication that they intend to take the land from us. So far, they have blocked our access to the sea and restricted our ability to move freely about the Island. We will have to strike them before they progress any further," she said.

"What do you want me to do, Nanya?" James asked.

"I don't want you to get involved, but I would appreciate it if you would leave before the trouble comes."

"Your niece is expecting my child, my only child. If I can't convince her to leave, then I will stay here and fight. I must protect her."

"Your concern for my niece is deeply appreciated, Mr. Gordon, but for you and Myka to die here is foolish. I cannot let her stay here and face the danger. However, there are other ways you can be of great help. You are too important of a man to engage in combat."

"She is right, sir, you are more valuable as an estate owner in alliance with the Maroons than a soldier fighting with them," Nev said.

"We could supply your fighters with weapons," James said.

"It is still too risky. If you get caught, you will lose what you have and be charged for treason against the British Empire," Nanya replied. "We have a favor to ask of you. It is not an easy task. Some of our women will stay and fight. I can't stop them. It would be disrespectful on my behalf, but the children and the villagers who are not able to fight, will have to relocate to the west in the Cockpit Country. Myka will be among them. The journey leads through the rugged mountain path into Accompong Town. I ask of you kindly to take my people to safety. Myka is willing to assist you, but she is not ready to lead. You will be honored among Maroons for a long time if you succeed."

"I accept the offer," James said. "Nev will need the help of some of your soldiers who can move fast and get to Rammy's place in Constant Spring. Tell him I need thirty to forty rifles and all the ammunition you can carry."

"I will send one of my best squads with you. It consists of seven men and five women. They hardly ever fail and they move very fast," Nanya said.

"I will take the squad and get the rifles, sir, and leave as soon as possible," Nev said.

"I will take the villagers to St. James," James replied softly to Nanya.

"I know that you are the right person for this mission, Mr. Gordon. The journey to the Cockpit Country through the mountainous interior of the Island is not to be taken lightly. It is most hazardous, and many have lost their lives traveling it. That is why I have requested your help," Nanya said.

"It's also an opportunity for you to convince Myka that you're the man for her," Nev whispered to James.

Two hours later, the villagers assembled for a meeting. They were told that they had to move fast because British soldiers were preparing to make an assault on the village. Nanya began to address the villagers in a speech.

"Travel light and take some food and water with you. The journey will take at least fourteen days. You will need to hunt and gather water, fruit, and ground provisions for food. Leave as soon as possible. In the west, there are no wars at this time. Our friend James Gordon will be leading the journey to St. James. Be respectful to him. When it is safe to return, I will send for you. The rest of us will stay here and we will bring the fight to the British before they bring it to us. Go in peace and God be with you."

The Maroons who would not fight—the children, some of the women, and the elderly—assembled for the journey. Most of the elderly men wanted to leave, but when one of them refused to travel and decided to stay and fight, many of the elders changed their positions and decided to stay and fight with Nanya.

"Just because I am old doesn't mean I can't fight," the old man said.

"James," Nev called.

"Yes?"

"I will update Hazel and meet you in Redberry. There is no need for me to return here after I get the weapons from Rammy," he said.

"I will see you at home in Redberry," James replied.

Nev knew that what he had to do was necessary, but he also knew that Hazel would not agree to let James travel into the mountains without him. Nev and the squad of Maroons left for the journey swiftly, while James and his party slowly marched out of the village.

"This way," a woman said, leading a donkey. "The journey is not as dangerous as everybody thinks, but it has many hills and gullies."

Nev and his squad were ten. James and his party were over 300, mostly women, children, and about twenty young men.

"I am glad you are coming with us," one of the women said to James.

"We will need three squads of seven persons each to watch over us. They will be our eyes in the forefront, middle, and rear. They will find the best location for us to camp at night, and if possible, they will provide meat from wild pigs. The seven persons in the rear will stay behind, approximately five to ten miles, and watch our backs. They will not hunt food for the multitude, but they will keep us informed," James said.

At that moment, Nanya and the Maroons who decided to stay behind prepared themselves to stop the British soldiers from advancing too far into the Blue Mountains. She formed divisions that positioned themselves strategically on the mountainsides. They waited patiently as they watched the British soldiers' every move.

The Maroons who were migrating to the west were three groups. James stayed with the first group in front, but at certain points, he would separate himself and wait for the last group. Myka was one of the leaders among the last group.

By late evening, they had completed fifteen miles, progressing westerly. Soon it was dark. James was concerned about everyone, but he was particularly concerned about Myka. When they stopped to rest for the night, James went to see her. He brought some jerk pork and coconut water for her. When they met, she was not angry, but happy to see him.

"I know," James said to Myka.

"What is it that you know?" she asked.

"I know you are expecting."

"The midwife told me that there were two babies."

"I didn't know you were expecting twins."

"James, I didn't know how to tell you, and I didn't know how you would react to me expecting your baby, so I decided to leave instead of facing rejection, which is typical for a person like me in this situation," Myka said.

"Don't worry; I am not typical. This is something good," James said.

"I just don't want to be a concubine. I will be the mother of your children and there is no reason I should not be your wife. This status I want and deserve. Any other way is unacceptable. If you are ashamed of me please let me know and I will stay away peacefully. We have to be true to each other if we are going to be together. I know our love will be tested, and contested by the authorities, and whosoever, but if you truly love me like I love you, we will prevail. You have to see it this way James."

"You feel that I will not marry you because of your heritage or because it's not legal?"

"I feel you will desert me or resent me when I need you most. This behaviour is common among men of your status. A woman in my position is always at a disadvantage because the law of the land currently supports this evil."

"Heritage is not a legitimate excuse not to marry. There has never been a time when love is illegal. I will never desert you, or deny you at anytime," James said.

Myka looked at him and remained silent.

"Return home with me and be the best wife and mother, and I will be the best father and husband. Let us not worry about the legalities. Our love will be bona fide and honorable once we are married."

"Let's eat what you brought for me. I can feel the babies moving," Myka said. "The food smells good too."

"It is a little spicy. Don't drink the coconut water too fast or it may upset your stomach," James said.

The next day, Myka traveled with James in the first group. James did not officially belong to any group because he kept circulating among them.

The second day they had covered seventeen more miles.

Approximately thirty miles away, Nev and the squad of Maroons were in Constant Spring. The squad waited in the woods as Nev took the urgent message to Rammy.

"I have fifty rifles and twenty pistols, and they are new. I have to report that they were stolen. The British allow me to trade guns, but if any discrepancies arise, I will be liable. I am not ready to be hanged. No sir, so I will say that the Maroons stole them," Rammy said.

"I understand," Nev said.

"You still owe me fifty pounds, but you can pay me later."

"Thank you."

"When it gets darker, that's when you should depart, and please stay off the roads. British soldiers have been patrolling the area frequently."

Rammy showed Nev the weapons. When it was dark, the Maroons secured the weapons for the journey into the Blue Mountains. They had three mules to assist them with carrying the load. Nev did not return with the Maroons. Instead, he went to Easington and informed Hazel and Albert about what took place.

"It's hard to say when they will return home," Nev said.

"The governor has implemented a curfew to deter rebellious activity. Soldiers are patrolling everywhere, especially in Spanish Town and Kingston," Albert said.

"I will have to go to St. Elizabeth, and from there, I will have to locate James and Myka," Nev said.

"Seems like you're worried about them," Hazel said.

"If they are taking the interior mountain path to the other side of the Island, they are safe from the British soldiers; however, the terrain is perilous," Albert said.

Later that night, Yanera and Nev sat in the kitchen of their small home. Nev was deep in his thoughts.

"Is there something worrying you?" Yanera said.

"I am all right," Nev answered.

"Nev, I had a strange dream last night. I dreamt that there was a war between the Maroons and the British. There were many casualties. All that time, James was negotiating peace between the two sides. Myka and James were married. Myka was expecting twins. They had many children and their children were of many races. They also became leaders of the Maroons. You, on the other hand, were a vagabond and a fugitive, and you stayed away from me. I feel your life will be in danger soon. I am afraid of losing you."

"Were the children good-looking or ugly?"

"They were good-looking. All of them were healthy," Yanera said.

"Then it's a good dream. I will be all right," Nev said.

Nev did not tell Yanera that Myka was pregnant because he did not feel that it was his responsibility to tell her. Nor did he want to confirm that her dream was reality unfolding.

The next day, around 10:00 a.m., twelve British soldiers visited the Easington estate.

It was an unexpected visit for Hazel and everyone else. The highest ranking soldier was Major Russell. He was seeking James to escort him into the Blue Mountains.

"James is in St. Elizabeth," Hazel said.

"Actually, his presence is not needed, just his permission to utilize the expertise of his servant Nev," Major Russell said.

"What do you want from Nev?" Hazel asked.

"Nev is the right person to take us into the Blue Mountains safely. All the trackers we employed have failed to take us safely into the mountains. He was referred by the governor himself."

"And what if Nev refuses this assignment?"

"A refusal would be an act of treason against the British government," Major Russell said.

At the same time, Nev entered the estate house premises.

"He is here," Hazel said.

"You sent for me, Miss Hazel?"

"Yes, Major Russell is requesting your help."

"It will be a pleasure to assist the major," Nev replied.

"I like your enthusiasm and attitude, Mr. Nev. The governor and Mr. Rammy were right," the major said.

Nev paused for a moment. "Is Mr. Rammy all right?"

"He reported a robbery at his store. Thirty flintlock rifles, twenty matchlocks, and twelve Dolep double-barreled pistols were stolen. The Maroons raided him and took all the arsenal they could. We know you know these mountains, Mr. Nev, and the governor of Jamaica has advised me to have open peace dialogues with the Maroon leaders before taking any other action. You and Mr. Gordon are our official ambassadors to the Maroons because of the solid relationship that this estate has established with them over the years."

"I will assist you in every way necessary," Nev said.

"We will depart tomorrow. Tonight we will be your guest if Miss Hazel does not object to the inconvenience," Major Russell said.

"Not at all, Major Russell, it is our duty to assist you," Hazel said.

"With your permission, can we rest here on the premises for the night?"

"Make yourself at home, Major," Hazel answered.

The major and the soldiers dismounted their horses and made sleeping provisions in the yard of the plantation house. They walked around the house, talking.

"This estate has never been raided. I don't feel it's coincidence or luck. It's close and it's an easy target for the Maroons. I feel Mr. Gordon and the Maroons have a strong, genuine connection that we can exploit effectively," Major Russell said to a few of his men quietly.

"Before you came, I overheard the major mentioning to the captain and one of the lieutenants that they have sent soldiers in pursuit of the Maroons who raided Rammy's place," Hazel said to Nev.

"I don't feel they will catch up with them. Those Maroons move very fast, but I am afraid they might pick up on the trail that James is on," Nev said quietly.

"I absolutely feel that the major is using us to locate where the Maroons live in the Blue Mountains, and his true intentions are sinister."

"I feel the same way also, but if I don't assist him, he will implicate us for treason, and I will definitely face the gallows."

"We have to be careful," Hazel said.

At that exact moment, high and deep in the Jamaican wilderness, James, Myka, and the migrating Maroons had covered three days of traveling.

Nico, one of the Maroon scouts from the front, had returned with good news. He reported to James. "Sir, another two days' journey and we will encounter a lake where we can rest and refresh ourselves for the rest of the trip."

Nico was a boy of extraordinary stamina due to the fact that he was always going a day in advance and returning with information. He never seemed to get tired. He was born in the mountains. He was fifteen years old, five feet five inches, and slim built.

There were also scouts who were staggering in the rear. Nina, a girl, would inform James of activities from the rear. She was fourteen years old and she was the sister of Nico. She was approximately five feet three inches, with a cool, dark complexion and thick black hair which she made into a ponytail. She was pretty and gentle as a dove. She also possessed outstanding speed and stamina. Nina was one of the best runners of the Maroons.

Later that day, two of the women came to James and Myka. They explained that the journey was rough, but they suggested not taking any more rest until they reached the lake. They said they would make it to the lake a day earlier and have more time to rest. Myka and James agreed, and the messengers were sent to inform the party leaders. Everyone agreed to travel throughout the night because the moon was full. Food supplies were rationed; however, water was abundant.

The next day, about five hundred soldiers descended on the Easington Sugar Estate, the home of Hazel and James.

Nev was ready to lead the way, and the major was eager to start the journey into the mountains. Before Nev departed, he consoled Hazel and reassured her that James and Myka would be safe. He also mentioned that the British had managed to employ trackers from Central America, and a number of Maroons had taken bribes to betray their own.

"I am afraid you might get hurt on this mission," Hazel said to Nev.

"Major Russell's expedition is to capture the Maroons and enslave them. As we speak, there are troops in the mountains, and I believe there is a party on the trail of James and Myka. James and the Maroons are still many steps ahead, but they will have to hurry or the soldiers might catch up with them. I will do my best to see that everything works out well, but I will need all the help I can get, so pray hard for me please," Nev said.

"I will," Hazel answered.

At the same time, a British private came to inform Nev that the major was ready to move.

"I will go now," Nev said as he went outside and mounted his horse.

"Forward, march!" the major shouted. The command was relayed down the line. The soldiers moved out slowly, all of them on horseback.

"With this many personnel, the Maroons will perceive us as a threat," Nev said to the major.

"We will scale down once we get to the foot of the mountain and establish a base camp. We will have the white peace flag flying at all times," Major Russell said.

"A blue and yellow banner signifies peace for the Maroons," Nev replied.

"We will fly a blue and yellow banner starting tomorrow," the major answered.

The British cavalry moved purposefully at a moderate pace towards the Blue Mountains. In less than two days, they were scheduled to arrive at the first area designated for a base camp.

Far away in the mountains, close to the center of the Island, James and his expedition arrived at the lake. It was a beautiful and very peaceful place. The lake spanned approximately five hundred meters in diameter. The water was cool and clear. The air was fresh and clean.

Early the next morning, at sunrise, the lake displayed a scene of many colors that sparkled continuously. It was special for everyone to see. The people enjoyed the moment. Myka's physical appearance was beginning to alter due to her pregnancy. She was very tired and extremely irritable, at times, despite being in a tranquil place.

"We should stay here for two days," Myka said to James.

"I agree because it's pleasant and beautiful here, but we must move on in due time," James replied.

The Secret Passage

Later that day, one of the Maroons returned and said the journey ahead was clear for now. Nina also returned from the rear. When Nina arrived, she was breathless, and all seven members of her party came with her. It seemed like they ran all night. The message was straightforward and clear.

"British soldiers are following us," she said.

"How can this be?" James asked.

"Do not be surprised. Sometimes our own turned against us, Mr. Gordon," an elderly woman said. Her name was Zefire. She was slightly petite, with a very dark complexion and long silver hair. She was a very attractive elderly woman. She carried a special wooden staff which was given to her by the Maroon elders in recognition and honor for skillful service rendered or special knowledege. A staff bearer was usually a councilor and a highly respected one.

"What do you mean?"

"It means we may have traitors among us," Myka replied.

"How far away are the British troops and how many of them are there?" James asked.

"There are about one hundred of them, and they are approximately one day away," Nina answered.

"If they capture us, they could almost guarantee Nanya's surrender, and that is a favorable speculation. We have to avoid being captured. Nina and her squad will not return to the rear. If we have a traitor among us, that person is behind us tainting our trail, and my great friend Nev is also in grave danger. I don't know the intentions of the soldiers behind us, but I believe it's not in our favor," James said.

"We will get ready to leave in the morning," Zefire said.

Everyone looked at her in surprise.

"Why not immediately?" James said.

"They will catch up to us if we stay here too long," another woman said.

"Don't be afraid. Get everyone ready to leave early in the morning. I have an alternative route—a secret which I will reveal in the morning. I don't feel the soldiers will get far traveling during the night," Zefire said.

On the eastern end of the Island, Nev, the major, and the cavalry that followed them were making progress.

"The Blue Mountains look closer than they really are," Major Russell said to Nev.

"A few more hours and we will be there," Nev replied.

"The British Empire wants to put an end to all rebellion in the West Indies," Major Russell said.

"When they put an end to slavery and the slave trade, then they might put an end to the slave uprisings," said Captain Mack, who was riding on the right side of the major.

The next hour, they came to a small village called Trinityville. The five hundred men cavalry did not stop. They marched on for another two hours until they reached their destination, a place called Maccer Succer, where several tributaries flow into the Rio Grande River. It was late in the evening and Major Russell ordered his senior officers to establish a wide perimeter with extra soldiers on guard. The rest of the regiment erected several tents and rested for the rest of the night.

In the central mountain, morning came and the Maroons were ready to move again.

"Make sure everyone is present and no one left here last night. If there is a traitor among us, he or she will try to establish some form of communication to the British soldiers, but it's all right, I want the solders to notice our trail," Zefire said.

The leaders reported that everyone was present.

"Tell everyone to tighten and lighten their load. On the other side of the lake, where the cliff meets the water, approximately ten feet below the surface, there is a cavern. In this cavern is a labyrinth of tunnels. Choosing the right ones is important for us to make it to the west. These caves connect through the mountains. If we follow the right path, we should be out within ten hours. We should cut our journey by three to four days. We have to travel while it's daylight. We cannot allow night to come upon us inside these caves. These caves are heavily infested with vampire bats. They are strictly nocturnal and they sleep while the sun is out. Even though there is little sunlight in these caves during the day, it's enough to keep the bats at bay. As soon as the sun goes down, they will awaken, and they will rise extremely furious if they find us in those caves. It is imperative that nightfall does not find us in the caves or none of us will survive. I am old and I get tired easily, but I'd rather take my chances in the caves than with the British," Zefire said to the leaders who assembled with her.

"Do you know the path to take once inside the caves?" James asked.

"There are markings on the walls that our elders from past generations left behind, and I have journeyed through them several times. I will lead the way."

"I will be in the rear. The sun has risen and it will not stand still. Let us go now. I don't want to be captured by the British, and I don't want to be eaten by bats either," James said.

"He is right, we should leave at once," Zefire said.

The Maroons went to the other side of the lake and disrobed to their bare minimum garments. Zefire and five Maroons were the first to enter the cavern. One Maroon returned to guide the others on the short underwater journey. James was the last to enter the underwater cavern. He dove into the water and followed a guide rope, going down about seven feet beneath the surface; then he went horizontal about ten meters and entered the cavern. It was like a large room with a pool. The room was not dark as expected, but some natural light seeped in through holes between large rocks. The spacious cavern had some stalactites and stalagmites connecting to form solid columns. The ground had fine white crystal sand. The ceilings were covered mostly with the multitude of vampire bats sleeping.

"This way. We have to hurry," a man said to James.

James was at the rear, and the multitudes were making their way through the caves. The pathway through the caves was marked. The older Maroons led the way and maintained a steady pace. Zefire and Myka were in front. Myka had mentioned that the traitor may not be among them at this moment, but that person may have informed the British soldiers of their movements. She stated that the traitor might be among those left behind.

Simultaneously, at the foothill of the Blue Mountains, Nev, Major Russell, and approximately two hundred soldiers were preparing to advance further into the Maroon territory. The rest of the soldiers were ordered to remain and establish a strong fort.

"Will the Maroons know that we come in peace?" Major Russell asked Nev.

"As long as we keep the yellow, blue, and white banner flying, that will signify our approach as peaceful," Nev answered.

The journey became more difficult as they ascended. They had to walk and lead the horses.

"I would like to have a cottage in these mountains one day," Major Russell said.

"I would like the same for myself," Nev replied.

"It is very peaceful here," Captain Mack said.

"When we make our cottages here, the tranquility will depart," Nev added.

It was getting close to midday. The men had not taken a break.

"We have to press on, even though we are tired. Two more hours to go; by tomorrow this time, we should be near the village," Nev said.

"These men are some of the fittest soldiers in the regiment. They should be okay at this altitude," Captain Mack said.

An hour later, Nev pointed out the rest area. It was far away, but it was within a reasonable distance.

Presently, in the central rural mountainous jungle, inside one of the mountain caves, the multitudes were making their way.

"We have to pick up the pace. We should have reached the central junctions already. When we reach the junction, wait for James and guide him through so he will not get lost. The largest cave facing west is the path to take. Please don't delay, for night will come quickly," Zefire said to Nina.

"Yes, ma'am," Nina replied and then remained at the junction.

An hour later, James arrived at the central junctions and met Nina.

"Time is running out, sir. Let us go swiftly," Nina said.

"Not before disrupting our trail so it will be confusing," James said.

"That's a good idea, sir."

It took them about an hour to cover and disguise the trails.

"I feel if we don't hurry, nightfall will catch us in here," Nina said.

At that exact time, the group of foot soldiers who were following the Maroons arrived at the lake. They followed the trail to the other side of the lake and entered the cavern.

"They will never escape from us. We will slaughter them all inside these caves," the leader and captain of the squad said once they entered the underground caves.

The Maroons had deliberately made the entrance into the caves easy to find.

On the estate in Easington, a letter arrived from England for James.

"I was wondering if I should meet with James and Myka in St. Elizabeth," Hazel suggested to Yanera, who was gazing out at the Blue Mountains.

"If you wait for them to come here, it might be better. James, Nev, and Myka are already gone, and we can't say when they will return. If you leave, this place can fall apart. I don't feel you should leave," Yanera said. "The letter that was delivered, who is it for?"

"It was for James, from Miss Ann," Hazel said.

In the Blue Mountains, Nev and Major Russell had arrived at their resting point. There was a small waterfall. The waterfall cascaded into a pool nearby. The water had a whitish appearance.

"This is a good place to rest for the night," the major said.

"We can also hydrate and replenish our water supply," Captain Mack added.

"I will make a campfire," Nev said.

The soldiers began to set up several small tents while Nev selected some dry wood for the fire.

"Why is the water so whitish?" Major Russell asked.

"The limestone dissolves into the water under the pressure of the water current," Nev answered.

Fifteen minutes later, Nev started a large fire in the middle of the camp.

The flames blazed bright and gave off a flavorful aroma. Most of the soldiers sat around it because it was comfortable and warm.

"I like the refreshing aroma the fire gives. What is causing it?" Captain Mack asked.

"It is the eucalyptus and sweet wood; when they burn together, they give off a special aroma," Nev said.

Some of the soldiers made tea and shared it with everyone. It was evening and the sun had begun to set.

On the other side of the country, the first set of Maroons had exited the caves, but James and Nina were still deep inside them, trying to make their way out before it got dark.

The vampire bats almost never attacked people on the outside. Sometimes they attacked livestock, but not as furiously as they would in the caves. Inside the caves, the bats would get the impression that they were under attack, and then they would defend themselves and their territory by swarming their attackers and biting them to death. Even if the victim survived the bites and bleeding, they would contract a deadly disease that would make them insane and very sick. Eventually, the victim would suffer and die. The Maroons were aware of this scenario.

"We have to hurry now," Nina said as they ran fast through the caves.

James was in the rear and Nina was slightly ahead.

"It sounds like someone is following us," Nina said.

"It sounds like the soldiers are in the caves," James replied.

The soldiers were advancing quicker than expected. They were close to the junction. James could hear them. He was running as fast as he could, hoping that when the soldiers reached the junction, they would lose sight of where to go. Nina was much faster than James, and she waited for him on occasion.

"Do not wait for me anymore. Night is at hand. Go quickly!" James told her.

By this time, the parties of Maroons had all exited the caves.

"Quickly, gather some dry twigs and fallen tree branches. We will start a fire after James and Nina exit the caves," Myka said to the people around her.

Inside the caves, Nina saw the opening to the outside, and just when she was about to sprint for the exit, she looked behind and did not see James. She slowed and halted.

"I can't leave him behind," she said to herself.

In a split second, she turned around and dashed towards the junction to find James. About 500 meters into the caves, she found him. He was out of breath, but still moving along. Nina went up to him and gave him water from her water bag.

"I told you to go ahead," James said.

"Save your breath, sir, and hold on to this rope," Nina said. She tied a small rope around James's right wrist and tied the other end on her left wrist. The rope was approximately four feet long. They rested for a minute or two to catch their breath. "Are you ready now, sir?"

"I have been ready," James replied.

"We will start slow, then we will gradually increase our speed. Breathe deep and slow. Breathe the same way as long as you're running. Your legs will get heavy and your chest will feel like it's going to burst, but the fatigue will alleviate if you breathe right. Drink some more water so you will not get cramps."

They started running again. This time, they stayed together, keeping a steady, moderate pace. James became tired again, but he kept on running although the pain in his legs was unbearable. His chest walls felt like they were going to explode. He tried hard not to think about it, but it was not easy. He knew he could not give up. Many thoughts ran through his mind. He thought about being a father and a husband, and being an advocate for the people he loved. He remembered when he was a boy, and the good times he shared with Hazel, who was like a big sister to him. He thought to himself, what if Hazel had not persuaded him to stay with her and how his life might have been different. Slowly, his tired lungs, chest muscle, and legs began to rejuvenate. His mind felt at ease. He was running easier now. He felt good. He kept in step and stride with Nina, who was a very conditioned runner. She did not leave him again. James did not fall behind anymore. Fifteen minutes later, they saw the exit. They were elated that they had made it to the end. When they went out of the caves, the people cheered. It was minutes before sunset.

"I felt we were being followed. If I am not mistaken, our pursuers saved us because the bats found them," James said.

"You're lucky and we are too. Light the fire! The fire will ensure nothing exits the caves here tonight," Myka said.

"We will take it easy from now on. Let us look for a place to rest because it will be too dark to do anything soon," Zefire said.

FABIAN COMRIE

In the Blue Mountains Nev, Major Russell, and the fifty British soldiers were high above base camp, approximately five thousand feet, but they were still a far distance from the summit. The soldiers ate dinner. Some drank coffee and some drank tea, but all of them had a piece of potato pudding.

"Captain Mack!" Major Russell said.

"Yes sir!"

"How is everything?"

"Everything is wonderful. We have several men guarding the perimeter round the clock with a shift change every four hours," Captain Mack answered.

"I am getting tired and I will call it an early night. We have to rise early," Major Russell said.

"Yes sir!"

Suddenly, a huge cloud, like a hand with its fingers pointing, arose from the eastern horizon. It spread across the sky in every direction, while moving fast towards the west.

"What a weird-looking cloud formation," Captain Mack said.

"I hope this cloud blows away soon. It's making the place darker than usual,"

Major Russell said.

"I have never seen a major storm in May. This is unusual," Captain Mack said.

"Does this cloud look like a storm to you, Nev?" Major Russell asked.

"I don't know, it might blow away or it might give us some torrential rain."

On the other side of the Island, James and the Maroons noticed the changes in the sky, and darkness came after.

"A powerful storm is coming," Zefire said.

"What should we do?" Myka asked.

"We may have to return to the caves," James said.

"It is an alternative, but there are safer caves in the hill approximately two miles ahead. These caves were the habitats of the Taino Indians. These caves are not infested with vampire bats. We will be safe if we make it before the storm comes," Zefire said.

"Let's go, everyone! Keep moving this way!" James announced loudly.

James and the Maroons descended to a lower mountain range while trying to get to the place called Cave Valley, where they would weather the storm safely. James and the Maroons knew that bad weather was approaching quickly, but the British soldiers with Nev were unaware of the impending storm. Nev knew that they were in for a terrible storm. He wanted to separate himself from Major Russell and his soldiers. He did not trust Major Russell because he was not fully clear about his intentions for the mission. He also knew that Major Russell had bribed some of the Maroons to spy for him. The storm was a perfect cover for Nev to escape.

Valley of Caves

"One more mile to go," Zefire said. "Keep moving, everyone." Suddenly, it began thundering, and lightning flashed everywhere. A strong wind came upon them. The people scattered and ran quickly into the nearby caves. Inside the caves, the people were cautious. They inspected them for insects and snakes. They quickly made the caves comfortable by making fires for warmth and light, and by padding rough floor surfaces with dry grass and leaves to lounge on. The perils of the journey, for the most part, were behind them.

A Moment of Terror

In the Blue Mountains, the storm fiercely confronted Major Russell and his men. Nev had separated himself from Major Russell's regiment. He confiscated many weapons and hid them as best as he could before leaving. The heavy rain and strong winds were accompanied by powerful lightning and loud, explosive thunder that frightened the soldiers who were newly oriented to the Island. Most of them had never experienced a hurricane. Most of them fled hastily as if they were being attacked by cannons. Some of them were confused. They did not flee to safety, and many fled to danger because they did not know where they were going. The storm was relentless. After a few minutes, showers of large hailstones came down on them rapidly. The forest trees began to fall left and right. Hysteria encircled them significantly. It was an intense moment of overwhelming terror.

"Organize the men and stay grounded!" Major Russell shouted to Captain Mack.

"I need everyone to get in an orderly formation!" Captain Mack yelled.

The storm muffled his commands and blew heavy debris and scattered them around him. The commanders were powerless.

After the storm passed, most of the men survived. A few were dead and some injured. Their immediate mission was to get everyone to the base camp before the sun rose.

In the valley of caves, in the northwestern region of the Island, James and the Maroons rested peacefully while the storm raged on and passed.

In the Blue Mountains, Nev found himself under a large tree trunk. The huge tree was down, but its powerful roots and branches and other trees that had fallen before it kept it from touching the ground. The huge tree had formed a roof that protected Nev underneath it. The morning had just begun. The darkness was dissipating. Nev crawled from under the tree trunks. He looked around to orient himself.

"Thank God I am not hurt," he said to himself.

He looked down the mountainside, and he could see the chaos. He could see some of the soldiers trying to get to the base camp at the foothills. Nev climbed the mountain to get to the other side. It was a struggle. When he reached the peak, he rested. The mountain peak was flat. He walked for over a mile until he started descending to the other side. The other side of the mountain peak was untouched by the storm. It was very steep. He walked slowly down the slope and into the valley in a diagonal direction. He knew his chances of finding fresh water were better in the valley than on the mountainside.

As he was going down the side of the mountain, he saw smoke and heard the seashell horn blow. He had no means to send a signal, but he knew his ordeal was ending. The signal was an alarm for food. He marked where the smoke was coming from and estimated its position because he knew the smoke would not be there for long. It took Nev another hour to cover two miles in the thick forest. He finally came to where he saw the smoke. He saw three men. He called out to them.

"Are you a slave that has escaped?" one of the Maroons said.

"No, I am not," Nev replied. "I am here to warn you that the British are coming to invade and occupy the Blue Mountains and the John Crow Mountains."

"Did you come to spy on us?" another Maroon asked.

"Nev is this man's name; he is a free man and a distinguished member of our community," a woman said as she came out of the jungle with two other men. She was the squad leader. Her name was Joanya. Nev remembered her traveling with Cojohn. Nev was escorted to see their chief leader, Nanya.

"Your Excellency. I was en route with Major Russell and fifty of his men to see you, but we took a heavy beating from the storm last night," Nev said.

"We know you did your best to slow them down by burning the sweet wood and eucalyptus together, and we laced the stream with the bitter cassava sap—measures that will not harm them but will cause them to sleep very soundly and be disoriented for a period of time when they arise," Nanya said.

"I managed to hide some of their weapons and ammunitions. I could not carry them," Nev said.

"What you did for us is greatly appreciated. As for those among us who believe it will be better when the British have total control over the Island, who are hoping to live in a better place and be at peace, they will learn soon that what governments promise can be deceptive," Nanya said.

"This is true, Your Majesty," Nev replied.

"The British are powerful. It will not be possible to fight them for long. The idea is not to drive them away, but to make them realize that we belong here. Our sovereignty must be recognized and respected. I will not give my honor away and be a slave," Nanya said.

Nanya knew that the Maroons could not match the firepower of the British, and it was only a matter of time before the British would subdue them. A few minutes later, Nanya told Nev to lead a party of men to the weapons he had confiscated.

"I don't want you to fight for us. Return to Mr. Gordon after you show us where the weapons are. We will attack the base camp tonight; then we will move on," Nanya said.

"After I reveal where the weapons are, I will go west to rejoin James. The major will be searching for me now. I cannot return home," Nev said.

Nev was eager to leave and reunite with James.

In the west, James and the Maroons had a good night's sleep in the valley of caves. It rained all night.

The Last of the First Jamaicans

In the morning, James and about twelve other persons organized themselves to hunt for food. They formed groups and went in three different directions. James and his crew went north, another crew went south, and another went west.

After a few hours, James and his crew came upon some cabanas inside a cleared and spacious forest. They were occupied by a small group of Taino people. They had chickens, goats, and pigs roaming about. They also had a large farm with banana trees, yams, cassava, coconut trees, and vegetables growing. James and the Maroons greeted them, but James was unable to communicate with them fluently because they spoke Spanish or Taino. One of the Maroons was able to communicate with them effectively. The Taino leader, an old man named Zeik, was short, medium built, muscular, and approximately sixty years old. He was bald.

"Who are you that speak for the Maroons? Are you a Maroon?" he asked.

"I am James Gordon."

"How many of you are there?"

"About three hundred."

"There are so many to feed. Bring them here, and I will prepare five pigs today and three goats tomorrow. We have green bananas and yams in abundance. Take as much as you need. When you prepare the food, waste nothing. My people will eat with your people at the feast," Zeik said.

"Thank you very much, sir," James said.

"You're welcome, Mr. Gordon, but remember; one kindness deserves another, and today is a good day."

"We came without an invitation and burden you with our hunger."

"The earth has yielded much more than what we expected, and your arrival is not encumbering to us. Everything has a purpose. Acts of kindness go for many generations, and cycle for centuries," Zeik said.

"Are you suggesting we were meant to be here and the ground provided food for us?"

"Perhaps. My people and I came here from Hispaniola. We never lived in one place for more than three or four years, but times are changing, and people are claiming the land they live on. The world will not belong to those who live in it, but those who have claimed it. If we move again, someone will claim this place, and we will lose the rights to live here again. Send for the people in the caves and stay here."

James sent for the Maroons who were waiting in the caves.

The Tainos lived in a beautiful forest where flowers, trees, and grass flourished. The tall trees made a high, sheltering canopy that provided exactly the right amount of shade and sunlight. There were many kinds of trees: cedars, mahoe, mahogany, coconut, pimento, cotton, plum, mango, and many other. The Tainos cultivated many kinds of fruit. There were bananas, citrus of all kinds, pineapples, roseapples, guava, custard apple, peas, beans, and corn. Their farms complemented the environment. Out of the valley, on the north side, was a ridge, and from that ridge, there was an ocean view. An average day, you would see a beautiful scenery of thick green forest land, bright blue skies with patches of white and gray clouds, and a golden sunlight that lasted a little more than twelve hours. The shores were approximately five to seven miles away. White powdered sandy beaches were common. Rivers, streams, and warm springs that provided water were many. The air was fresh and clean. The place was peaceful and conducive to healthy living.

The Fugitive

At this time, Nev was making his way from the Blue Mountains following the path James and the Maroons had taken. He had a knife, he was alone, and he was moving fast.

Major Russell postponed the mission of meeting the Maroons. However, that night, the Maroons found the base camp and dealt them a devastating blow by burning it and driving the soldiers out of the mountains. The soldiers retreated to Spanish Town. Two days after, Major Russell met with his superior, Governor Hunter, who replaced Governor Ashcroft. He explained to the governor that a storm had set them back. The Maroons attacked after the storm and stole some of their weapons. He also stated that he was betrayed by Nev.

"I hope you learn from this experience. If you fail the next time, I will relieve you of your duties. Your men have to be ready. Presently, they are like boys up against hard-core, well-seasoned Maroon guerrilla fighters. What should I say to my fellow superiors and the powerful sugar estate owners? Should I say, a handful of Maroon women drove a regiment of British soldiers out of the Blue Mountains? If the military doesn't perceive the Maroons as formidable, then we might as well surrender. The Maroons will come at us with everything, even magic, and we must confront them with our best. I will give you an opportunity to redeem yourself. This time be ready, and get this situation under control! I really don't feel good about fighting the Maroons either, but a directive has been given to me by my superiors to suppress all threat to the British Empire. So far, the estate owners believe the best resolution is waging war," Governor Hunter said.

"What about Nev, sir? He was responsible for killing one of the trackers, and now he has joined the Maroons," Major Russell said.

"Placing the blame on Nev should be the last thing on your mind. One man is not the problem. Please dismiss yourself immediately out of my sight!"

Major Russell was ashamed. And from that moment on, an intense hatred grew in him for Nev.

James and the migrating Maroons had spent two days with the Tainos. One evening, James and Myka were together roasting corn and potatoes on a small fire. Then Myka retrieved a book out of a crocus bag. It was a Bible and she began to read softly to James. James listened as he gently massaged her neck, back, and shoulders. Zeik was with another group and noticed Myka reading to James. He was amazed that she could read. In the morning, when James and the Maroons were ready to leave, Zeik was sad and wanted to talk to James and Myka alone. While everyone was preparing to leave, Myka, James, and Zeik separated themselves from the crowd to converse privately.

"I have a big favor to ask of you," Zeik said.

"Tell me and I will do my best to see it through," James said.

"Yesterday, I noticed your wife reading for you. I have always wanted to learn how to read, but I never acquired this skill."

"It is never too late to learn."

"It's too late for me, but I want my children to learn these ways. I want them to go with you. Teach them how to read and work with numbers."

"Being literate is a key element for survival these days, but it will take a long time."

"Take as long as you want. There are four of them, two girls and two boys. The girls were eight and seven. The boys were six and five."

"It won't be easy, and they will miss their parents. Their spirits will be down for a while."

"They have no parents. They are the orphans of my people. Take them and be like a father to them. You can care for them better than I can. These children may survive with me, but with you, they will prosper. You're not obligated to grant this favor. However, I will be forever grateful to you,." Zeik said.

"I will do whatever it takes to help them."

Zeik was very happy when James accepted his proposal.

Later that morning, James and the party of Maroons left the Taino village. The Taino children traveled with Myka, with whom they had connected very quickly. They respected her and obeyed her commands, although they spoke only Spanish and Taino.

"The Taino children seem to like you," James said.

"I want to go home. I miss my parents, and I miss sleeping in a bed. I feel like an old grandmother already. My legs are sore and weak," Myka replied.

"One week more; this journey will be a memory."

"I am so sorry. It's because of me that you're here."

"There are many reasons why we are here. It would be wrong to blame anyone," James said.

Nev was making his way west on foot, but he decided to change his course after a day and follow the North Coast route because it would be easier for him to find food and water. He planned to travel mostly at night and remain undetected. Nev headed for the small town of Port Maria. It was night when he arrived. The town was desolate. The next day he walked to a place called Oracabessa, where he rested. There was a cornfield with green corn. He ate green corn and then he rested all day in the nearby woods. Night came and he was well rested. He resumed his journey all night. The next place was Ocho Rios. He rested in the woods near a surging waterfall that emptied into the sea.

By this time, James, Myka, and the Maroons had entered the mountains of the Cockpit country. Their journey was on the final leg. Some of the Maroons began to sing. The songs energized them as they walked. The next day, the leader of the western Maroons and a party of Maroons met with James and his migrating refugees. Hiljoe was the leader of the Maroons in the west. He welcomed everyone with open arms. There were several Maroon villages scattered in the western mountains of the Cockpit Country. The Cockpit Mountain range occupied two parishes: Trelawny to the east and St. James to the west.

James and Myka spent two more days in the village with the Maroons. They felt safe and comfortable, but during this time, Zefire and Hiljoe were planning to send a reinforcement to the Blue Mountains and also commence some raids on the eastern sea coast.

"What day is today?" Myka asked James.

"I don't know," he answered.

"I know we are in the month of June. The year is 1733, but I don't know what day it is."

"It is Thursday. Today is my birthday," Nina answered.

During the journey, Nina had been very helpful to Myka and James.

The next day, James and Myka were getting ready to leave the Cockpit Country for his newly acquired property in St. Elizabeth. Joining him were the four Taino children.

Zefire also asked James to take Nina and her older brother Niko and their younger sister to live with him, and teach them how to read and write.

James and his crew bade good-bye to the Maroons. Seven Maroon warriors were assigned to guide them to St. Elizabeth safely. The Maroons had bestowed on James the rank of a commander for leading the Maroons safely across the Island. This was a very respectable position that had many favorable implications.

In Ocho Rios, after Nev rested, he followed the waterfall into the mountain approximately one mile from where it came. He was tired and decided to rest for a while before moving on. When he had rested, it was evening. It was getting late, but he moved on. The next two days, Nev traveled day and night. When he reached his landmark, before going south into the Cockpit Country mountains, he decided to rest on a beach near a lagoon.

On the western side of the lagoon was a small port town called

Falmouth. Nev decided not to enter Falmouth. There was a land mass that stretched out into the ocean in a westerly direction and formed a cove. It seemed like the perfect breeding ground for many fish. The forest on this cove would provide enough concealment for Nev to be active and still be undetected. A river also flowed into the lagoon from the hills. Nev was drained, but most of all, he was very hungry. He planned to get a lot of rest and eat a healthy fish dinner before moving again.

He found a comfortable place and he slept all night. In the morning, he made a fireplace and a shelter with coconut tree leaves. Then he tied his dagger on a stick and walked slowly out into the sea, searching for a fish for a meal. Most of the fish he had seen close to the shore were very small, and most of the big ones were still nursing their offspring. He had no choice but to go into deeper waters. He swam out further into the sea and looked down, where he saw many fish. He dove quietly so he would not startle them. Then he went to work. He got four large yellowtail snappers. It was enough for him.

Nev prepared the fish on the beach a good distance from his resting place. He buried the guts in the sand; then he went to his shelter and made a fire using flint stones and dry leaves and twigs. He seasoned the fish with lime juice from the limes he gathered from the journey. When the fish was finished roasting, he said a prayer and ate.

The fish was delicious and satisfying. Then he rested on his bed of coconut branches and leaves. When he arose, it was dark. He had three more fish left. He ate two and decided to save one for breakfast. He planned to spend the night at the cove because it was too dark to travel in the mountainous forest. While he sat on the beach, he thought of many things and felt many things, but most of all, he felt something precarious was going to confront him. He was temporarily in a state of urgency.

Suddenly, he saw a vessel far offshore heading in his direction. It docked in deep waters. Nev thought a vessel so close to Falmouth would see the lighthouse and know where to go. Approximately twenty minutes later, two small boats appeared. They were heading to the shores close to his location. Fifteen minutes later, the two small boats landed ashore. Nev hid between two big boulders on an elevation, carefully watching and listening. There were six persons. One of them was a woman. One of the men and the woman were blindfolded, with their hands tied. The other four men were armed with pistols. It was clear to Nev that this was a hostage situation. The victims were most likely being held for a ransom, and the culprits were pirates of the Caribbean.

Nev had no intentions of getting himself involved, but their intrusion on the Island had ruined his night for a good sleep. The only reason why the hostages were alive was for money. If Nev was discovered, he would be killed immediately.

"Tie the bastards up and let's have a drink," one of the pirates said loudly. He was tall, muscular, and he had a mean demeanor. "Separate them. They are too close. Don't want them to be cozy and close."

"They might find us too hospitable, boss. You're too nice," the smallest of the pirates said.

"Shut up! One more fancy word from you, and I will sever your tongue. I definitely will not be nice to you," the tall pirate said. He carried a sword and a pistol.

The short pirate was about four feet. Two of them were medium and over five feet. Their leader was over six feet tall. "You heard what the boss said. Tie them up and hurry up," the short man said.

"I need a moment of privacy," the young woman said. She was very pretty, with black hair, and she spoke with a French accent.

"Escort her to those rocks over there and let her have her privacy; make it quick! Any foolish moves and your father dies," the tall pirate said. "That goes for you too, Selvan." He was referring to the pirate who was escorting her.

Nev was watching. He became more afraid when the tall pirate pointed to the rocks near him. One of them grabbed the girl's right arm and started leading her Nev's way. Nev realized there was a very good chance of him being detected. Little by little, the pirate and the girl were getting closer to Nev. They came near the rocks between two short coconut trees and in front of the boulders.

"I will be okay from here. Give me some more space," the woman said.

She walked between the boulders, but Nev had already slipped away and hid in the bushes nearby. She noticed the area was recently occupied, but she didn't see Nev. New was almost naked. He knew his complexion would be a camouflage in the darkness. The woman started her business, and Nev was in the bushes where no one could see him.

"Let me see you closely and watch what you are doing," the pirate said as he walked towards the girl.

"How very rude of you!" she shouted.

In one bold move, Nev sprinted and leaped in the air and landed behind the man, simultaneously locking the pirate in a sleeper hold. Nev's grip was tight and powerful. The pirate did not have the opportunity to make a sound. In less than a minute he was out. The young woman saw him, but Nev signaled her to be silent.

"Don't be afraid," he whispered. "I will not harm you."

The woman was afraid, but she remained silent.

Nev bound the unconscious pirate's arms and legs and stuffed his mouth with sand so he could not speak.

"What's taking them so long?" the tall pirate said.

"Go see what's going on," the short pirate said to the other medium-sized pirate. "They must be doing the hanky-panky, boss. He was kinda sweet on her."

"Shut up!" the tall pirate yelled.

The other pirate went over to the rocks to investigate. He saw the girl, but he did not see the other pirate.

"Where is Selvan?" he said to the girl.

"Don't you see I am not decent yet? Don't come any closer! Selvan is in the bushes over there, doing his business," she said.

The other pirate went to investigate.

As soon as he went into the bushes, Nev swiftly emerged behind him and applied the deadly sleeper hold. The pirate was out cold and most likely seriously injured. Then Nev bound his hands and legs and put sand in his mouth.

A few minutes later, the tall pirate said, "Something is wrong!"

"Maybe they're taking advantage of the young woman in a threesome, boss," the short pirate said.

"Be quiet! All you ever have on your mind is hanky-panky," the tall pirate said. He went over close to the tied-up man and looked around. He was a little unbalanced from being drunk. Then bang! A shot rang out from beyond the rocks, and the tall pirate fell on his face.

"Boss, get up, boss!" the short pirate cried as he knelt over the tall one's body. Then he took out a pistol, threw it to the side, and raised his arms up and yelled, "Don't kill me, I surrender!"

Nev and the woman ran towards him. The woman quickly cut the ropes off her father.

"I will not kill you, but I will not let you go free," Nev said to the short pirate. "Give me the ropes so I can bind him to a tree."

They quickly tied the short pirate to a coconut tree.

"One word from you, and I will put sand in your mouth," the woman said.

"Yes, Miss Boss," the short pirate replied.

"You and the lady are free to go now, sir," Nev said.

"We wouldn't know where to go," the man said. "We don't even know exactly where we are. I am Jack Bolden. I am a planter and investor from Tortuga. I was on my way to St. Lucia when our ship was attacked by pirates. We were separated. They made most of the crew walk the plank and drowned, after they robbed them. They held us for ransom because they said I was rich. They demanded money. I told them they would have the money delivered in less than ten days. They took us here and promised to release us when the money was delivered." Mr. Bolden was sixty-five years old, with short white hair.

"If we take the lifeboat, we can make it to Montego Bay in the morning. There is a small British Navy fleet that is stationed there. State your position with them. If they move fast enough, they can capture the pirates that abducted you, sir," Nev said.

"What is your name, sir?" the woman asked.

"My name is Nev."

They got in the boat and paddled away heading west. Nev paddled the boat for two hours continuously.

When he arrived in Montego Bay, they searched for the British Naval station. Within a few minutes, they found it. There were several guards on duty. Nev docked the rowboat and helped Mr. Bolden and the woman onto the docks.

"Take me to your commander, I have urgent matters," Mr. Bolden said to one of the sailors on guard.

The woman turned and looked at Nev and smiled after he lifted her onto the dock. Before she could say a word, Nev was already departing.

"Wait for us please," she said.

"You're in good hands. I have to hurry. Take care, ma'am," he replied.

Nev was out of sight shortly after. It was almost daybreak. He decided to stay on the sea coast and row the boat south and then east to St. Elizabeth.

When the sun rose, he was south of Montego Bay. The water was clear and he noticed an abundance of conch. He dove and retrieved a few of the shells. Then he cracked one open and ate it. He had to get to St. Elizabeth soon, where he hoped to reunite with James and Myka.

James was already in St. Elizabeth. Lord Mans was still living on the property; although he had sold the land to James, he stayed in the house. He was relocating to England in three weeks.

"I am afraid that something has happened to Nev. He said he would be here waiting for me," James said to Myka.

"I hope he is all right," she replied.

"I have to get back to Easington fast."

"When are you planning to leave?"

"Tomorrow."

"I don't mind staying here without you, but I feel you should wait here a little longer," Myka said.

In the evening, Nev had reached his destination—the town of Black River, off the coast of St. Elizabeth. He managed to trade the boat for some working clothes and some boots. Slowly, he continued his journey without delaying too long. He wanted to be on top of the mountain before nightfall.

At the Easington estate, Hazel, Yanera, Albert, and almost everyone on the plantation were worried about Nev, James, and Myka. Hazel called a meeting.

"James and Nev have never been gone this long," she said, "and there is much unrest on the Island. In five months we have to resume sugar production again. Still, I don't know if James, Nev, or Myka are okay."

"Do you want me to get a party and search for them, Miss Hazel?" Albert asked.

"And where would we start?" Hazel asked.

"We could send a few servants to St. Elizabeth and see if they are there. It would take them at least ten days. My husband can take care of himself, and I feel James is okay," Yanera said.

"I feel we should wait at least one more week, Miss Hazel. In the meantime I will prepare the land for growing sugarcane. A crop of coffee will be ready this year also," Albert said.

"All right then, we'll wait another week before sending out a search party," Hazel said.

Time to Run

It was dark before Nev made his way on top of the hill and into the savannahs of northern St. Elizabeth. He was determined to reach Redberry. He had approximately twenty miles to go, and he kept on walking. He thought about what happened the night before. He would never forget the beautiful woman and her father. Hopefully, he might see them again, he thought to himself. He was also looking forward to the end of this ordeal and to be united with his family.

Nev walked all night, and when it was morning, he was in Redberry. He was on the trail, but he felt he would reach the house faster if he took a shorter path through a cattle pasture. He would save a lot of time. As he walked, he passed several herds of cattle feeding in the tall pangola grass. The cows saw him and ignored him. The house where James stayed came into view, and he gave a sigh of relief. The journey was done, he said to himself. However, he saw something among the grass that made him curious. He looked more keenly and noticed a cow giving birth. He stopped momentarily to look, but he did not want to interfere.

Not too far away was a large, muscular, mean-looking bull. The bull seemed displeased with Nev's curiosity and most likely presumed that he was a threat. The bull started advancing towards Nev in a steady trot and, at the same time, poising itself to make a powerful charge. Nev immediately recognized what the bull had positioned itself to do. In an instant, he started running. The furious bull started after him, matching his increasing speed. The pasture was surrounded by a wooden fence enclosure.

The closest fence was 250 meters away. Nev knew if the bull struck him, he might not be able to walk again. He felt the bull gaining speed, so he made a sharp right turn, and then another to the left, but the bull made the adjustments quickly. His knife fell when he tried to retrieve it. His only means to defend himself was gone. He was moving at full speed, but it was only a matter of moments to the fatal outcome because the beast was so fast.

I am going to die, he thought.

Suddenly, the fence was close, and Nev, at his own power, quickly went airborne like a flying fish. High up he went, and then he stretched out and maintained a horizontal position while flying forward swiftly until he cleared the fence. The bull halted and watched the amazing feat. The animal was disappointed, yet amazed and humbled by Nev's extraordinary escape.

"Ha ha ha! Nev, are you okay?" James shouted.

Nev looked at James, out of breath, and smiled. "I am perfectly all right, but why the loud belly laughs? I could have died if that bull had caught me," he said.

"I have never seen anyone move so fast or jump so high!" James said.

Nev did not respond. He got up and settled himself.

"Where were you going?" he said to James.

"I was going back to Easington to find out what happened to you, because I was expecting you here," James said. "I have many things to tell you."

"I just want to forget most of the last two weeks," Nev said.

The men shared some of their stories of traveling across the Island. James postponed returning to Easington on that day. However, after a week in Redberry, they decided to return to Easington together. They agreed that the trip to Easington was too perilous for Myka, and they promised to return to Redberry soon.

In three days they arrived at Eastington. At first, Albert and Manwa were worried when they did not see Myka, but they were glad when James updated them. Hazel also gave James the letter from Ann. He was eager to read it. In the letter, Ann stated she suffered many days of what she thought was seasickness, but when she arrived in England, she realized she was pregnant. She broke off the engagement with her fiancé. Her son's name was Mathew Gordon. She also stated she wanted to return to Jamaica and start a family with James. The letter brought mixed feelings to James. He did not know how to respond, so he wrote Ann a letter that stated he was happy she had their son, and for them to be together was not possible because he was engaged to another woman.

James only shared the news with Nev. Nev said that James was in a lot of good trouble.

"What's good about the troubles I am going to face?" James asked.

"You will have many children, and they will need a father like you. The problem you are going to have now is raising them. That is a good thing. As for me, I feel that there are hard times ahead of me, James," Nev said.

Guilty Until Proven Innocent

For the last two weeks, Nev had been having nightmares and moods of despair.

That evening the family had dinner together: Nev, James, Hazel, Manwa, Albert, Rayne, and several others at the plantation house. Dinner started at around 6:00 and ended about 7:30. At that time, Major Russell and twelve soldiers invaded and surrounded the estate house.

"How can I help you, Major Russell?" James said loudly.

Major Russell was in the front yard, mounted on a white horse with a horseman to his right and one to his left. "We would like you to hand over the fugitive and traitor, Nev!" he said.

"Why?"

"He is wanted for aiding and abetting the enemy, and carrying out acts of treason against the British Empire."

"This is rubbish. Where is the proof? You can't arrest him without valid evidence," Hazel said.

"My soldier saw him stealing our muskets. Muskets the Maroons used against us," Major Russell said.

"My husband was your guide to the Blue Mountains, and now you seek to kill him. Is this the way you pay for his services?" asked Yanera.

"If it's me you're here for, Major, here I am, but please, do not hurt the others," Nev said.

"Arrest him," the major said.

Three horsemen dismounted and bound Nev's hands with ropes.

"I will ride with him to ensure that he will not be abused," James said.

"Stay here, sir. Whatever happens, look after my wife. Weep not for me; God is with me. If I die, I will be with him," Nev said.

Nev mounted a horse, and the major and his posse rode off with him to Spanish Town. Nev offered no resistance. The next day, James went to see the governor of Jamaica in Spanish Town. Governor Robert Hunter was an ex-military leader, and James felt that he would be sympathetic to Nev's plight. He was a governor in the United States previously. James arrived at Spanish town early that morning. He waited two hours before seeing the governor.

James was waiting in the courtyard at the executive manor in Spanish Town.

"The governor will see you now, sir," a soldier said.

James followed the soldier to the governor's office.

"Mr. Gordon, sorry for making you wait so long," the governor said.

"Your Excellency, please call me James."

"What can I do for you, James?"

"Nev has been placed under arrest by Major Russell. He claimed Nev led him and his men into an ambush," James said.

"I understand Nev is a free man, and he is also a British citizen. He will be subjected to a fair trial. If he is found guilty of treason, he will be executed. If he is innocent, he will be freed," the governor said.

"Governor, Nev is innocent. He does not deserve to be sentenced to death."

"Such a thing is dreadful. I know Nev is a loyal comrade, but the law must take its course. He will be given a fair trial," the governor replied quietly. "All executions will be carried out by the state publicly to set an example and give a satisfying closure to the victims and their family."

"Can I see Nev before the hearing?" James asked.

"No one shall see him. If you have any evidence, take it to our constabulary department. I will grant you one favor. I will have the hearing a week before the execution. Everyone who is related to him can come to the hearing. The hearing will be the last Wednesday of June, when all substantial evidence will be examined."

"Governor, Nev is not a traitor. Please take into consideration the position he was in."

"You seem more worried about Nev than he is worried about himself. I will inquire thoroughly into the reason why the major accused him of treason. Believe me, James. It will not sit well with me to execute an innocent man," Governor Hunter said.

"Thank you, sir."

James felt he had done what he could to influence the governor of Jamaica to take an interest in the case. He returned to Easington, where the rest of his family and everyone on the plantation awaited him.

"The governor said he would examine the case to see if the charges against Nev were valid. On the last Wednesday in June, there will be a hearing, which we are allowed to attend. There they will announce whether Nev is innocent or guilty," James said.

"What if he is found guilty?" Hazel asked.

"I can't say what will happen. It will be hard to watch. I will take it as very personal between the major and I," he said.

"Sir, avenging Nev if he is executed will cause more problems. If he dies, it will be his time to die. It's not that I don't love my husband. I love Nev very much, but if you avenge his demise and kill the major, the British authority will turn on us and consume us. Everyone will suffer. Please reconsider and do not set your mind on vengeance," Yanera said.

"She is right, James," Hazel said.

"I know she is right," James replied quietly. "Myka is in St. Elizabeth. She has many tasks at hand, and she needs all the help she can get. Albert, take your family and go to St. Elizabeth and start constructing three cabins. Make them large and spacious on five-acre parcels. Laz will tell you where to build them. I will give you the house plans before you leave. Take some of the servants and their families with you. Please take men that are skilled in carpentry. The rest of us will stay until Nev's plight is decided," James said.

James felt responsible for what had happened to Nev, but there was not much he could do. The Blue Mountains had become a war zone. The major and the Maroon leader, Nanya, were very reluctant. They were also formidable warriors. The British and the Maroons knew that it was a matter of time before the British conquered the Blue Mountains. The Maroons were not capable of withstanding a superpower like Britain for long.

The Maroons in the west were watching, but they were not physically taking part in the battles.

A week later, the major met with the governor in Spanish Town.

"Your Excellency, we have made significant progress on the Maroons of the Blue Mountains. We are capable of wiping them out in a few weeks," Major Russell said.

"Quite an accomplishment, Major. We have the Blue Mountain Maroons close to submission, or extinction. Now tell me, how will the rest of the country feel when they hear that we have wiped out the civilization of the Blue Mountains?" Governor Hunter asked.

"The planters will know that, once and for all, the British military is here to protect and serve them against all foes," Major Russell replied.

"And fulfill their sinister deeds," the governor answered.

The major turned away as his face hardened in a loss for words.

Then the governor spoke. "On the other hand, many plantation owners are mostly absent. They reap the profits that are created here, but they live in England. They care about their British bank account more than the welfare of Jamaica. They don't need military protection. Furthermore, the slaves and freemen that live here are not supposed to be Britain's enemy. They should be our allies.

"Nanya had held back from fighting in full force because her reservation was a deliberate tactic. If they can't fight us now, they will fight us later, in the next generation, and into the next century. Do you know why the Maroons in the west have not participated in the wars? Yet, they communicate with each other often, from here to Cuba, Hispaniola, and Tortuga. We might have an edge with modern technology and education, but their ancient ways and their abilities to apply them are superior. Our abilities to properly use the technology we call modern are unsteady. Why did your men become hysterical and confused in the mountains during the first campaign? Have you ever thought that Nev might have saved you and your men from being massacred after the storm? Why are you so anxious to kill him? Is it because you realize that he is far more intelligent and capable than he is alleged to be? I have reconsidered my position! I will only enforce what's best for this nation! War is not a good option."

"But, Governor…"

"Be still, and listen for a minute, Major! It's not polite to interrupt!" Governor Hunter said. "I am not looking for a military resolution that will cause a genocide. You will not destroy Nanya and her village. You will approach her respectfully, and negotiate a peaceful settlement. If she accepts our diplomatic resolutions, then we can say it's a victory. But if she does not, brace yourself, because there will be bloodshed from coast to coast.

"There might not be any gold on this Island, but it's full of other valuable resources that we can all benefit from. I am sick and tired of harassing poor people. None of us will live forever, but we are in a position to set the country on a course that will make it a place suitable to live for everyone for a long time."

"I will proceed as you order, Governor," Major Russell said.

"Use the head that's on your shoulders this time, Major. Nev, who has been charged with treason—do you have any solid evidence against him?"

"He is responsible for misleading and causing the death of many of my soldiers. Also, he has being charged with supplying the Maroons with weapons and ammunition, sir. I have several witnesses."

"If he is guilty, then he will hang alongside Lincoln Jack, the pirate, and five of his men," Governor Hunter said.

"Lincoln Jack has been captured?" Major Russell asked.

"He is in Montego Bay under the custody of the British Navy," Governor Hunter answered.

That was good news and a big blow to piracy in the West Indies.

The Execution

On the last Wednesday in June, 1733, James and Hazel went to the hearing that would decide Nev's fate. The governor and Major Russell were present.

"Let the hearing begin!" a military officer announced. "All rise," he said as the military judge entered the room. The jury selected consisted of plantation owners and some high-ranking soldiers.

"The proceeding is the trial of Nev Teachman for treason against the British monarch. I am Judge Jenman Jackson presiding," the judge said.

The hearing began and Nev told his story. His hands were still bound in ropes. Nev had no one to testify on his behalf, and five soldiers testified against him.

They took a break before announcing the verdict. Approximately one hour later, they assembled to hear the jury's decision.

"We, the jury, have found the defendant Nev Teachman, a freeman and a British subject, guilty of treason," the foreman said.

Then the judge said, "The jury has found the defendant Nev Teachman guilty of treason for aiding and abetting against Britain in a situational crisis. I hereby sentence you to hang until death on Monday, July 12, 1733, at noon."

Hazel burst out into a scream, and James took her outside the courtroom.

"He doesn't deserve this, not Nev. Tell me this isn't real, James!"

Hazel wept all afternoon. When Yanera heard the news, she wept also. Almost everyone on the Easington estate was unhappy. July 12th was near, but no one wanted that day to come.

Yanera requested permission to see her husband before the day of hanging. Her request was denied. He was under military custody.

James told her to leave Easington and go to St. Elizabeth. It would be best to get things off her mind. Hazel decided to send her daughter Rayne with Yanera.

On the day of July 12, 1733, there were seven gallows, six for the pirates and one for Nev. There was a crowd of dignitaries from plantation owners to free persons and slaves. There were many government officials present. The stage was set for the public execution.

A soldier addressed the crowd on the event of the day. It was like an outdoor amphitheatre concert waiting to start.

"Today is a day of justice that will bring a conclusion to some of our enemies. Lincoln Jack and five of his vicious associates will face justice today. Lincoln Jack terrorized, killed, and robbed many citizens he and his crew encountered on the seas. He also held many persons hostage for ransom. He showed no mercy in his pillages. Today Britian will show him justice. Lincoln Jack abducted the fiancee of Lord John Aschroft, a former governor of Jamaica, but she managed to escape and summon for help. The prompt response of the British Navy resulted in the capture of Lincoln Jack. The honorable John Ashcroft and his fiancée are reunited and are here today.

"Next, we have an ex-slave who led some British soldiers into an ambush and traded their weapons to the Maroons. Today, we will bring justice to a traitor called Nev Teachman," the soldier announced to the waiting public.

"Did he say the ex-slave's name was Nev?" Lord John Ashcroft fiancee asked.

"Yes, are you ready for this, my dear?"

"The men who violated me and my father deserve what's coming to them, but the man who rescued us, his name is also Nev," Lord Ashcroft's fiancée said.

"Elizabeth, that name is very common. When the prisoners take their places on the gallows, you will know. Do not interrupt unless you are sure the man is innocent," Ashcroft said.

"Let's get closer so we can see better. Let's sit near the governor," Elizabeth said.

In a single file, the assailants were marched out and led up a stairs to the gallows. When the prisoners took their places on the gallows, Elizabeth recognized Nev immediately.

James and Hazel were there and called out his name. "I love you and God bless you, Nev!" Hazel shouted.

"I will do everything for your family!" James yelled.

At the same time, the fiancée of Lord Ashcroft said, "I know that man!"

"Which one?" Governor Hunter said.

"The black man," she replied. "He is the one who rescued my father and I. I can't watch him die. He is Nev and I owe my life to him. If it wasn't for him, I might have been killed by those pirates. Something is wrong! This is not right!" Elizabeth said loudly.

"Are you sure of this, my dear?" John Ashcroft asked.

"Yes, I am sure that he is the man who helped us. I can't believe this is happening. We are going to kill the person who saved me and my father. I wish my father was here to verify what I am saying is true."

"Governor, we have a problem!" Ashcroft said loudly.

The governor stood and raised his right hand and walked to the gallows. "Captain!" he called out.

"Yes, sir?"

"Return the Negro prisoner, Nev, to his confinement immediately, until further instructions from me only!" the governor said.

"What did you say, sir?" the captain said.

"I said, return the black man to his quarters now! He will not be executed today!"

At once, Nev was taken from the gallows and escorted to his prison quarters.

James and Hazel were equally surprised that they were leading Nev off the gallows.

"Proceed with the execution of the other six men as scheduled," the governor told the commanding officer.

Governor Hunter realized that he had to thoroughly investigate the added dimensions regarding Nev's situation. Elizabeth, Lord Ashcroft's fiancée, was the daughter of a wealthy and influential British business-man who had made a substantial number of investments in the British Caribbean islands, especially Tortuga and Jamaica. Lord Ashcroft was the owner of many estates throughout the Caribbean and the owner of the logging company that exported wood for furniture from Central America to England. He was also a former governor of Jamaica.

"What happened?" James said to Hazel.

"I don't know, but I feel Lord Ashcroft and his fiancée had some-thing to do with it," Hazel said.

James and Hazel went to the governor and requested to see Nev.

"After the execution of the pirates, we will see him," the governor said.

The six pirates suffered the fate of the gallows. The governor, Hazel, James, Lord John Ashcroft, and Elizabeth, went to see Nev, a few hours later.

Lord Bolden, Elizabeth's father, was summoned from Montego Bay to give his account. His story was verified by the coast guards in Montego Bay.

"I have heard many bad things about you, but I was doubtful. If it was not for Elizabeth, I would have killed a man who is more patriotic than any government official I know," Governor Hunter said to Nev.

"It is good to see you again, madam," Nev said to Elizabeth.

"I didn't get a chance to thank you or say good-bye. You helped us and left. We went back to the beach and arrested the pirates we left there, and captured the rest of them in Tortuga," Elizabeth said with tears in her eyes.

"Governor," Lord Ashcroft said.

"Yes?"

"If he was an enemy of the British Empire, Elizabeth would not be here, nor would we have captured Lincoln Jack."

"Set him free immediately. I will give him a full pardon and reinstate his freedom as a citizen of Great Britain," Governor Hunter said.

Elizabeth and Hazel cried because they were happy, and Nev went home with James and Hazel.

"Mr. Gordon."

"Your Excellency?"

"There will be a ball at the House of Parliament on Friday afternoon. I will expect you and everyone here to be there. If you don't come, I will send my guards to arrest you, and later I will try you for the gallows," Governor Hunter said with a smile.

"We will be there, Governor," James said.

James, Nev, and Hazel left for Easington soon after. The rumors spread quickly that an innocent man was almost executed.

Strange Suspicion

"Nev, after a situation like this, it would be wise to be secluded for a period of time. Yanera is on her way to St. Elizabeth. I feel you should be with her. We cannot trust the major or the governor. They could devise other means and come after you. We have to be a step ahead in order to live with what's going on now. You're a lucky man. It was a miracle Elizabeth was present at the execution," James said.

"I will leave before nightfall. James, I believe some of your luck rubbed off on me," Nev said.

"Why are you leaving so early?" Hazel asked.

"Just a strong feeling that there will be no better time than soon," Nev replied.

"Something doesn't feel right to me either," James said.

"If the major is going to come after me, sir, he will go to Easington first. If he does not find me there, then there is no telling what he might resort to," Nev replied.

"I fear this is true. We have to prepare ourselves and be ready," Hazel said.

"Our hunches might not be right, but it's safe to be prepared," James said.

That night, Nev left Easington for St. Elizabeth with sixteen women and their children and four wagons with horses. They would travel night and day until they reached St. Elizabeth. Friday came and Hazel and James went to the ball at the House of Parliament. Hazel, James, Lord Ashcroft and his fiancée, Elizabeth, Rammy, Major Russell, and many guests were present. The best of foods, wine, and beverages were provided and lavishly laid out for the feast. Before the ball started, the governor called James and Hazel into a room. The major and Lord John Ashcroft were present.

"Where is Nev?" the major asked.

"I don't know. He left Wednesday after he was released from prison," James replied.

"Mr. Gordon has never suffered a loss by rebellious slaves or by the Maroons," the major said.

"He is lucky," Lord Ashcroft replied.

"Not luck, but we give the slaves optimal support. We try to make them feel good about themselves," Hazel said.

"Treating everyone fairly goes a long way. The slaves are human, and their rights must not be ignored," James added.

"The reason I am holding this ball is to discuss a treaty I want to propose with the Maroons of the Blue Mountains. Major Russell has to meet the Maroons and propose a civil offer that is conducive to peace. In that offer is freedom to travel, access to the sea, and the rights to conduct commerce, but they cannot provide refuge to runaway slaves. When a slave seeks refuge with them, they must return the slave, and a reward should be paid to them for it," the governor said.

"I feel it's a start," John Ashcroft said.

"How do their leaders feel?" James asked.

"They don't feel the British should decide where they live. To them, no one is a slave, and the Blue Mountains belong to them," the governor replied.

"Conflicts and rumors of unrest will project Jamaica as unfriendly," Ashcroft said. "In order for us to move forward, we have to embrace a better relationship with everyone, a relationship that fosters trust and equality. The old ways and policies must be abandoned for Jamaica to advance."

"I agree with what you say, Lord Ashcroft," James said.

"Myself as well," the governor replied.

The major was silent.

That evening, James and Hazel stayed at the ball for two more hours before leaving. They talked with Rammy about many things; then he bade them good-bye and left.

"Take care, my friend, and be very careful of the major. He is very spiteful," Rammy whispered to James.

Starting Over

James and Hazel headed straight home that night from Spanish Town to Kingston and then to Easington.

"What is that glow? It is not time to burn the sugarcane fields yet," Hazel said.

"The estate is burning!" James yelled.

James rode off in a hurry when he saw the estate was on fire. When they arrived at the plantation, he quickly looked around the house to see if anyone was around, but he did not see anyone.

"Quickly! Ben, go and see if the slave quarters are okay. Massu, check on the livestock," Hazel shouted to the men who had escorted her to the governor's ball. She entered the plantation yard.

"Stay away!" James yelled.

Suddenly, the house was completely engulfed in flames. The stables were on fire, and a few of the slaves' houses were burning.

"The animals are not in the stables, sir," Massu reported.

"There is no one in the village, sir," Ben reported.

"My servants have scorched my property and left with our livestock," James said.

They watched the house burn until morning. The next morning, one of the slaves who took care of the livestock returned. His name was Michael.

"Micheal, what happened?" James said.

"Nev told me to evacuate the stables and take the animals to the east side across the river, sir," Micheal answered.

"Where is everyone? Nev is in St. Elizabeth," Hazel said.

"No ma'am, Nev sent me here this morning. Yesterday in the evening we relocated the animals. Last night everyone evacuated the plantation," Micheal explained.

"We have to see Nev at once," Hazel said.

When Hazel and James went to the east side property forest across the river, they met Nev. He explained to them what happened.

"While you were at the ball, some of Major Russell's men came and set the estate on fire. The major has recruited a few Maroons that are no longer in allegiance with Nanya. These Maroons work for pay and the promise of fortunes. I was on my way to St. Elizabeth when I was intercepted by a band of Maroons who informed me that the major had paid men to burn the estate after I was hanged. I returned to warn the people, and we relocated the animals."

"What we have lost is incomparable to what we could have lost if you had not returned," James said.

"The major has become our adversary. It will be difficult to know his intentions and how to counter what he has planned for us," Nev said.

"Keep the animals here for now. Tomorrow, some of us will return to the plantation house to assess the damages," James said.

"Lately, it has been one problem after another. What should we do?" Hazel said.

"This incident will set us back, but we will rebuild and pretend as if we were not hindered. We will outfox the foxes and manage our business more cleverly. I will not be discouraged. Keep your head up, my sister, for we will start rebuilding soon," James replied.

The following week, James started the cleanup and rebuilding of the estate house. He made an appointment to see the governor, Lord John Ashcroft, and the major. He explained to them that he was in need of investors because he was planning to expand in livestock, venture into other areas of farming, and open a marketplace for commerce in Kingston.

"I don't know who burned my estate, and I don't care to know. The sugarcane fields were untouched. My servants did not run away. I am motivated to rebuild and forgive," James said to the governor and Lord John Ashcroft.

"Can you relate to the Maroons after they burned your place?" the governor asked.

"Is there a better option, Governor? The Maroons have unique skills that we could benefit from. Not only are they the best guerrilla fighters, but they are also expert farmers and fishermen. Trading with them is essential, and we can benefit from each other. We can grow foods that will thrive here from other countries with similar climates. We can expand, improve, and diversity our production."

"I believe this will work," John Ashcroft said.

"I believe we can work together, slaves and freemen," James replied.

"I feel this will begin a new era of prosperity for the country," the governor said.

"I like his ideas, they are fresh and uplifting," John Ashcroft said.

"I would like to have the major bring this idea forward through the peace dialogues with the Maroons," the governor said.

"I would like the major to be an investor also," James said.

The major visited James and Hazel in Easington a week after.

"Major, it is good to see you," Hazel said.

"It's good that you're rebuilding quickly," Major Russell said as he held his head down. A feeling of guilt overcame him and he seemed remorseful, but he did not admit his involvement with the burning of the estate house.

"We still have a lot of work to get done. When we first planned to build this house, we decided to use bricks and blocks of stones for the foundation, so the house withstood the fire much better than we thought it would," Hazel commented.

"It will be better than before, and so will everything else," James said.

"I have read the proposal you sent me. The governor and I have fully approved of your suggestions. In a time of war and tension, the resources and fabric of the society will diminish, but a time of peace usually brings prosperity with hard work and unity. The Maroons are more intelligent than I had perceived. However, the one thing they will not agree with is returning runaway slaves that seek refuge among them. They say it is not their way," the major said.

"That's a delicate issue. Your job is not easy, Major. We would like you to join us as an investor as soon as you can. It is important to us. You have an army to feed, and we can provide the food for them," Hazel said.

"My salary is not substantial. I have no income to invest," Major Russell said.

"You don't need money to invest, just your efforts to provide some security and endorse us to your connections," Hazel said.

"In twelve years, you will be in a position to retire comfortably, like a man who has found a treasure," James replied.

"Jamaica has some of the finest beach properties, and I would like to retire and live on one of them," Major Russell said while laughing. "Count me in, and from now on, you can count on me."

James and Hazel felt the major probably knew who was responsible for the arson, but it did not matter now; the past was unchangeable. They wanted to make the major an ally and move on.

The three days after, the major made a desperate and brave move in order to end the disputes between the Maroons and the ruling British. Major Russell went on a mission into the Blue Mountains alone to see the Maroon leader. He made his way in the heart of the mountains and navigated his course close to the village where he was captured and held hostage until his plea was relayed to Nanya.

"I admire your bravery to enter my garrison alone. You left yourself to the mercy of the lowest ranking Maroon fighter," Nanya said.

"Pardon me for intruding like this. I took the risk to inform you that there is a better way for both of us," Major Russell said. "The British government's ways are laced with deceptions. They have shown me that their intentions are not going to benefit Jamaica now or in the future. It's like a person who promises love and devotion, but has no heart to begin with. This is my perspective and what I really feel. Yet, I know there is a better way.

"My superiors in England sent me here not to maintain the peace, but to destroy anyone and anything that stands against them. In other words, the British government sent me here to kill you and the rest of the Maroons. I have come to realize that if I kill you, it will not bring peace. The uprisings will continue. I have been a soldier most of my life. Being a soldier in a time of peace is better than being one in a time of war. Peace will bring prosperity with work and collaboration—prosperity that will involve the Maroons in every way: free trade, land to farm, cattle to raise, and the right to partake in fishing off the country's coastal shores without harassment. The time has come for us to put aside our differences and bring together what we have in common to better ourselves."

Nanya was relaxed as she listened attentively. "What about the slaves who come here seeking refuge. Will you still force us to turn them over?"

"Their owners will pay you handsomely when they come for them. The governor and the land owners have agreed that the Maroons cannot harbor any runaway slaves. I know this is a major problem."

"Do you feel if we don't provide a haven for runaway slaves, the revolts will end?"

"I don't know."

"Your offer of peace is reasonable, but it must be done officially so everyone knows that this agreement is true. Some of us are doubtful of the ways of the British. Some of my people want to repatriate to Africa because the Ashanti are the dominant tribe at present. It will be difficult to please everyone or even the majority. I am also weary of fighting," Nanya said.

"How do you know the Ashantis are ruling in Africa?" Major Russell asked.

"We know our people," Nanya said. "The ships arriving recently with the African slaves are of the Kromantie tribe and not Ashanti. The Kromanties will not be so eager to dwell with us when they run away because we are not Kromanties. We are Ashantis.

"The British government will eventually assign more soldiers to Jamaica to suppress any uprisings and control the people. This action will therefore result in a state of tension that will set the foundation for a revolution. I believe the Kromanties are natural warmongers who seek to fight when there is no conflict. They embrace war and look forward to it as a rite of passage. They will rebel in slavery and freedom. It's just a matter of time.

"If Britain wants peace, I suggest they end the slave trade abruptly, and if they intend to maintain peace, they must start treating their foreign subjects and citizen properly. So far, the practice is to dominate, exploit, and humiliate the poor. As long as this practice continues, there will be disagreements. Africa was once our home, but not anymore. Jamaica is home, and we want to feel at home here. We should have equal access to the privileges that a government enables. The British Empire should treat us with dignity, and not try to obliterate us. There is enough land here for everyone to live on and prosper," she said.

"I understand your position. I will make a plea on your behalf to the governor," Major Russell replied.

"I have considered the options and decided to give what you have suggested a chance," Nanya said.

"Thank you. I will leave now before it gets dark," Major Russell replied.

Nanya ordered a squad of Maroon soldiers to escort the major to the nearest British post.

The major returned to the governor's quarters in Spanish Town with the information. The governor composed the documents that would grant the Blue Mountain Maroons land to live on and privileges to travel and trade freely. For the most part, the documents had many conditions, but it was a start.

The major met the governor to discuss the treaty.

"Major Russell! The government of England wants Nanya dead, but those in the British parliament in London are far from understanding the continuous turmoil that would engulf this country if Nanya died by our hands. Britain would realize that they are not invincible. This action will never sit well with the Maroons. The retributions would cause hell in Jamaica. I haven't felt well these past few days either. My health is failing, but I feel I must set this country on the right path before I go. I will relay to England that the Maroon leader, Nanya, has met her fate in battle and is no longer a threat," the governor said.

"Yes sir."

"Russell!" the governor called out loudly.

The major paused to listen.

"You will be rewarded for your gallantry."

"Thank you, sir."

Later that year, 1733, the governor sent a proclamation to the government in Britain stating that Nanya, the Maroon leader, was killed in battle. The major was promoted to Lt. Colonel, and he remained in Jamaica. Jamaica experienced a time of peace and prosperity. Nanya, the Maroon leader, was alive and well. She turned her efforts to farming and commerce. Months later, Governor Hunter became very ill, and Lord John Ashcroft became governor again.

"James, I don't like being interim governor. To tell you the truth, I took the position again because none of these other plantation owners has enough common sense to drive a bunch of chickens off their roost. I would sincerely recommend you for this position," Governor Ashcroft said.

"I am deeply honored that you would see me fit for the position, but I am not motivated to be governor, and I don't want to disappoint anyone. I don't even have a formal education," James said.

"All right, man, but I want you to stand by me and help me with the tough decisions. I want to do my best and complete the good work Governor Hunter started."

"I will stand by you in everything that is right and that you can guarantee. I will not attend the long, pointless meetings and debates that are conducted every quarter in parliament. Nor will I squander myself in any lavish feast on the weekends."

"These things are necessary for the state of affairs and to appease the wealthy," Governor Ashcroft said.

"I understand, but I don't need to partake of them, Your Excellency," James said.

James returned to St. Elizabeth and completed three more cottages and quarters for the servants. During this time, Lord Mans returned to England and shortly after died in Wales. Rayne, the daughter of Hazel, was at this time preparing to attend school in England the following year. The father of the Taino children never visited them. The children from the Maroon village never returned to live with the Maroons again. The children were very contented, but they needed a teacher. Someone with a well-rounded education and a desire to teach. Yanera and Myka were doing a good job of teaching. Myka was almost nine months pregnant, and Yanera was also helping Hazel manage the two estates' finances. James wrote Ann and requested her to return to Jamaica and manage the school and a library. Six months later, she responded with some interesting news. Ann was married and had no desire to return to Jamaica soon. As for their son, he was thriving very well, and he was comfortable with his stepfather. She stated she was expecting again. She insisted that she would send some necessary teaching material to help with the school.

Hazel had a hunch that the sugar industry would decline and livestock would thrive. Governor Ashcroft was very interested in purchasing the whole property at Easington, but Hazel wanted to keep twenty-five percent.

"The governor is a tough businessman. I wonder when he will agree on our proposal," Hazel said.

"He is certainly a well-tuned capitalist of a higher order," James replied.

Rayne was a schoolteacher, but she was still very young. Hazel did not want to delay her much longer from getting a tertiary education. Hazel had started arranging for her to attend a boarding school in England. Seven months later, the estate house at Easington was completely rebuilt.

Parenthood

"**M**ommy, come quickly!" Rayne shouted from outside the cottage.

"What is it, girl?" Hazel replied.

Hazel ran down the stairs and outside as fast as she could. She and James followed Rayne to the other house. Myka was having strong labor pains.

"It's all right, she is going to have a baby. Go and get Yanera and Manwa," Hazel said to Rayne.

"Be calm and don't act so outrageous," James said to Rayne as she ran.

James was uncomfortable.

"You are about to deliver the baby," Hazel said to Myka. "James, wash your hands; get some towels and a basin with water for me to wash my hands."

Hazel spoke with authority. James realized it was time to listen and follow her orders.

"Straighten up, Myka, and walk to the bed." Myka did exactly as Hazel said.

"James, if you can, get two or three more pillows," Hazel said.

James brought the towels, basin of water, and then went to get the pillows.

"Breathe deeply and slowly. This will help you relax. There is no need to be afraid. The pain is intense but it's tolerable," Hazel said to Myka quietly.

Yanera and Manwa entered the room. James returned with the pillows and towels. Yanera had a small box with a pair of scissors and several pieces of white cords, like shoe laces, and a bottle of alcohol. Manwa took the pillow from James and set them under Myka's shoulders, elevating her shoulders approximately thirty-five to forty degrees. Hazel took off Myka's bloomers, pushed her knees up, and spread her legs apart. James was walking out the room. "Don't leave, James!" Myka said. James turned around immediately.

In a matter of moments after positioning herself, fluid exploded into Hazel's face and chest area. The amniotic sack had ruptured suddenly.

"She is crowning," Hazel said.

"Wipe Hazel's face with a towel, James," Yanera said.

James dried Hazel's face.

"Get ready, Myka, take a deep breath and push," Hazel said.

Hazel supported Myka's pelvis and pubic area with her left hand. With her right hand, she formed a "U" with her thumb and index finger, supporting the southern borders of the vagina. This measure helped to sustain the uterus and vagina from injuries while she pushed.

"This time, wait for the contraction, then push," Yanera said.

"All right, I am ready again," Myka said.

"One, two, three, and push," Hazel said. "The baby is coming!"

The baby's head was visible. With the next push, the baby's head exited face down. Immeadiately after, its body rotated sideways which made it easy for the shoulders to pass through the vaginal passage.

"It's a girl!" Hazel said. Yanera quickly opened the baby's mouth and cleaned it. Next, she put her mouth over the baby's nose and gently aspirated some debris. The baby began to cry. Her color brightened into a beautiful pinkish color that signified good health. Manwa opened the box and grabbed two of the strings and gave James the scissors. "Clean the scissors with the alcohol," she said to him.

She tied the umbilical cord approximately three inches from the baby's navel, and another a few inches after.

"Cut the cord right here between the ties," she said to James, pointing to exactly where she wanted the umbilical cord cut. James did as she said precisely. Yanera dried the baby and wrapped her neatly in a dry blanket.

"Women, brace yourselves. She is about to deliver again," Hazel said.

Quickly the women cleaned away the area under Myka's hips to make way for the next baby.

"Once again, Myka, gently push," Hazel said.

Myka took a deep breath and pushed. The baby's head came through, but this time, a portion of the umbilical cord was wrapped around the baby's neck.

The umbilical cord was still an important part of the baby's cardiopulmonary system until complete delivery. Compromising the cord could endanger the baby.

"Stop pushing!" Hazel said. "The cord is around the neck. Do not push until I tell you to do so!"

Yanera quickly cleaned the baby's mouth and nostrils, repeating the same technique she did for the first child. Manwa tied off the cord in two places and cut between them.

"Ready, once more, slowly push," Hazel said.

Myka followed Hazel's instructions, and the rest of the baby's body eased through the birth passage without difficulty. Suddenly the baby started crying.

"It's a boy," Yanera said.

Manwa cleaned and wrapped the boy in a blanket, and Hazel continued to gently massage Myka's lower abdomen.

Myka was tired. She stretched and took another deep breath while relaxing her knees.

"She is having another baby!" James yelled.

"No, honey, this is the placenta. It means the end," Myka said with a pleasant look on her face. Everyone laughed except James.

"The babies are laughing at me too," James said; then he smiled.

The next year, 1734, Rayne left Jamaica to attend school in England, and former Governor Robert Hunter passed.

In 1735, a man named John Gregory became governor of Jamaica, replacing John Ashcroft. John Ashcroft, James, Nev, Hazel, and Rammy became business partners and established a logging company that successfully ventured in Georges Cayes. This place was located off the south eastern coast of Mexico. James and Hazel sold the Easington estate to the new governor. For several years, incidents of civil unrest in Jamaica were few.

James and Myka were married in December, 1735. Many attended their wedding, but the government ruled the marriage as unlawful because Myka was of African heritage. They had five more children, but more than twenty children called James father and Myka mother. In that time, the land had many orphans. Today, the Jamaican motto is "Out of many, one people." However, to many, it is the land of the fatherless.

References

JAMAICA in SLAVERY and FREEDOM. Edited by Kathleen E.A. Monteith and Glen Richards.

THE STORY OF THE JAMAICAN PEOPLE. Philip Sherlock and Hazel Bennett.

BIRDS OF JAMAICA. Ann Haynes-Sutton, Robert Sutton, Audrey Downer.

The Village Policeman

By Fabian Comrie

Barranco is a small village located on the southern coast of Belize. Living here is good but there are challenges. This serene, remote, beautiful village, is inhabited by a people who are truly committed to each other when it's necessary. Vulnerable to the strong elements of the Caribbean sea, nestled comfortably on the edge of a dangerous jungle, and welcoming to unpredictable strangers, the village of Barranco has withstood many difficult obstacles with impeccable resilience.

The Village Watchmen

For many years the village of Barranco had no official police officers or firefighters. They had instead what they called "the watchmen"—two or three people who volunteered to provide security at night, working together from sunset to sunrise. This tradition had been in existence for many generations. The watchmen surveyed the village, the seacoast, and the jungle lines. If danger threatened, they would alert the villagers.

My grandparents were watchmen. Many women and young adults participated in this group when it was necessary. Young men had to partake of this responsibility.

The watchmen were disciplined and adhered to strict principles. No consumption of alcohol and unnecessary noise were allowed while on duty. If a significant incident occured that was not reported, those on duty would be responsible.

Many problems the watchmen encountered were as a result of robbers who came from as near as Guatemala and Honduras, and as far away as Suriname. Wild animals such as Jaguars occasionally preyed on livestock and staked out the village. Stringent precautions had to be enforced whenever these circumstances occured in order to protect the villagers.

The village was situated directly in the path of hurricanes. Every year several came. The strong ones were distructive. Droughts, during the dry summer months, created the conditions that made it feasible for wild fires to ignite easily. Wild fires where especially a danger to barns and homes made of lumber.

The watchmen had an outstanding reputation that was renowned throughout the region. This reputation was a strong deterrent to those with ill intentions.

Home Sweet Home

Our home was situated on a hill close to the jungle line in the northwest corner of the village. From that location, almost the entire shoreline was visible. I lived with my grandparents and my two sisters, Krystle and Tristie. Krystle was the eldest and Tristie was the youngest. I was three years younger than Krystle and four years older than Tristie. They called me Mays.

We hardly knew our father. He went to Germany to work in an automobile factory and never returned. He wrote a few letters and then stopped. Our mother was a schoolteacher in the village, but when I was eight years old she left to further her education at the University of Florida. She visited us at least once every two years. She eventually remarried and became a professor at the University of Miami.

My grandparents were in their late sixties and very active. We maintained a small farm with vegetables, coffee, pigs, and goats. It kept us busy and provided us with sufficient food and income. This was very helpful, and even though we worked very hard, my sisters and I looked forward to playing with our friends on the beach. The beach was our playground, the place for recreation and fun. Soccer, cricket, volleyball, and swimming were some of our favorite pastimes. We maintained excellent physical condition as we grew.

Early one morning in the summer of 1980, when I was 16 years old, my best friend James came looking for me. He was two years older. He said to get dressed and follow him to the docks because he had a job offer for me.

"What kind of job is it?" I asked.

"Come and see," he replied.

I followed him to the beach. A small fishing boat was docked on the south side. The blue, white, and yellow boat had only one crew-member. He was the captain and the owner, a tall brown skinned muscular man about 40 years old. He said his name was Iman. Iman had dreadlocks, looked to be about 220 pounds, and seemed to be in good physical shape. He was looking for two men to help him fish. He hired us on the spot without a single question and offered to pay us $300 each at the end of seven days, almost six times the going rate. We were happy, and from that moment on I was looking forward to payday. We set sail before sunset and cast our fishing nets.

The next morning we went back and the nets were empty. James felt the sea current was too strong in the area where we set the nets. However, Iman did not want to retrieve or relocate them. James and I felt he was just lazy. The following day was the same. There were no fish in the nets, and Iman was not too concerned. We realized our suggestion to relocate the nets was insignificant to him, so we remained silent thereafter.

Iman always kept the radio on, day and night, and whenever the weather report was broadcasting he turned up the volume. He never called us by our names or talked too much. He called us "youth man," and it meant either of us. Iman was an unusual person; he was always talking and laughing quietly to himself.

Early, on the morning of the fifth day working for Iman, I brought him breakfast—beans, fried fish, fried dumplings, and coffee. He enjoyed it and was very thankful.

"Where are you from?" I asked him.

"I am from Jamaica," he replied.

"You have any relatives or family that you correspond with?" I asked.

"My family migrated to the United States and left me with this fishing boat. I never saw them again," Iman answered with a smile.

"Do you have any children or a wife?" I asked.

"No, I have none," Iman replied.

"Do you always travel alone, and do you ever feel like settling down?" I asked.

"I have always wanted a nice house, a beautiful wife and children, and to live in a village like this," Iman said. "But for many years I was incarcerated unjustly, which has set me back. But I haven't given up."

"Some of the young women in the village are curious and would like to meet you," I said. "They said that you are very handsome."

Then, quite suddenly, his face hardened, his eyes widened, and he seemed very upset, as if I had provoked an unpleasant emotion in him.

"Please don't ask me any more questions," he said. "There is a lot of work to be done today."

In the afternoon, the clouds darkened. The weather report forecast heavy rain and a thunderstorm. We thought Iman would send us home, but he said it was the best time to reel in the nets.

"Let's go now!" he said loudly.

As the rain came, we sailed out into the ocean. Iman was laughing and singing. Then suddenly he started crying, and after a breif moment of silence, he started laughing again. It seemed humorous, but James and I never laughed, fearing that Iman would get angry.

"He has been alone too long," James whispered to me.

"He seems to want us around," I said, "but doesn't want to talk to us very much."

"After he pays us I will be happy. We will never work for him again," James replied.

Iman knew exactly where the nets were. When we approached them, he slowed the boats and came to a stop before we lowered the anchor. We hauled in the first net, and to our surprise, it was full of fish. The rain was pouring hard, but we kept on working.

"Let's go, youth men!" Iman shouted.

The second net was also full of fish, and so was the third. Iman was right. The catch was big. We worked for two straight hours until everything was organized. Then the rain abruptly stopped and we took a short break.

When our break was over, Iman started the boat and we were heading south instead of northwest.

"You're heading in the wrong direction!" James shouted.

It seemed as if Iman did not hear. Then James went and tapped him on his shoulder. Iman brought the boat to a slow stop.

"Why you touch me?" he yelled angrily. "You trying to hurt me, man!"

"No, I am not trying to hurt you," James replied. "I am letting you know that we have to go back to Barranco, and you are going in the wrong direction."

Iman stared at James as if he saw a monster.

"Devils from the deep blue sea!" he yelled.

Then he went below deck and returned with the largest handgun I had ever seen.

"Painful rass pirates!" he cried. "Get off my boat!"

I looked at James, but saw only his feet as he penetrated the water with a perfect dive. I didn't hesitate to follow. *Boom! Boom! Boom!* Iman was shooting at us. As if we had propellers on our feet, we swam away without resurfacing. I thought I was going to die. The gun blasts were enormous.

We swam very fast for a while, surfacing only to catch our breath. We were terrified. When we were at a safe distance, I looked back and saw the boat heading in the opposite direction. Iman, for unknown reasons, did not pursue us, but left us to the fate of the ocean.

Land was out of sight. We had no idea where to go.

"What will we do now," James said, treading water.

"Pray hard," I said.

We were lost. Death was certain if we did nothing, and it was crucial that we did the right thing in order to survive.

It was still cloudy. Then, at once, the clouds opened and sunlight beamed from one corner of the sky.

"That's it," I said to James.

"What!"

"The sun sets over the jungle in the west."

"What do you mean?" James asked.

"If we follow the sun, we will be inbound for the shore," I replied.

"You're right," James said.

We started swimming toward the sunset at an easy, steady pace. We could not waste time because nightfall was coming. After an hour I was tired to the point of giving up. I needed a break, just a short one. James was an excellent swimmer and he sensed that I was fatigued. He turned on his back and shouted.

"You have to try harder and keep moving! She is probably wondering where you are!"

I could hear the urgency in James' voice, and although I was tired, it motivated me to try harder.

We could completely lose our sense of direction if night came upon us in the sea. I was tired and afraid, but from that point on, I had to optimise my swimming. After a while I caught up with James and passed him, but he was never far behind. We swam without talking, but kept watching each other and watching out for sharks. We did not intend to give up.

Fifteen minutes later land was in sight. We had about another mile to go, but were confident we would make it. As we struggled to reach the shore, James took the lead once again. By this time the sunlight was dissipating, and it was becoming dark quickly.

When we finally reached the shore we had no energy to stand, so we crawled from the surf and rested for almost an hour. Then we arose, washed the sand out of our clothes, and twisted and squeezed most the water out until they were partially dry. We knew where we were, but it was far—about five to six miles south of the village. We had to walk home.

"What girl were you talking about, James?" I asked.

"You have nothing else on your mind after we almost died?" he replied. "You talk about girls too much. No wonder they don't like you."

James made it seem as if it was my fault that Iman didn't pay us and tried to kill us instead, but since we had survived, I had forgiven him and Iman. We arrived home very late that night. I was happy and slept well until morning.

As for what happed that day, we never told anyone and seldomly mentioned it to each other. We never saw Iman again.

Changes

In the following months James and I became village watchmen. We worked together most of the time. A year later, James joined the medical division of the Belize Defense Force. He wanted to be a doctor. Three years later James married my older sister Krystle. They went to medical school overseas. They wanted to return to Barranco after school and open a private practice.

Tristie was preparing to attend nursing school in Florida and lived with our mother. I was still a village watchman and a farmer most of the time. I was 20 years old now. Most of my friends were relocating and migrating for opportunities. I felt left behind.

At that time, a civil war had erupted in El Salvador. Guatemala was in dispute with Belize over territorial sovereignty. British soldiers had set up observation garrisons at various strategic locations deep in the jungle as if an invasion was pending.

I wanted to join the British navy and attend a university to study like James, Krystle, and Tristie, but I had to wait. My grandparents were older and needed my support. During this period, my grandmother became ill and passed away.

A Career Not of Choice

My grandfather encouraged me to pursue my goals even if I had to leave. I enlisted in the military, but did not get into the British navy's medical corps because I scored very low on the military comprehensive test. The only position available to me with a low test score was the infantry.

"You can always earn the money and pursue your dreams later," my grandfather said.

In two months I was ready to depart. It was hard leaving my grandfather, but he had many friends in the village and was still capable of taking care of himself. Also, I would be able to help him financially.

The military life was fast paced and training was constant. It was a culture that admired discipline and adhered to strict regulations, but it also despised justice and self-reliance.

It wasn't easy. I had to rise very early and work very late. Everything was a challenge, but I learned a great deal, such as how to use various kinds of handguns and rifles. I practiced shooting constantly until I became good. Tracking and navigation were enjoyable. After we learned a skill we would master it under stressful conditions, like shooting in the dark or blindfolded, swimming in very cold water, or working long periods without sleep or food.

I also learned a great deal about boats, jeeps, and generators. I spent many days in the jungles of Belize, using and fine-tuning the skills I had acquired. After two years I wanted to leave. I anticipated the end of my enlistment with excitement.

After the military I returned to Barranco, worked on the farm, fixed cars and boats part time, and volunteered as a village watchman occasionally, while searching for a job in law enforcement.

One year later the call came to attend the police academy. I was 25 years old.

First Assignment

L aw enforcement was unfamiliar to me, but I felt it was a job I could do. The principles of law enforcement were not easy to grasp. There were many things to learn in a short time. Being an ex-military person helped very much.

After the police academy I went straight to my first assignment, a precinct in northern Belize City. My partner was Carlton Briggs, a renowned and well-respected police officer.

The community we worked in was peaceful. However, this was not the case the year before I arrived. The neighborhood had been crime infested, and progress was gridlocked by illegal activities. Violence ruled and the people lived in fear, but Carlton Briggs came and turned it around. He used all the resources he could to clean the community of crime. He made many arrests and outgunned the gunslingers. With the help of community leaders, Carlton started new programs to deter crime, maintain peace, and foster growth.

As a result of his relentless hard work, many new businesses were established and began to prosper. The crime rate declined remarkably, and the community became a boomtown for opportunities and investments.

For the first time in a long time there was little to do for a police officer, and routine patrols became boring.

After a month, Carlton and I were summoned to the captain's office.

He commended Carlton for a job well done. He mentioned that crime was down 80% in our precinct. He added that Carlton was one of the best police officers he had ever seen, but his skills were needed elsewhere.

The following week we were transferred to a precinct in southern Belize City where the crime rate was high. During our first week on the job there were five fatal shootings, eight robberies (two of which were home invasions), and numerous cases of domestic unrest. The crime rate was attributed to many factors, such as poverty, corruption, unemployment, and illiteracy. Southern Belize City was a fertile ground for criminal activities.

Our work was difficult and extremely dangerous. Carlton's request for three more officers was denied. Nevertheless, we threw ourselves into the work and became very busy. I patrolled nights and afternoons while Carlton gathered information. He also worked with community leaders and citizens to find ways to improve conditions.

I made myself very visible during the hours I patrolled, yet this was barely effective. It was as if the criminals were tracking my every move on radar.

After the third week Carlton and I met to share the information we had gathered. We concluded that the community did not trust the police, who had a reputation for being corrupt and unable to provide adequate security, especially for witnesses who were willing to testify against serious criminals. Local gangs, such as the Blue Rag Gang and the Black Palm Society, seemed unopposed most of the time. The Blue Rag Gang was made up of street thugs. They made their money from robberies, selling drugs, and carrying out assassinations.

The Black Palm Society was the more powerful of the two. Their leader was unknown. They exploited the Blue Rags and used them to sell the drugs they smuggled. While the Blue Rag Gang worked the streets and cause unrest, The Black Palm Society profitted extensively and remained mostly undetectable. They were the corporate criminals—they made the rules and the Blue Rags followed. If they didn't follow the rules, they suffered brutal consequences.

One night when I returned to the station after a patrol, I found that Carlton had arrested a 15-year-old boy for shooting out the lights in a park and on nearby streets.

"Are you going to keep him in jail?" I asked.

"No," Carlton replied. "I have to let him go."

"Did you find the weapon?" I asked.

"Yes," Carlton replied. "It's a nine-millimeter Glock."

Carlton seemed very worried because he knew the boy's life was now in danger. Whoever gave him the weapon would suspect him of informing the police because he had been in our custody and questioned. We did not have the facility to keep him, so that night we returned the boy to his home. His family was angry with us. Even though we had found a weapon in his possession, they said that we planted it.

That same night when we returned to the station, we had a call from the local pastor. We went to his house immediately. The pastor was terrified. He had received a blackmail letter, stating that he had to have $10,000 available in two weeks, and $1,000 for every month thereafter if he wanted to keep operating his church. A child had forwarded the letter to him, which had a palm print on it in black ink. The pastor said he wasn't going to pay. Carlton and I asked him to take some measures to enhance his security. We would also do our best to provide him with some degree of protection.

A few days later, heeding Carlton's request for help, the Captain sent us a secretary. Her name was Jane. She was a big help right from the start. Jane was a tall woman, about 5' 7", with a captivating smile, big brown eyes, long curly hair, and a dark complexion. She was charismatic and friendly.

A month passed and we had very little time off.

Mission at the Harbor

"This Sunday, let us attend church and go to my parents' place for dinner," Carlton said.

"Thank you very much," I replied.

"Tonight we have a dangerous mission," Carlton added. "How well can you shoot a rifle?"

"I'm all right," I replied.

"Well, tonight I don't have a choice. The Black Palms are smuggling weapons and drugs, and we have an opportunity to put a dent in their illegal operations."

It was a Friday, and Carlton gave Jane the afternoon off since it was also payday.

That afternoon at the station I cleaned the 30-30 Winchester and my Colt .22 revolver. I zero sighted the 30-30 as best as possible, the unofficial way, without going to a range or firing a shot. I did not have a night vision scope, which would enhance my ability to see targets in the dark, and there was not enough time to obtain one. Later, Carlton and I went over maps of the port and some scenarios.

At around 8:00 p.m., we left the station, out of uniform, in an unmarked small car. Heading for the port of Belize City, we were as ready as possible. Carlton and I arrived at the port. We left the car a half a mile from where we entered the compound.

"I received information that an illegal cargo would be in this area," Carlton said.

We positioned ourselves a good distance from the dock, where we had a good view of the area. We waited for over an hour while maintaining our silence. Then we heard the noise of a small boat approaching the docks. Smugglers sometimes operated boldly, seemingly not concerned about security or customs (which might have been paid to look the other way).

As the boat approached the dock from the sea, a white van was also arriving in the same location from the south side. Carlton and I briefly went over our communication signals—folded arms, no worries; hands on hips, caution; one hand on hips, one on chin, prepare for action. Carlton moved in closer and I took position on one of the containers approximately 150 meters away. I had to keep a sharp eye out for Carlton's safety.

We were in place when the boat docked, and the white Ford van pulled up next to it. About half a dozen men worked fast to unload the boat. Carlton moved in. In less than a minute, he signaled me to join him with caution.

As I was getting ready to descend from the container, I glimpsed a silhouette with a rifle moving quickly on the north side, approximately 100 meters from where Carlton was and about 175 meters from where I was. When I looked at the shadow again, it had assumed a prone shooting position. I felt Carlton's life was in imminent danger.

I immediately took aim with the 30-30 and fired three shots. Then I turned to see where Carlton was. He was not hurt, but I felt he was still in danger. I fired six times at everyone near him, one bullet for each target. It was over in no time.

Carlton gave the signal to cease firing. I went over to where he was. Two of the men were injured and four were dead. Carlton was shocked but unharmed.

"That was excellent shooting," he said.

After calling for backup and ambulances, we went to investigate the shadow on the container and discovered a dead man. He had a new .30-06 Colt rifle with a night vision scope, and two brand new 9 mm Berettas. The .30-06 was a very powerful weapon. Carlton told me to keep the rifle and Berettas as personal weapons because they were much better than the ones we had. The rest of the night was taken up by a lot of paperwork and statements. The boat was filled with weapons, drugs, and ammunition, including 12, M16 rifles, a dozen AK-47s, and approximately 200 kilograms of cocaine.

Good Day for Dinner

The next day was Saturday. We went back on the job as if nothing had happened. This was a good day. I made two arrests for drug sales.

Sunday came. We went to church and then to the home of Carlton's parents in Salt Creek, a peaceful and beautiful village. Carlton's parents were farmers. They raised chickens and goats, and cultivated various kinds of vegetables.

I was hungry and longed for a good, home cooked meal. The food they prepared looked and smelled good.

"I am so hungry," I said to Carlton.

"You did a good job Friday night. You shoot so well. Where did you learn to shoot like that?"

"Just luck," I replied.

"Incredible, Carlton said, so precise, and so fast with an old rifle. I can imagine you with the new .30-06."

I was silent and did not want to elaborate on the subject. The killings bothered me. I wanted to forget the incident completely.

"Let's eat, man," I said.

"The food will be gone soon," Carlton's father said, "if you don't start eating."

He was already serving himself.

"It's stew chicken with rice and peas," Carlton's mother said.

"Can I take some back?" I said.

"Yes, of course," Carlton replied.

"Who wants to say grace before we start?" Carlton's mother asked.

"Let us pray," Carlton said. "Thank you, Lord, for the food. Amen."

"I have never had a meal like this since I left Barranco," I said.

"Well, eat all you can," Carlton said.

While they were talking, I was busy eating.

"What a wonderful dinner," I said.

They laughed. The dinner was delicious.

We stayed for a while and had a pleasant conversation. I learned that Carlton had a fiancé who was about to finish law school at the University of the West Indies.

We said our goodbyes shortly before sunset. I was on duty that night and Jane was at the station covering for us. While we were heading home, Carlton told me he would retire in less than a year. He said that he wanted to take over his father's farm and expand it. Being a devoted husband and a dedicated police officer was going to be too much for him. If he retired, he could focus more on raising a family and being a farmer. However, he wanted to get the precinct on the right path. He was confident he could do it in a short time.

Uncertain Dilemma

Shortly after we arrived at the station, Jane had terrible news for us, and especially for me. My grandfather had passed and my presence was needed in Barranco. The other news were, the three dogs the pastor had aquired for his protection were poisoned, and the juvenile who was apprehended for shooting out the streetlights had been fatally shot, in the park, near his residence. I told Carlton that I was able to work until 5:00 a.m., but he insisted that I should leave immediately for Barranco and return in five days. It was a tight situation. However, because Carlton was a very good crime fighter, I decided to leave for Barranco as he had ordered. He was also my boss.

Reunited Once Again

Traveling on the southern highway was peaceful. I reminisced about some of the wonderful moments my grandfather and I shared. His life was not easy, but it was exciting and adventurous. His time was now over. I cried silently, not because I was sad, but in reverence and respect for the man who helped raise me.

The drive to Barranco was long and without incident. When I arrived home, everyone was there—James, Krystle, Tristie, and our mother. No one was really sad. We were happy to be together. The funeral service went well the next day.

The third day James and I visited some of the villagers, especially the older folks. He was planning to return to Barranco to start his medical practice within a few months. He was a doctor now.

In the evening we sat on the porch, looking out at the ocean in the distance.

"So tell me, Mays, how do you like being a policeman?" James asked.

"I don't know," I replied. "I haven't thought about it very much. I like everyone to be safe and secure, but I really don't like being a police officer."

"It's not easy being a police officer these days. The bad guys usually have good lawyers, and they get away with many things. Even when they go to prison, the sentences are too light for the crimes."

"Sometimes witnesses disappear and the cases are nullified," I added.

"Seems that it's always a struggle," James said.

"I don't know what to say, it's easier said than done," I replied. "The course that crime and corruption take is similar to the path of an unchecked, deadly disease. Crime consumes, and as it consumes it spreads."

"I will agree with that," James replied.

"The watchmen here said you were one of the best on the job," a villager said, overhearing the conversation. "You were very talented but a litte too crazy," he added.

"Being a police officer is unnatural for him," Krystle said from the kitchen door, looking at us.

"He was lazy, and nobody liked working with him," Tristie said as she walked onto the deck, smiling.

"Tristie, you shouldn't even say that," Krystle said. "You liked being with him when he played watchman here."

"We tracked and captured a jaguar when it was taking the villagers' livestock," Tristie said. "Capturing that jaguar wasn't easy. But that big cat left a significant trail of footprints that were different from goats, cows, or pigs."

"That cat was sick and wanted to be captured," I said. "It was harder to rehabilitate than capture."

"Yeah, if it wasn't injured, it wouldn't have preyed on the livestock," James added.

"The jaguar came for help," I said, "and I believe we did a good job of helping it get to the zoo."

"Yes, I wanted it for a pet," Krystle said.

"So did I," Tristie said.

"Right! A pet jaguar!" James said. "As soon as it regained its health, it would have had us for a meal. That jaguar was very strong and highly unpredictable."

"Well, where is the comparison between wild animals and criminals?" Tristie asked.

"Who said there were any comparisons? Criminals have lawyers," said Krystle.

"Criminals are more sophisticated," I added. "Not much to compare."

"That is true," James replied.

"I wish the medical community would invent a medicine that made criminals tell the truth," I said.

"I have a suggestion that may help," James said. "The basic medical skills you learned as an infantry soldier, like starting an I.V., will be very helpful. I have the recipe for getting the truth from any bad person who will not confess. It is liquid nitrous oxide and sodium pentothal. Put the nitrous oxide on a handkerchief. If inhaled, it will render you unconscious. The next step is to start an I.V. with saline and then administer the sodium pentothal slowly. By then, the biggest liar will want to preach the truth. I have a kit ready for you."

My sisters, James, and I spoke of many things that beautiful day. However, at sunset, we were interrupted by a phone call from Jane.

It was bad news. Carlton had been seriously injured in an ambush. She said I was needed urgently. I gathered my belongings, including the truth cocktail James gave me, and departed.

I arrived at the station and Jane told me the details. There were no witnesses to the crime, but I knew the two men who survived the shooting at the port were already out of jail. I went to the hospital to see Carlton, and he did not look good. The doctors said his prognosis was poor.

Somehow, I felt responsible. Carlton was an excellent police officer. I should not have gone to Barranco.

Bad News and Disappointments

I went back to the station and rested for a while, but I could not sleep. Morning came quickly and I went to the pastor's home. I felt he was a target. I told him to pay the extortionist when the time came. The pastor was upset and remarked that I was the cause of Carlton getting hurt because I was not there to back him.

After, I went to headquarters to see the precinct Captain. I asked for more help, but he said it was not in the budget to provide any additional assistance at that time. He also added that I was one of the worst police officers he had ever seen and that he had just received a complaint from the pastor.

Reconciliation

I went back to the station. I had my issued revolver, but it was a disadvantage compared with the newer handguns on the street. I retrieved one of the 9 mm Berettas and a Glock with a pair of magazines that we had confiscated from criminals. In the back of the station there was a trail bike and a regular bicycle, both in good condition.

At approximately 4:00 p.m., Jane went home. I waited until twilight. Then I adorned my dark blue sweat suit and armed myself with a Glock and a Beretta. Both handguns were ready. I left the station and headed for the park on the trail bike. I had a soccer ball with me also. No one was at the park and there were no lights on. I played alone, juggling the soccer ball and kicking it around.

From the park I could see the street where the boy who had the Glock lived. I continued to practice and exercise for approximately one hour. It was getting darker. When I was about to leave, I saw four men approaching from about 175 meters away. I pretended not to notice them. They seemed very threatening as they approached quickly. When they were about 30 meters away I turned towards them. One of them reached into his waist and pulled out something.

That's when I dropped to the ground while retrieving the Glock. By the time I hit the ground, he had fired one shot and missed. I returned fire quickly and continuously with a steady aim. The one who fired first received his portion of bullets, and then the others respectively. Three of the men were down and one was on the run. I steadied the Glock once more and fired twice in his direction until he fell. Then I checked all the men and found that they were armed. I took the money they had. One of them was still alive and in severe pain.

"Help me, please," he said. "The pain is too much."

"This pain you're feeling is the same pain you and your associates inflicted on others," I replied. "You will not bear this pain for long, because in a short while you will die. Your bleeding is too profuse for you to survive. Rest in peace."

I cleaned the Glock and left it on his body. Then I retrieved my soccer ball and left the scene.

After 20 minutes at the station, I was summoned back to the scene on an emergency call. I went there slowly, wearing my uniform.

An ambulance was there and another squad car. The man who was injured eventually died. Spectators had gathered. One woman said that the men were terrorists and deserved what they got. An old man came forward and said he had witnessed the incident. He said Carlton Briggs shot these men. He said he saw Briggs exercising in the park. I filled out a report as best as I could and went back to the station to sleep.

In the morning, Jane confirmed that the men were infamous members of the Blue Rag Gang. That day I passed by the pastor's home frequently. There were no major incidents, but that night I disguised myself in ragged clothes and staked out the pastor's home from a hidden location. I stayed at the position all night, and in the morning when I was just about to leave, a new black BMW 750i pulled up to his house. Four men exited the car, but one stayed next to the vehicle while the others went inside the gate.

I had the two Berettas in my position, so I decided to move in closer to the house. I approached the man next to the car and asked if he had a dollar to give me. He said no. Then I called out aloud "pastor!" several times and he answered. I felt relieved that he was safe.

The pastor and the men came outside the house.

"What can I do for you?" the pastor said.

"Can you give me some food or ten dollars?" I asked.

"No, go away!" he replied. He didn't recognize me.

I turned to the three neatly dressed men leaving the house and said, "Can I have some money for food, gentlemen?"

One of the men had a large envelope.

"What's in the envelope?" I asked loudly. "Can I clean the car?"

Suddenly one of them yelled out, "Don't touch the car, stinking boy! You don't have anything to do! You smell like shit!"

As they left, I memorized the BMW's license plate. I turned toward the pastor and he said, "Don't disturb me, man. You are so annoying and nasty."

"You have any leftover breakfast for me?" I asked.

"Go away now!" he replied. "You ugly, smelly, bad jackass!"

I wanted to laugh, but couldn't at that moment.

The pastor was not the only one being extorted, but he was the only one willing to report it.

The car was the property of the Olive Tree Club. This nightclub was well known to everyone. It was situated on the outskirts of the southern end of the city. The next day I went to the precinct headquarters to submit a progress report to the Captain. It was paperwork that the supervisors required. I turned in the report. When I was about to leave, the Captain saw me.

"Officer Mays," he called out.

"Yes sir," I replied.

"I want to tell you that we might be able to provide four more additional officers in your precinct," he said.

"Sir, that is wonderful news," I said.

The Captain was silent momentarily, and then said quietly, "I don't feel that Carlton is going to make it."

I did not know what to say. I didn't want to talk to him for long, so I remained silent.

"You're dismissed," he said. As I turned to leave, he said, "Good luck, and be safe."

When I returned to the station, Jane was crying. She said Carlton was dead. She cried intensely for a long time. I was very sad, but did not cry.

In the following days, after patrol, I staked out the Olive Tree Club. I noticed that a police officer frequented the club almost nightly and always left with a package. He was not a high-ranking officer and was never in uniform. I followed him one night and he went home. But when I followed him on his day off, he dropped off the packages in a safety deposit box. For a week I staked out the place where the box was. I found that the packages were being collected by another police officer, who delivered them to a police superintendent's residence. What was in the packages did not concern me at that time. I felt it was money.

I had to make my move soon, and so I planned it for the next Saturday night. The Olive Tree was a busy place on Saturday nights, and it was the right time to make my move.

One Friday when I was at the station, a storeowner named Bustamante came to make a complaint about being threatened. He said he couldn't pay the Black Palm Gang the regular extortion tax of $500 that month, but had to pay $2,000 the next month or both his businesses would be burnt to the ground.

"I am very discouraged to hear this, Mr. Bustamante," I said. "As of tonight, I will keep a close surveillance on your places."

"I may have to close my businesses and move away. I don't have $2,000 to pay a criminal."

"How much do you have?" I asked.

"Man, put fun and jokes aside," Mr. Bustamante said. "That's why people don't like you. Carlton would never make a joke like that. I am absolutely bankrupt."

Mr. Bustamante was in a predicament and obviously did not want to lose his businesses. That is why he came to me.

That night I cleaned and oiled the .30-06 Colt rifle with the night vision scope and the two 9 mm Berettas. I gave the bike a quick tune up. Then I put on the black sweat suit and black helmet and headed out for the Olive Tree. My arsenal was packed neatly in a backpack. If I waited for Saturday night, it might be too late.

The night was foggy and the roads were wet. It had just finished raining. I arrived at the club and waited at a distance behind some trees. I had a clear view of the club entrance and parking lot. The black BMW was there. I waited for a long time, to the point of falling asleep and almost giving up, but at about 3:00 a.m. the music stopped and the people started leaving slowly. Little by little the crowd dissipated until almost everyone was gone. Three cars were still in the parking lot, and one of them was the BMW 750i. Later, some men that I recognized exited the club. This was the opportunity I had waited for. Now was the time to make my move.

I pulled slowly into the gate with my one of the Berettas pointing at them. "No one move," I said. "Give me that case."

I grabbed the black briefcase and sped off on the bike. I fired twice over their heads and they took cover. This would buy me some time.

They returned fire, got in their cars and began pursuing me. I quickly got out of danger, but I also wanted them to follow me. Their cars were faster than I expected. They gained speed quickly. If it were not for the potholes on the road they would have caught me.

I was heading further out of town when I noticed a cemetery on one side of the street. Then I saw a little street that led into the cemetery. I turned off my headlights and immediately turned into the graveyard. A bullet took out one of my rearview mirrors as I headed down the dark, narrow street. I managed to slow the bike significantly before falling off. Then I got up and ran into a dark area of the cemetery. I left the black briefcase next to the bike, but did not forget my backpack arsenal.

The tombs were above ground. This was helpful for my concealment and cover. Suddenly, the three cars pulled up. I immediately took cover behind a tomb, undid my backpack, and quickly assembled the rifle. They were laying down heavy fire in my direction, so I had to be careful. As soon the bullets ceased, I positioned my rifle, aimed steadily, and squeezed off a shot. I saw a man's head explode as he fell backwards in instant death.

Another man with a rifle took cover behind some tombs. I had the night vision binoculars attached to my rifle and it was working well. I fired two rounds and two more men cried out in agony. Then I rolled quickly to regain cover at a different position. There were about seven men and three were already dead or hurt. One of the cars started to move. Someone was leaving.

"No one must escape," I said to myself.

I took aim at the silhouette driving and squeezed off two rounds. The car slowly came to a stop. I took cover again. The rifleman fired back a single shot that came very close. I felt he knew precisely where I was.

As I positioned myself to fire, the rifleman laid down a heavy suppressive fire. I had to crawl away from that location. The rifleman knew that he might also reveal his location when he fired, so he relocated himself just like me. It was a tactic soldiers and police used. I felt he was a trained rifleman.

There were three of them left. Two men were stationary, because the flash from their guns told me where they were, but the rifleman concerned me the most. He was a good shooter. The other two men were just hiding and waiting to escape.

I felt the rifleman knew my general location and proximity because his bullets were so close. I wanted to set him up.

I set the rifle stock firmly on my right shoulder and took one of the Berettas in my left hand. I inclined to my right and relaxed while looking through the rifle's sight and night scope. I could see clearly. I stretched my left hand away from me as far as I could and fired two shots. He fired back once. The Beretta exploded from my left hand. His bullet had snatched the gun from my grip precisely. It was a perfect shot, but when he took that shot his head became visible.

It was my turn to shoot, but in that instant my scope went dark.

The batteries were dead. I fired two shots and repositioned myself. I knew my shots were off target. I crouched behind a tomb as a barrage of bullets rained in my direction.

The rifleman was formidable. I was afraid. I had met my match, and my edge, the night vision scope, was gone. It was so dark that I could not see my fingers ten inches away. Then it came to me. I remembered when I practised shooting blindfolded, as a soldier. The mind and ears could perceive and locate a target like a sonar device. It took great concentration and a keen ear. Blind persons usually developed this skill. I had not practiced this skill much, but if I tried, it might save me.

I figured the rifleman had a night vision scope that was working, so I maintained my cover and remained silent.

I could hear my heart beat as I listened intensively. I took a few slow deep breaths and my heart rate decreased. I closed my eyes and listened a little more. Then, moment by moment, I could hear all three men, but I focused on the rifleman. He was the quietest. I could hear him as he crawled very slowly, moving sideways to his left. He had an advantage now. I knew that he knew exactly where I was. Then I heard him grip the rifle and shuffle to acquire leverage. He was preparing to shoot. Like an animal pursued by a predator, I sensed imminent danger.

Instantly, with one swift move, I aimed the rifle in the direction of the sounds and squeezed off three rounds. I heard his rifle fall as the bullets penetrated his body. He took his last breath. The sharpshooter was no more.

Suddenly, two men scrambled from behind a tomb and started running. They got into one of the cars and were quickly heading out to the main road. I ran as fast as I could out of the cemetery to the small main road. I took aim, but pulled the rifle down. Too many killings for one night, but then I remembered Carlton. So I aimed again and fired several times. I thought I missed, but the car zigzagged, flipped over, and burst into flames.

I went back to the bike, recovered the briefcase, and left for the station. I returned in no time.

Soon after, the darkness gave way to the break of day. I slept until Jane arrived for duty at about 8:30 a.m.

"You look so tired and ugly," she said.

"I was up all night, and you're the second person this week to say I was ugly," I replied.

"Get some more sleep," she said, "and I will wake you if anything comes up."

I went back to sleep and woke at noon very hungry.

"How about lunch," I said to Jane.

"If I get it, you will have to pay for it," she said.

"Okay," I said.

I understood what that meant.

I had no money, but curiosity led me to my locker, when I looked in the briefcase that I took from the men, it was neatly packed with money, both Belizean and U.S. dollars. I grabbed a few of the large Belizean bills, approximately $250, and secured the briefcase back in my locker again. I gave Jane the money to buy lunch that day.

"Mays, this is more than enough money," she said.

"Well, I owe you because you have bought all the lunches recently."

"It's still too much," she replied.

"Please buy lunch and keep it. You deserve it."

"Thank you," Jane replied. "I felt you were a cheapskate, but today you convinced me to believe otherwise."

"Yeah, you girls believe every single working man is rich and selfish."

The cemetery incident hit the evening news. One man said he saw everything, and when the reporter inquired, he replied that Carlton Briggs was responsible. The reporter asked the witness where Carlton went after the incident, and he said, "Carlton went underground."

It was not over. That night I kept surveillance on the superintendent who was receiving the envelopes. I suspected he was involved with the extortion of the small businesses, but I had no proof. Constables were taking the packages to him indirectly.

The superintendent lived in an upscale neighborhood with his family. He had a beautiful wife and two daughters. One of his daughters was a teenager and the other was in her early 20s. Both daughters were attending college in Miami. His wife visited them frequently.

I was patiently gathering the information I needed. The community was safe since the ghost of Carlton patrolled at night, and no one had harassed the businessmen recently.

I discovered that the superintendent had a mistress. My opportunity came three weeks later when his wife left on a trip to Miami for the Labor Day weekend. That Friday evening I watched him closely. As soon as it was dark, he left his house and drove his Mercedes to meet his sweetheart. She lived in a condominium not far from his home. He pulled into her apartment complex.

While he was exiting his car, I snuck up, grabbed him from behind, and covered his nostrils with the handkerchief dampened with liquid nitrous oxide. He passed out immediately. I placed him back in his car. Then I accessed a vein in his right hand and started to slowly administer the dose of sodium pentothal James gave to me. By this time, he was unconscious, but he was breathing.

I drove the Mercedes to a place they called Yaughbaro, known locally as Ybarra. Ybarra was an encircled cemetery of vaults with a playground in the middle. I was disguised and wore a mask. In the car I administered more sodium pentothal, and as he awoke I began to ask him some basic questions that he answered truthfully. Then I started inquiring about the Black Palm Society. The information was disturbing.

When I had enough information, I administered more sodium pentothal until he passed out. I drove the car into the middle of the playground and laid him down outside on the grass. I covered him with a blanket and a large poncho so he would not get wet or too cold. I removed the IV and left him there to sleep it off. Next, I drove his vehicle back to his mistress's place, got on my bike, and went to the station.

The next day he was found in the cemetery walking around, talking of many things. He even proclaimed that he was the one who took out a contract for the hit on Carlton Briggs. He was admitted to a mental hospital the same day, and soon after was forced to take a medical retirement. He was never charged with any crimes and his sanity was questionable from then on.

A New Era Begins

The following weeks were peaceful. The storeowner, Mr. Bustamante, and the pastor claimed that no one had been extorting them recently. I counted the money that I had discovered in the briefcase and the package. The total sum was approximately $270,000, with $50,000 in Belizean money and $220,000 in U.S. currency. I did not know what to do with the money. Returning it would certainly implicate me and blow my cover, so I kept it.

A month later, five new police officers were assigned to the station, four men and a woman. For three weeks I was busy orienting them to the locality. They were excellent officers and the community loved them. Jane was reassigned to headquarters and promoted. She was now the Captain's secretary. The community was also changing for the better. The park and streetlights were fixed, the school painted, and a community center was being established with the help of community donations and volunteers. One anonymous person donated $20,000 U.S. Another anonymous person also donated $40,000 BZD to the local church.

Two weeks later, I was summoned to the Captain's office at headquarters. He said that I could not resign at this time, but he could reassign me. He also had a Sergeant due to replace me in two weeks. He would manage the other officers. We talked pleasantly for a long time.

"Your jurisdiction has gotten quiet," the Captain said.

"Yes sir," I replied.

"Why is that?" he asked.

"It's the four new recruits, sir, and your leadership," I said. "The recruits are excellent. Their presence has had a profound impact on deterring crime."

"Well, it is a new start for the community and it feels right," the Captain commented. "Your next assignment starts in one week in northern Belize. A place called Blue Lagoon. It's a small, vibrant village with many farms and forests, a big area to cover, but your skills will come in handy there. You will be alone due to the location and population."

The Captain paused.

"By the way, one of the men in the cemetery was a police officer, the one with the rifle. He was a formidable rifle expert and won sharpshooter of the year three times. The ballistics from his rifle matches the ones that injured Carlton. I know who is responsible for the change, but I can't prove it."

"Who is it, sir?" I asked. Jane entered the office and the Captain waited before speaking again.

"Your next assignment will be confidential," the Captain said, "but if I need you I will bring you back. You are obligated for four years, and then you can resign. I had the wrong impression of you, until I saw your records and noticed that the Blue Rags and the Black Palm were either dead or running scared."

"Running scared?" I asked. "If no one is chasing them, sir, then why are they running?"

"I wish I knew," the Captain replied. "It must be Carlton's ghost."

I felt the Captain was aware of my vigilante activities, but he made no indications or comments. I also felt he knew about the corrupt police officers in the department. However, he received all the credit for turning the community around, and was promoted to superintendent.

Blue Lagoon

My next assignment was in the village of Blue Lagoon. It was ten miles away from the closest town. It was a vibrant farming village accessible by boat or car, with a population of approximately 500. The police station was situated near the lagoon on a three-acre parcel of land. I had brought a new jeep, a small speedboat, and a horse for transportation. The village was peaceful. Crimes here were minor offenses, such as fights, domestic quarrels, marijuana vending and smoking, and theft. There was a small jail at the station, a telephone, and two CB radios. There was also a large living quarters for an officer and his family.

My usual day in Blue Lagoon began with a walk through the main streets. I never displayed a gun. I wanted to look friendly and approachable. Many of the villagers talked and walked with me frequently. I also attended the primary school for morning devotion whenever I could. My presence was a mark of civil respect.

The chairman of the village was Dr. Mitchell, a retired veterinarian. He was about 78 years old and had been chairman for the last 10 years.

The chairman was the village's elected leader. It was a position of honor that required prudent management skills. A salary was not included, but the benefits were priceless. Dr. Mitchell visited frequently, just to talk, mostly in the evenings. Sometimes we talked until it was late at night.

Water to Drink

One Saturday morning at around 5:30 a.m., a loud knocking on my door awoke me. It was two young women on horseback. They wanted me to follow them. I quickly got dressed while the two girls waited with their horses inside the compound.

"We will ride with you, sir, because our horses are tired," the youngest one said. They left their horses at the station.

They led me on a farm road outside the village on a northwesterly direction. It was dark because we were going through a forest. About four miles into the journey, the forest gave way to a vast grassy savannah with scattered large trees of various kinds. In the distance there were two houses on two separate small hills.

"Is that the place we're going?" I asked.

"Yes," they replied.

We followed the road until it curved to the left at a slight upgrade. Then we were on a hill with a spectacular view of where the lagoon made a cove. The houses were far apart but visible. The women directed me to the farthest one. There were two men there who were arguing. One of the men was complaining that his neighbor's cows had destroyed his bean fields. The cows had escaped in search of water, and had stampeded through his bean fields.

"Due to the scarcity of water, the cows have no choice but to go to the lagoon," one of the men said.

"Everytime I try to improve my farm, this man spoils it with his ugly cows!" the other man replied.

Then they turned to me.

"We would like your help in solving this matter," the bean farmer said.

The men introduced themselves to me as Fabian and Teddy. Fabian was the livestock farm owner, and Teddy was the cultivator of fruits, beans, and vegetables. I listened to each man's complaints.

"It would be better if we called a meeting for another day and returned with some ideas for a resolution," I said. "Taking this matter to court will be time consuming and expensive."

"Yes, I agree," Fabian said.

"The animals need the water," I said.

"Yes," Teddy said, "but if he kept the troughs full, they would not have tried to get to the lagoon."

At this moment, the sun rose and morning came over the land. A cool and gentle breeze circulated. It was going to be a hot day, but the breeze made it tolerable.

This was an important matter but not an emergency, so I agreed to return when they had decided on a resolution that would endure and stand in accord with everyone's satisfaction.

The two men had families, and although they lived close to each other, they were not related. The women who rode the horses to the station were Teddy's daughters, Melanie and Anita. Melanie was a year older than Anita. They told me that they had tried calling me by phone, but did not get an answer.

"It's time for me to return to the station," I said.

The women were not ready to retrieve their horses from the station. They said they would return for them by noon tomorrow.

"Give them water and keep them in the shade," Melanie said.

The women directed me in another direction back to town. It was a longer way, but the roads were better. On the way back I saw more of the farms and the surrounding lands. After two miles I encountered a sign that advertised fruits and vegetables for sale. I turned into the small driveway on the left and followed the road. It curved to the left until a house was visible. Then I entered a large grassy yard where the lagoon beached once more.

The yard had several dwarf coconut trees scattered about evenly. There were fowls running about in the yard, colorful roosters, hens, and chickens. A neat row of hibiscus about four feet high lined the back portion of the yard. This home was very attractive, with an interesting landscape.

As I exited my jeep, two ferocious barking dogs, in the yard, charged me, but a tall, brown complexion man, came out of the house and shouted, "Stop!" The dogs obeyed immeadiately. A petite woman followed him.

"Good morning," I said.

"Morning officer," they replied.

"I just want to know if I could buy some fruits and vegetables."

"Yes, man, I have plenty," he said.

"I am Mays," I said.

"I am Ken and my wife is Nancy," he replied.

We walked alongside the house to a wide door that opened into a large kitchen, which adjoined the dining room. It was a very spacious house that made good use of natural light. In the middle of the kitchen, upon a plank table, were a variety of fruits and vegetables arranged in neat rows.

"What a colorful display. Did you grow these here?" I asked.

"Yes, officer," Ken replied. "All these vegetables and fruits are grown in this area."

"I need some of the spinach, scallions, yams, some oranges, and a pawpaw," I said. "Just give me a reasonable amount of each."

Nancy came inside while we were selecting the produce.

"I am glad we have a police officer in Blue Lagoon now," she said.

"I am glad to be here," I answered.

"Someone has been raiding our farm as if they were going to the supermarket," she said.

"That is very unfortunate," I replied.

"When you have the time, please check it out for us," Ken said.

"I have the time and I will start right now."

Nancy was willing to give me a tour of her vegetable gardens and greenhouse. She showed me the yam fields that were located on the other side of the main road. I followed her as we walked and looked at the many different kinds of vegetables, mints, herbs, and spices. She showed me the places where the thief had been. She said the yam field was frequently raided. I told her I would try to search for some clues. I noticed a fresh trail and wanted to follow it.

"I will be all right from here," I said.

"Okay," she replied.

I followed the trail until I was far away from Nancy. Minutes later, the trail led off the farm and into the woods. After a mile or more I came out of the woods and into an open meadow. The grass was heavy, and there was a small wooden house in the distance with smoke rising from an exterior stone fireplace. A two-foot high stone-wall surrounded the half acre yard, in which two small children were playing.

They saw me as soon as I saw them. They looked a me momentarily and fled into the house. A puppy and a dog came charging at full speed, barking wildly. I stopped at the entrance to the yard. The dog kept a safe distance, but the puppy was furious and kept coming closer, trying to bite me.

A young woman came out the house with the two children. She seemed frightened. She was also very attractive.

"Hello," I said.

"Yes officer?"

"I am Mays, the new policeman here in Blue Lagoon."

The evidence was all around. The yams roasting on the small fire were ample proof that the thief lived here. She seemed intimidated by my presence, but I was not about to make an accusation or arrest. She was poor, from what I had observed.

"How can I help you, officer?" she asked nervously.

"I am just making a friendly visit and introducing myself to the villagers."

She relaxed a little. All the while the children hung onto her dress, one on each side, staring into my face. The dogs had stopped barking, but the puppy maintained a resentful gaze.

We talked for a while. Her name was Millicent. I knew she lived with a man from the clothes hanging on the line to dry. I wanted to know where her husband was, but I did not want to ask her upfront because it would have implied some degree of suspicion. From her accent I knew she spoke Spanish, and her choice of words during our conversation told me she was very intelligent. She had long curly black hair that seemed almost blue. She was approximately 5'5" with a dark brown complexion, thick red lips, and brown eyes. She looked strong and innocent. She was neither fat nor skinny. She was beautiful.

"I have to go now," I said.

"Please return," she replied. Then she smiled.

I enjoyed the moment, and although stealing was wrong, I could not find it within myself to accuse her of stealing. Some women marry into poverty, and whomever she lived with was lucky.

I left and walked back the way I came to Ken's place. When I arrived, I didn't tell Ken and Nancy what I had discovered. My purchase was ready, but I bought more. When I was about to leave Ken stopped me.

"Wait man," he said. "Don't leave yet."

Then he brought a box with him.

"I know where you're going," he said.

"Where am I going?" I asked.

"You're going to Millicent's house, man," he replied.

"How you know?" I asked.

"Just feelings man. Give me a ride."

I had a feeling that Ken knew the thief all along, but didn't want to reveal it yet. In a few minutes we arrived at Millicent's home. The dogs barked again and this time the children playing in the yard did not run to their mother. However, they were surprised to see me back so soon.

Ken brought out the box and presented it to them. It contained toiletries and canned foods. I gave her most of the fruits and vegetables I bought. She was grateful, and I offered her a job as an assistant at the station, to help clean it and do the laundry, which she accepted.

On the dirt road leading to the house, we saw a slender Spanish man approaching.

"Papa," the little girl said and ran towards her father. The two dogs followed her. The younger boy stayed by his mother, but he was happy to see his father coming.

The man seemed a little apprehensive as he approached, but Ken started speaking to him before he reached the entrance. Millicent had already started cooking some food from the box and it smelled good with all the seasonings.

"I've been looking for you to help me with the farm, man," Ken said loudly. Then Millicent introduced her husband William to me and he relaxed.

"They brought food for us," she said, "and the officer is looking for help to clean the station and wash his clothes, honey."

William seemed to be a man of few words. He was about 5' 11" and a little over 30.

"Thank you very much," he said. "I need the work."

"Come by my house around eight in the morning," Ken said, "and we will talk more about the job."

"Okay, Mr. Ken, I will see you later," William answered.

Millicent was willing to work for me if I helped her with transportation. I promised to give her my horse. She said she would pay me for it soon. Ken and I bid them goodbye. I was glad the situation turned out well. William was desperate to feed his hungry family and he needed a chance to become a legitimate provider, but I would keep my eyes on him.

I brought Ken back to his house and then I went to the station. It was already almost six p.m. Melanie, Anita, and a young man driving a jeep similar to mine were waiting for me. He introduced himself to me as Dale, a son of Fabian. They brought some food for me, beans with fish and rice. I was quite hungry.

"Thanks for the food. How are you guys going to solve the water problem?"

"If the animals had water, there wouldn't be a problem," replied Dale.

"Can Mr. Fabian dig another well or two?" I asked.

"Well, whenever we try to dig more wells on our property, we never find any water," Dale said, "and the local drill does not go farther than 120 feet."

"What about pumping the water from the lagoon?" I asked.

"The water in the lagoon is mixed with sea water," Anita replied. "Sometimes it's fresh, but most of the time it is too brackish."

"The animals would eventually get hypertension from drinking the water from the lagoon," Melanie added.

"Hope you guys come up with a solution soon," I said.

"I hope so too," Melanie said.

The girls left on the horses and Dale drove the jeep. I was tired and ready to take a nap, but as soon as they left Dr. Mitchell, the village chairman, showed up.

"Mays, how are you this evening?"

"I am doing fine, Dr. Mitchell."

Dr. Mitchell walked everywhere he went. He was energetic and seemed to be in very good physical shape. There were two hammocks hanging on the back porch that faced the lagoon. The chairman sat in one of them, making himself comfortable as if he was going to visit for a long time. We shared the dinner the girls gave me.

"Mays, how do you like the village so far?" he asked.

"So far, so good," I replied. "I like the tranquility."

"Yes, I like it too, but you will find that it takes some work to maintain," Mitchell said.

Dr. Mitchell was relaxed as he talked about many things. He talked about the people and how they had progressed. He talked of when he was a boy and how the village was only accessible by boat. He also mentioned times when hurricanes and heavy rains crippled the village. Dr. Mitchell said the hurricane season was close and he wanted to be well prepared. He talked about the shelter, food supplies, water, and other necessities needed to survive a hurricane and its aftermath. He said the village was inaccessible by road for weeks after a hurricane. I promised him I would help in the preparations if a hurricane threatened.

Night came, and the full moon rose and reflected its light upon the lagoon. It made me feel good and I thought about having a home here. I was glad Dr. Mitchell visited me. He gave me insight into what was expected of me. I was still learning, and he was a man with a wealth of information and understanding. He left me around 10:00 p.m. and I hoped he would return soon.

The next day was Saturday, a day that felt peaceful and easy. The people were at work preparing for Sunday, but in a relaxed way without the pressures of the other days.

At about 9:00 a.m. I went over to Fabian's house to see what resolution he had planned for providing water to his cattle. He needed a well, but the water table on his property was very deep. I went to Teddy and told him what was needed, and he said he would let Fabian dig the wells on his property. The requirement was that Fabian dig three wells and that Teddy own two of them. He also said that Fabian would have access to all the water needed after he finished the three wells.

I brought the two men together and they agreed on the proposition. They also agreed to put the proposition on an official affidavit. The final resolution was to dig four wells and use them to supply water to both farms equally. However, Teddy wanted to own two of the wells because they were on his property. Both men finally came to a comfortable agreement

Fabian said he was ready to start drilling the four wells as early as next week. Fabian would pump his water into tanks on his property, and have it available for distribution through pipes to various locations on the ranch when the dry times came. Teddy wanted his well to expand his vegetable farm. Both men were planning to expand their farms.

I was happy with the resolution, but before I could leave Melanie invited me for lunch. Melanie was a good cook. The food was delicious. After lunch I headed back to the station. Millicent was there and working already. The station was immaculate when she finished.

In the afternoon, Dale, Anita, and Melanie visited.

"Hey, who cleaned the station and arranged your furniture so well?" Melanie asked.

"Millicent did all this work," I said. "I don't like to clean, but I like a clean and tidy place."

"Send her over to my place," Dale said. "My mother has been looking for someone to help her with the housework for a long time."

"I will let her know when I see her," I said.

The following week Fabian hired a crew and started digging the four wells. The news spread rapidly when all four hit the water table at less than 80 feet. Final construction features were being added to make them safe, secure, and accommodating. Fabian had also erected two large-capacity water tanks.

Above the Law

One evening while making my rounds, I noticed a black Land Rover recklessly speeding down the village main street. Two evenings later, the same Land Rover, at around the same time, sped through the village, on the main street, even faster. The driver either did not realize he was driving recklessly or didn't care. I wanted to catch him.

The next day I waited for him. At about six p.m. that Friday evening, I heard the distinct sound of the Landover. I didnt want to race through the village after it because that could cause a fatal accident. The Land Rover passed and I started to follow it with flashing lights. It slowed down but kept driving about 200 meters before stopping near the village store. I pulled up behind the vehicle and copied the license plate. The driver got out.

"You have a problem, officer?"

"Yes, I do. I have noticed this vehicle speeding through the village several times now. The posted speed limit is 25 miles per hour. At the speed you were going, you would not be able to react safely if a child wandered in your way. Your license please."

He handed me his driver's license. His name was Gerald and he was 35.

"How long are you going to keep me here? I have to go! No tickets, please, just a warning!"

Gerald was giving me orders as if he was my boss.

"You deserve a ticket this time, Mr. Gerald. Anymore comments from you and I will impound this vehicle. You can contest this citation in the Orange Walk District Court. Next time you drive like this, I will take away your driving privileges."

Gerald then reached into his pocket, took out his wallet, removed $150, and handed it to me.

"Sorry sir, I can't accept that," I said.

He was very upset.

"Just follow the speed limit when you're driving through the village, pay this ticket, and you will be okay."

"Boy! I have connections. I will have you transferred out of this village soon. Just wait and see!"

I did not reply and he left, driving away slowly. I should have taken his money and still give him the ticket, but one bad deed follows another. After that, Gerald obeyed the speed limit.

High Winds and Rain

June came and went quickly. It was now July. Schools were on summer holiday and there were children everywhere. The days were hot and humid, and the news reported that there was a hurricane gaining momentum on a course towards Belize. It was forecasted to arrive in seven days.

It was my responsibility to prepare the villagers to weather the storm. Dr. Mitchell, the village chairman, had many years of experience in getting prepared for a disaster. He was already making plans to inform the villagers about the location of the shelter and how to prepare themselves. He posted signs, and notified the local radio station in Orange Walk to make frequent announcements. Those citizens who had strong houses were encouraged to stay home, and if they were able, take in a neighbor who lived in a weaker dwelling.

The only shelter in the village was the primary school. I wanted it to be an optimally comfortable shelter. I started to get all the necessary amenities, like non-perishable foods, toiletries, fuel, generators, and lots of potable water. The next evening we had a community meeting and Dr. Mitchell laid out his plans. Most of the villagers agreed to cooperate and help as much as they could.

On July 7, two days before the hurricane was schedule to arrive, Mitch and I met again. We sat on the porch at the station looking out at the lagoon. It was about 6:30 p.m. He had brought some seasoned yellow rice, fish, and yellow watermelon. Before we began to eat, Ken, Dale, Melanie, and Anita also came to visit. Melanie and Anita brought some ackee, salt fish, and fried dumplings. We set a table on the porch, shared a delicious meal, and talked about the approaching storm.

"I am not worried about the storm itself," Mr. Ken said. "It's the aftermath and getting the resources to recover."

"Yes, that is true," Mitch said. "Usually we get cut off and isolated, and no vehicle can come in or out of Blue Lagoon."

"Yes, you're right," Dale agreed. "Only by boat can we access and exit the village."

"Ann and I will be using our boat strictly for medical emergencies," Melanie said. "We are ready in case someone is injured or sick." Melanie and Anita were registered nurses and Dale was their designated driver.

"My boat and I are also available for any worthwhile purposes," I said.

"This ackee and fish is the best," Ken mumbled, as he polished some off with a piece of Johnnycake.

"It's good, man," Mitch replied.

"We need to have some accountability records of where everyone will be staying during the hurricane," I said, "even those who are staying with neighbors."

"Oh! Millicent and her family will be with us," Ken said.

"We have two elderly persons staying with us already," Anita remarked.

"We can never be too prepared for this storm," Melanie added. "The last I heard it was upgraded to a category five with winds at 250 miles per hour. It was southeast of Kingston, Jamaica,"

Except for a higher tide, there were no visible signs that a hurricane was threatening. The sunset was as beautiful as ever. The sky was clear except for a few nimbus clouds that curtained the horizon, and the cool, gentle breezes came and went as usual.

"Melanie, Dale, and I have to leave now," Anita said.

"Thank you for the food and for stopping by," I replied.

"You're welcome," they said and left.

"I gave a speeding ticket last week to a man named Gerald. Either of you know this man?" I asked.

"That's Dale's brother," Mitch said, "and that man is a very arrogant fellow."

"He's a real estate lawyer slash politician wannabe. He's not like his daddy Fabian or his brother Dale," Ken said.

"He's like his mother," Mitch remarked.

"He's a loan shark, too," Ken said. "Whenever he lends any money, he holds on to his clients' titles for collateral."

"Now he has more land than anyone else," Mitch added.

"But if you're stupid enough to borrow money from him at 35 and 45 percent interest," Ken said, "you deserve to lose your land and be his servant."

"He is legitimate, but tough," Mitch said.

"Despite all that, he is well educated and getting richer every day," Ken said, "but we have to realize that he has a cruel business nature."

Mitch and I laughed.

"This is serious, but funny," I said.

My mind drifted back and forth on what everyone had said. This was an independent community for the most part, and much more peaceful than a big city. They were organized and unified. Most of the wealthy in Blue Lagoon were willing to help the poor, and a meal, no matter how small, fed many. It reminded me of my home, Barranco. My job as a peace officer here seemed easy, but, as Mitch said, that tranquility was not easy to maintain. Occasionally the community's solidarity would be threatened, and how committed we were as a community would be tested.

Gerald, a man I recently met and hardly knew, troubled me. He seemed to be a vindictive person, capable of becoming a disciple of evil.

"Tomorrow, I'll get some more propane and gasoline," I said.

"Let's have a drink, man," Mitch said.

"I have some coffee wine," I replied.

"That sounds good," Mitch said.

"Love it, my brother," Ken replied.

"The shelter is fully stocked, and I don't like to worry too much," Mitch said.

We sat on the porch, sipped the wine until the bottle was empty, and then fell asleep. It was a peaceful evening.

The following day was Friday and the people was preparing as much as they could to weather the storm. By mid-afternoon we had the school shelter ready. There was still no indication that a storm was threatening; however, the singing birds that usually adorned the lagoon's coastline were gone, and the farm animals were restless and had a sense of urgency about them.

That Friday a few volunteers started relocating the senior persons to the shelter. The animals were taken to high ground in case of flooding. Most of the villagers tried to secure their homes, boats, and farm equipment.

The storm had devastated the southern coast of Jamaica the day before, leaving most of the country without electricity and many towns isolated due to road damage. It was now on its way to Belize, picking up speed and strength.

Saturday morning came and there was a complete change in the weather. The day was cloudy and overcast. I visited Mitch again and he assured me that the village was prepared. He urged me to fortify the station and stay at the shelter. With the help of some villagers, we did work on the station and moved my boat out of the water. Later that evening I decided to patrol the village in my police jeep one last time. I visited the villagers who lived on the outskirts of town. They were well prepared.

Before nightfall that Saturday, I went to the store to get some personal items. The store stayed open late for procrastinators like me and for those who were paid late. There were only a few customers. I noticed a small boy waiting outside. He had a bicycle and a bag. I had seen him before, but did not know his name. He appeared frightened. By now it was dark.

I got the things I needed and, while paying for them, asked Mr. Lloyd, the storekeeper, if he knew the little boy outside. He took a glance and said his name was Enrique. I got my groceries, went outside, and asked Enrique if he wanted a ride home. He said yes and smiled. Enrique lived two miles north of the village.

"Why were you afraid to go home?" I asked.

"If the storm caught me in the streets, it would pick me up and blow me away," he replied.

Enrique looked about 10 years old. He had seen the devastation of past hurricanes and knew how powerful they could be. When we arrived at his small place, I retrieved his bicycle from the back of the jeep. His mother heard the vehicle outside and opened the door.

"What took you so long, Enrique?"

Enrique paused as if he did not know what to say.

"He was held up at the store," I said. "That's why I brought him home. There were too many last minute shoppers."

"Thank you, sir," she replied.

"Is everything okay?" I asked. "You have everything you need?"

"We are good, Mr. Mays," she replied.

"Okay, take care," I said and left.

I continued to patrol the village. The streets became empty. It was getting darker earlier than usual. It was approximately eight p.m. I did not feel like going to the shelter as yet, so I drove to some of the areas that were far from the village. I went by Ken's place and Millicent and her family were there, along with the dogs, too. I went by Fabian's place and he was there with his family. I didn't see his son Gerald, and his whereabouts were not my concern. I went to Teddy's place. He and his family had guests.

The hurricane was scheduled to reach the coast at around 1:00 a.m. Sunday. It was now 10:30 p.m. on Saturday night. I headed back towards the village from Teddy's place. I drove slowly. I was tired. The winds intensified, but it was not raining. The trees, the sugarcane fields, and all the tall grasses and plants were dancing in the strong winds and holding their ground, resisting being uprooted. No one was on the streets and the stores were closed.

I was satisfied that the village had prepared well for the storm. However, as Ken and Mitch had said, the aftermath and recovery always required more effort and labor, especially if the preparation was poor. By the time I reached the village, the wind became stronger and it started drizzling. Just as I arrived at the school shelter, lightning and thunder began. I climbed the steps to the school's main door, and before I could knock Mitch opened the door.

"Where have you been?" he asked. "Backside, look here! If you start with the worries, I will lock you outside, man."

Clearly, this was a joke. They were happy to see me and I was glad to be there. He showed me a desk that had a radio, telephone, and CB radio. The desk was in the northern right corner of the large hall.

"That's our area," Mitch said. "The hurricane has been upgraded to a category five. They called it Gilbert."

"Nice name," I replied.

The chairman had taken a census of the villagers here at the shelter and those staying in their homes. After the storm, he would recheck and verify his census for accountability.

It started raining heavily, pouring down furiously in sheets and buckets. There were many families in the shelter. Some were sleeping; some playing cards, some reading, and some were just observing everybody else. I listened to the radio to get as much information as I could. The chairman gave the order to turn the breakers off and use lanterns and flashlights.

Within an hour the storm intensified. The powerful winds and heavy rain roared like thousands of lions. It blew for a several minutes in one direction, and then changed to another. Relentless, powerful, and fast, this was one of the stronger ones. We prayed for the building to hold up. We prayed that this monstrous beast would depart quickly.

After an hour and a half it calmed down, as if it were going west over land. Everyone was quiet. I thought the worst had passed, but it was yet to come.

"This is the eye," an old woman said.

"Is it watching us," a little girl replied.

After ten minutes we heard another monster coming from the sea. The eye had given us a break, but the other side was arriving now with a dreadful roar. Families clung to one another; children held onto their mothers, mothers embraced their husbands. The wind crashed into the shelter with tremendous force, trying to uproot the entire foundation. The building held its ground, until gale force winds attacked the roof. Back and forth it swayed, to and fro. A few windows failed and part of the roof gave in, but the main hall remained intact. Another two hours passed. The force of the storm had dissipated, but it kept on raining heavily. One single raindrop was enough to leave you soaking wet. Morning finally dawned on us. What I saw from the window was not good.

Mitch gathered the volunteers. He ordered a few to remain in the shelter to make sure no one was missing, injured, or sick. The others were ordered to assess the damage to the village. I was ordered to account for those villagers who lived the furthest away. Everyone had an assignment, and they all cooperated.

Mitch opened the main door of the shelter and I was one of the first to exit. Many trees had fallen. There was no electricity. A few power lines were down, rendering some streets unsafe. My jeep was damaged superficially but drivable.

First I went to the house where Enrique lived. They were okay, except their latrine was blown away. Surprisingly, the streets were not flooded. But many trees were down, which created some roadblocks. Next I went to Ken's place and everyone there was also okay. William and Millicent were worried about their home, so he came with me to make a damage assessment.

We spent almost an hour clearing the road that led to his place. When we finally arrived we found his house demolished, as if an explosion had occurred. William looked surprised at first.

"Now I have to build a new home for Millicent and the kids," he said.

"Build a good strong one this time," I replied.

"But I have no place to live while I build my house," William replied.

Next we went over to Fabian's home. Everyone was okay, but he said he would feel a lot better when he got hold of his brother Joe.

"I never heard of Joe before," I said.

"He lives on the mouth of the cove," Fabian said, "where the sea and the lagoon meet."

The Missing Fisherman

The mouth of the lagoon had a cliff on both sides about 20 to 30 feet high, like two peninsulas that formed a natural cove. The cove opened into a vast and dynamic lagoon system. The waters came in and out. On the top of the cove were spreads of grassy, spacious land with coconuts and mango trees. Both sides were designed like a state of the art golf course and garden in one. Joe's house was situated on the northwest plateau.

"Joe is a solitary man," Fabian said. "I may see him tomorrow."

Next I went to Teddy's place, and all his family members and guests were present.

"Anyone hurt from last night's storm?" Anita asked.

"I don't know yet," I replied. "Fabian is worried about Joe, and if anyone sees him, please let me know."

"Uncle Joe is always hard to find," Melanie pointed out. "Maybe he went fishing. Wait until tomorrow. If he doesn't show up then, we start looking."

I returned to Ken's place and William told the bad news to his wife. Ken offered them his place to stay until they could rebuild their home. Millicent did not seem too upset that the storm destroyed their small dwelling place. She was even happier when William said he would start building the new house soon.

"This time, let's build a bigger and better house with concrete and logs," she said. "A three bedroom house with three bathrooms, if we save, we can do it. We are working."

Millicent was enormously excited dreaming of her new home, but William looked as if there was another hurricane coming.

When I returned to the village shelter, the chairman informed me that the shelter would remain open as long as necessary because many villagers had lost their homes. Those who could return home went home. Recovery workers were organized. The next day everyone worked hard and cleared the roads, but the village was still isolated due to flooding in other villages. The news reported that the storm had died over Guatemala, but it had flooded many villages and towns in its way.

I went to the chairman and told him about Joe, but Mitch said that Joe was the last person he was worried about. "Don't worry about him. He's a survivor. It would take more than a storm to make that man disappear."

The next day the villagers focused on repairing each other's damaged homes while the chairman brought in more supplies via boats. The farms had taken a loss in provisions, fruits, and vegetables, but most of the animals survived. Electricity was restored in two weeks. The shelter remained open, and the recovery work continued at a remarkable pace. However, during this time, no one had seen Joe.

The investigation was now official. I went to Fabian's house to inquire about his brother. He was now very concerned about Joe's whereabouts.

"Dale has been over to his place many times to feed the dogs, but he hasn't seen Joe," Fabian said. "Joe is a loner, but he always lets you know when he's around."

"Dale is here," I said. "Let me ask him."

"One of Uncle Joe's fishing boats is missing," Dale told me. "He might be at sea."

"Did he have any problems with anyone?" I asked.

"Not that I know of," Fabian replied.

I went to Teddy's house and the family was home. Melanie and Anita were cooking. They had a friend with them named Jennifer. She was from another village, but sheltered with her family during the storm. She was at Joe's place two days before the storm, but that was the last time she saw him.

We talked about Joe, and they were beginning to worry, too. He did not have any foes they knew of, but recently had some strong words with Gerald. Gerald wanted to purchase his property, and Joe might have had some property tax problems.

It was a busy week. I had to do some repairs to the station, but the work was too much for me so I paid some men to do it.

It was Saturday again, three weeks after the storm, when I went to see Dale. We decided to go to Joe's place and take a closer look for any signs of him being missing. Dale had visited Joe's home almost every day. The watchdogs were there, and no one could enter the property without either Dale's or Joe's permission.

We went by boat because Joe's place was very far by road. When we arrived, three Doberman dogs came to greet us. Dale took out a whistle and blew it a few times.

"Without the whistle," he said, "the dogs would tear us apart. I have to blow a special code too."

"Why all the security?" I asked.

"Joe is an ex-veteran of the French Foreign Legion. He also trains horses and dogs."

"I thought he was just a fisherman," I replied.

Joe had a beautiful home and a five-acre grass yard that was well kept. I looked around the yard to see if there were any indications of foul play.

"What are you looking for?" Dale asked.

"Nothing," I replied.

"I just recalled that the day after the hurricane, I found several sardine cans with holes in them, wired," Dale said.

"Someone tried to distract the dogs," I replied.

"These dogs only eat with the permission of Joe and me. They have to be really hungry to eat from anyone else."

All three dogs played vigorously around the yard. While they showed no signs of aggression, I knew they were watching me. We eventually went inside the house. There was a small swing door in the back, and the dogs could go in and out as they pleased.

The house was neat, clean, and spacious, with few pieces of furniture. We went outside again to look at Joe's fishing boat. He had two and one was missing. Still, I found nothing out of the ordinary. While everyone had begun to worry about Joe, I felt he wasn't dead but wanted people to think he was. I couldn't dispute what other people thought, but I had to follow my hunches.

That night after work, I changed into a camouflaged outfit and took my boat out on the lagoon to where I could stake out Joe's place. I did this for two nights, but saw nothing unusual. On the third night, around midnight, a boat boldly docked at Joe's place and four men got off. They went on Joe's boat and it looked like they were searching it. They did not enter Joe's fenced home.

One of the men was Gerald, Dale's older brother and Joe's eldest nephew. The other three I did not know. I remained undetected until the men left.

The village of Blue Lagoon had recovered remarkably from the hurricane. Home rebuilding was almost completed because the local government provided some essential aid.

One day Gerald came to the station. He inquired about the search for his missing uncle. I told him that a missing persons report had been filed the previous week, and that an investigation was in progress.

"He went fishing before the hurricane, got in trouble, and died," Gerald boldly stated.

"It seems like that is what happened," I replied. "Did he have any children or immediate family?"

"None whatsoever, he was single," Gerald answered. "Hurry up with the investigation because my family needs closure! Instead of wasting time fleecing revenue by writing false traffic tickets, you could be working on finding Joe's body or evidence of his death."

I felt Gerald was trying to see if he could influence me on the case, or find out what I already knew. I wanted to make him feel that he was influencing me, but every case is different, and to draw any immediate conclusion was not wise without substantial supporting information.

"I have already notified the coast guard to submit an all points bulletin for his fishing boat," I said.

"Great. My father and I will send a search party to sea tomorrow."

"That is wonderful," I said. "Let me know what you find."

"Another thing," Gerald added. "I have filed a complaint against you for harassment and I have also requested your transfer. You are absolutely no good for this village. I will see to it that your time here is short."

Gerald talked some more in a very condescending tone until I could not listen to him anymore. I looked out on the lagoon and watched the intense orange sunset over the horizon that was reflected in the clouds. Gerald was talking but I did not hear.

"You're not listening to me," Gerald said. Then he left the station in a hurry.

That night I went once more to stake out Joe's place. Just after 2:00 a.m. I noticed a small canoe coming from the sea, staying close to the banks for concealment. The canoe docked and a man came ashore. He entered the premises and the dogs greeted him. I could not identify the man, but I had a strong feeling it was Joe. He had not broken the law, but I wanted to know why he was hiding. I was glad he was alive yet concerned for his safety. But I couldn't approach him at this moment. I now realized that Dale and Fabian knew more than they were revealing about Joe.

He stayed about one hour and then left. I went back to the station. The next day I met with Fabian and Dale and asked them what was really going on.

They said Joe was part of mercenary group that had worked for the Sandinistas in Nicaragua. After the Nicaraguan civil war ended, Joe and his friends smuggled drugs from South America and traded weapons with the Sandinistas. It was a risky business and Joe left it before most of his veteran associates. He made a lot of money. He got out while he was still ahead.

Some of his colleagues, however, stayed in the business and became very rich and powerful. But when the United States DEA and Interpol started cracking down, friends became enemies and treachery replaced camaraderie. Some of the members became witnesses. Lately, for some reason, a few members of the group had been assassinated. Although Joe left the drug business a long time ago, he wasn't taking any chances. Most of the properities Joe had, had been recently transfered in Fabian's name for protection.

Dale and Fabian said that Joe had dangerous enemies because of what he knew. Dale emphasized that highly efficient assassins might have been dispatched to terminate Joe.

Lust and Desperation

Later that day, Millicent came to work at the station very late.
"I am very tired. Please forgive me if I am not able to complete all my tasks today. I would greatly appreciate it."

"No problem," I replied.

She appeared to be exhausted and very angry.

"Is everything okay?" I asked. "How is the new house?"

"Well, that's the problem," she said.

"What's wrong with it?"

"It's Will," she said.

"What's going on with William?" I asked.

"Everyone who lost their house in the storm has completely rebuilt, except us," she said, as her eyes filled with tears. "I work very hard and all I ask of him is that he does his part, but he constantly avoids his responsibilities. We have been together for a long time, but I am getting weary of him now. It's hard to understand why he is not receptive to me. I gave him so much and received so little, and you have given me so much in such a short time. What if you had not come here?

Everyone has started treating me better because of you. How will I ever repay you?"

She reached out and gripped my right hand in desperation.

For a moment, I was also very tempted to touch her. Her dress was shorter than usual and it was transparent at close look. Her shape was perfect and her gentle touch was firm and strong. She was adorable, and even though the lovemaking beast within me raged, I had to keep it caged.

Many men would give a fortune to be with her, but whatever

the case may be, she had given her vows to William. I had to respect that.

"What can I do for you?"

"Whenever William gets any money, he goes away and cannot be found."

"I will try my best to help you," I said.

"I don't want to live with Mr. Ken longer than I should, but Will seems not to care," she said. "He would like us to live there as long as possible."

We were close. Her body radiated a warm invigorating sexual energy that overcame me. It felt good. I could not resist. I did not know what to do. With one last effort, I step away and created a larger space between us.

"I forgot to do something," I said. "I have to go. The money you paid me for the horse is under the Bible on my desk with your regular pay. The horse was a gift. You don't have to work today. I have some dirty clothes but they can wait. I will return soon."

I left in my Jeep and went to Ken's place. Him and William were there. We talked for a while. I asked William how the house was coming along and he said it would be completed by December, but then a sense of uneasiness came over him.

"Oh, I have to tend to the baby calves," he said. "They might need water and shade. The sun is hot today." Then he left abruptly.

I told Ken what Millicent said.

"He wastes his money every payday, man," Ken said.

"On what? Drinking?" I asked.

"No man!" he said.

Then he began to tell me quietly.

"William wastes his money at the Blue Oasis," he said, shaking his head. "The man has a weakness for women."

The Blue Oasis was a famous brothel situated in the free zone between Mexico and Belize. Men from all occupations and classes frequented it. Women from Belize, Mexico, and many other countries worked there, making more money than any other job could offer them. Prostitution paid well for these women.

"Well, William has a remarkable wife and two healthy children," I said.

"He does not realize how lucky he is," Ken added. "No woman at the Blue Oasis can compare to Millicent. That woman is a hell of a woman."

"She is definitely a woman of immense beauty," I remarked.

"William better be careful," he said. "She has an eye for you, and Gerald has made several moves to win her over. As a matter of fact, Gerald sold them the land where they lived very cheap."

"Love is kind and cruel at the same time," I replied.

"My brother, I feel I have to pray for him a little, and hope he changes," Ken said.

"I can't arrest him for wasting his money on other women," I added.

The Blue Oasis

After meeting with Ken, I visited Millicent briefly. I asked her for some of William's photos in order to help her. She agreed and gave me a few.

I went back to the station, dressed in a suit, and headed for the Blue Oasis. In 45 minutes I was at the border in the free zone. The Blue Oasis was not hard to find. It was a modern, state-of-the-art nightclub, casino, restaurant, hotel, and brothel. The bright blue neon sign was visible from a far distance.

I went to one of the security guards at the front entrance. I showed him my professional identification, introduced myself politely, and requested to speak to a supervisor on matters of urgent importance. The security officer notified his supervisor and the two of them escorted me to his office. The supervisor was a tall, muscular man of dark complexion who introduced himself as Sergeant Lloyd.

"How can I help you today," he said.

"I am here on behalf of the Department of Health to inform you of a man with a deadly and highly transmittable disease. This man has frequented this establishment many times. Here are some pictures."

"I may have seen him before," Lloyd said. "I will need to make copies of these pictures. Janet, take these pictures and make three copies of each." He handed the photos to his assistant Janet, a petite Spanish security officer.

"So what kind of communicable disease does this healthy looking man have?"

I pondered what to say and in a split second came out with it.

"He has a rare strain of Opportunistic Emphazematic Tuberculosis."

"I have never heard of such a disease. Where did he get it from?" Lloyd asked.

"Animals," I replied. "From a jungle when he worked overseas."

Sergeant Lloyd turned his nose and hardened his face in disgust.

"How nasty!" he exclaimed.

"This disease can be spread rapidly via contact and through the air at close proximity," I said.

"What! I will alert all staff and call a meeting on all shifts immediately. I have to protect this establishment."

Lloyd seemed more frightened than serious.

"William Rocio is his name," I said.

"Thank you very much, Mr. Mays," Lloyd said.

"If he enters this building and coughs, everyone might get infected," I added.

"Mr. Mays, this is dangerous shit. My security teams will double check the identifications of everyone entering our resort."

Lloyd returned the photos to me. He had more copies than he really needed.

The Blue Oasis was a relaxing, superbly decorated venue, with soothing soft music playing continuously, and beautiful women lounging everywhere. Everyone was adorned in impressive apparel. Since I was looking classy myself, I decided to stay for a while.

There were several bars situated in the big lobby. I walked up to one of them and ordered a fruit punch, but the bartender gave me a glass of cherry juice instead. It was good. While having my drink, I turned to look at the beautiful women all around. I noticed their eyes were on me, too, and one woman dressed in red approached me.

"Care for company?" she said.

"Absolutely," I answered. "It's hard to refuse your company."

She smiled. She was very attractive and wanted the same drink I had, but it cost me three times more when I bought it for her.

"This is your first time here," she said.

"Yes, it is," I replied.

"You like the girls here?" she asked.

"Yes, I do. I like the place, the girls, and especially the one talking to me now."

"That's good. I like you too."

She sat on the barstool with her legs crossed. The red dress was split high on one side, leaving her legs mostly exposed. Her knees were touching mine. She was beautiful, captivating, and I was having fun.

"I could be your companion for the evening if you like, she said, but you have to take care of some expenses."

"That's not a problem," I answered.

"Would you like another drink, sir?" the bartender asked.

"Yes," I replied. "Make one more for the lady, too."

"I can show you a good time for the right price," she said. "I have a hotel suite with a Jacuzzi, and I will definitely need some company this evening. Kelly is my name. Have you ever had a service like this before?"

"This is my first time here," I replied

"What brings you here, if you don't mind me asking?"

"I am here on business."

"You should treat yourself to an unforgettable time," she said. "It's worth it, and I am very good."

She looked straight into my eyes with an honest plea. She reached over and touched my hands.

"Let me know when you're ready," she said.

She had me in her palms and I was ready, but I had no money on me to cover the expense.

"Is there a restroom?" I asked.

"Yes, over there," she answered.

"Please excuse me," I said.

I headed for the restroom, then made my escape to my vehicle and went home.

I hoped my scheme would work in helping Millicent. The Blue Oasis was an entertaining place. I could see why William liked it, and also why he did not have any money.

I was happy to return the photos to Millicent.

"Let me know if there is any progress," I said to her.

Remnants of Closure

When I returned to the station, there was a large crowd there. I was wondering what caused the commotion. I saw a salvage boat. The people said that the remains of Joe's fishing boat had been recovered. Gerald had hired the salvage crew. He declared that since the police were not capable of conducting a thorough investigation, he had to take the responsibility upon himself in order to provide closure for his family.

"We now have proof that Joe died in an accident at sea," Gerald said.

Some of the villagers cried. They said Joe was a kind man.

Time of Urgency

The next day Fabian paid me a visit. We sat on the porch at the back of the station that overlooked the lagoon.

"There is something that is worrying me," Fabian said.

"What's the matter?"

"I'm not so sure Joe is dead, and I am getting suspicious. Joe is my younger brother and I have custody of his property, with restrictions. Gerald is certain that Joe is dead, and he wants me to give him a portion of his inheritance as soon as possible."

"Talking about the will already?" I replied.

"Gerald said he has partners who are willing to help him with his plans for a new housing scheme called Blue Lagoon Heights," Fabian said. "This is too quick for me. I believe he had this all planned long ago."

"What does his mother say?" I asked.

"Josephine is not his mother. Josephine is Dale's mother. Gerald's mother lives in California. She had some property in Dangriga that they developed together and sold. Now it seems that they are after Joe's and mine. I am very concerned for Joe.

"Joe has a son in the South, in Barranco," Fabian went on. "His name is Ali and he's 14. The boy and his mother recently moved from Honduras. His son was born here, but his mother is Honduran."

"I am from Barranco," I said. "I know Barranco very well."

"That's good. Can you help me find him?" Fabian asked.

"Yes, I can."

"This boy is the rightful heir to Joe's property, if Joe is gone," Fabian said in a low tone.

"We have to find Joe's son," I said.

"Yes," Fabian answered. "The way Gerald has been behaving, this boy's life might be in danger."

"If we find the boy first," I said, "we will be a step ahead. You never know until you follow your curiosity, and your hunch is as good as mine."

"Gerald is my son, but he can be deceptive and inconsiderate. "

"Ha, I thought his father was worse," I said.

"I can be," Fabian said with a smile. "Can we leave tomorrow night, no later than 7:30?"

"Okay, but I have to return as soon as I can after the trip."

"Sure, we will take my Land Rover," Fabian replied.

"See you tomorrow night at seven," I said.

The next day was Friday, September 1st. I made preparations for the trip, as well as preparations to do some fishing around the lagoon when I returned.

In the evening I went to Fabian's house and he was already waiting for me.

"Are you going to use your jeep or my Rover?" he asked.

"You said you were going to drive the Rover," I replied.

"Well, we can take the Rover if you drive the first few hours," Fabian said.

Fabian was an easygoing person but somewhat lazy. I grabbed my bag out of the jeep and placed it in the Land Rover. It had been a long time since I went home, and I looked forward to being there again. Fabian bid goodbye to his wife Josephine, who was on her way to see Vicky, Teddy's wife and the mother of Melanie and Anita.

We started the journey nice and easy. The Rover was new and drove comfortably. We took a shortcut that ran alongside a sugarcane field not too far from the lagoon. It was a dirt road, and we had at least eight miles to go before we entered the highway.

Fifteen minutes into the journey, Fabian's seat was all the way back and he was asleep. I was relying on his conversations to keep me awake, but this was not going to happen. I reached into my bag and grabbed a pack of chewing gum. I tried to open it with one hand, and it fell on the other side next to Fabian's feet. As I reached over to get the packet without disturbing him, there was a loud crash and pieces of the windshield were all over us.

There were more blasts that took out the back glass. I knew immediately it was a high-powered rifle. I stayed down and floored the accelerator. The vehicle hit the embankment and went airborne into the sugarcane field. The Rover hit the ground hard and rolled several times before coming to a stop. We were upside down.

I managed to crawl out after cutting the seat belt with my pocketknife. It was dark. I realized Fabian was not inside the vehicle. I looked around but didn't see him. As I crawled away, I glimpsed him crawling away too.

"Are you okay?" I asked.

"Be quiet man," he whispered loudly, "someone is trying to kill us."

"Burn it!" someone yelled.

"Oh shit!" Fabian said. "Let's head for the lagoon."

The lagoon was nearby, and I have never seen anyone crawl so fast. Fabian scuttled like a frightened alligator and I understood his urgency. A few moments later, the entire sugarcane field became engulfed in flames.

"Mays!" Fabian called out softly. "You okay?"

"Yes, I am," I replied.

"Let's swim up the lagoon on the left side," he said. "Ken's house is about two miles north of here."

"Okay," I replied.

"We have no time to waste. Let's go now. Move your ass!"

He grabbed onto a big log and paddled his way out into the lagoon. He placed himself well to one side of the log to give me room to join him. I did so, and off we went.

Fabian was in better shape than I expected. He paddled his feet effortlessly and nonstop.

"Who is trying to take us out?" I said.

"I cannot say until I am sure," Fabian answered. "Maybe Joe's old friends. I look like him."

We swam for almost two miles with the aid of the big log.

"Whose house is that?" I asked.

"It's Ken's house," Fabian answered.

"But it's on the other side," I said.

"I made a mistake. Why don't you swim across and get his boat and return for me?"

"What if the snipers find you here alone, waiting?" I said.

"Let's go now," he replied.

After I mentioned snipers, Fabian was determined to cross the lagoon.

"Whoever tried to kill us could see us on that side, where the road is," Fabian said, "that's why I chose to swim on this side."

"Very clever," I said.

It was about one mile across the lagoon to Ken's house. We recognized it because it was the first southernmost house. We could see the lights from far away, which guided us. Fabian was a good swimmer and I was confident he would cross the lagoon. He was not tired as he held onto the log and pushed his way across. Since he knew the area very well, I followed him.

In less than 20 minutes we arrived on shore. When I stood up, the water was at my waist. However, when Fabian tried to stand he experienced an intense pain in his left ankle. He thought he had been shot, but on further examination it was not a bullet wound. His left ankle was broken or sprained. I alerted Ken. He came and assisted Fabian out of the water.

"I need a ride to the station as soon as possible," I said to Ken.

"No problem. I will take you in my small boat."

Fabian stayed at Ken's place. Nancy and Millicent tended to his injury. Ken and I left for the station in his boat.

We arrived at the station quickly. I changed into my uniform. At the same time, Ken checked the boat to make sure it was ready for the long journey. I opened my safe and grabbed my loaded Berettas and the bag with the deadly .30-06 Colt rifle and the night vision scope.

"Let me top off your engine oil," Ken said, "and you'll be ready."

"Thanks man," I replied.

I boarded the boat. When Ken finished topping off the oil he left. He knew I was in a hurry.

"Be careful," Ken said.

I started out slowly and then gradually increased speed. Once again I was on my way to Barranco. I felt Joe's son's life might be in danger, so time was of the essence. I headed north until I reached Corozal Bay. The Bay had two names. If you lived in Mexico it was the Bay of Chetumal, and if you lived in Belize it was Carozal Bay.

I followed the coast to the right until I arrived at the Point of Sarteneja, and then I veered south. If I made it to Belize City within one hour, I would be doing okay.

The sea was calm and the moon shone brightly, just enough for me to see safely ahead. All along the way I kept looking at the boat compass to make sure I was going south. Many things were going through my mind—Joe's motive for disappearing, and the thought of his only son being in imminent danger. Forty minutes went by quickly. I could see the lights of Caye Caulker Island. Another 25 miles and I would be in Belize City.

My boat was an 18-foot Nautique with a 260 horsepower engine. It was very fast and reliable, but drank a lot of gas. When I was within three miles of the Belize City port, I slowed down tremendously to avoid drawing any attention to myself. I continued at a slow pace until I approached Rider's Caye, then stopped, refueled, and checked the oil. I was now inside Belize City's harbor, where the coast guard could stop me and seize my boat if I aroused any reasonable suspicions. I was also far outside my jurisdiction.

When I was far south of the port of Belize City, I accelerated the boat again. Still, I had to be cautious. There were many small islands to navigate. I had many miles to go. I stayed clear of the small port town of Dangriga because I was moving very fast and did not want to stop. Belize had a large coastline and it wasn't easy to navigate.

About three hours into the journey, I decided to head straight south into the open sea from Placencia instead of following the coast, hoping to reduce travel time and hit the peninsula of Manabique. I was taking a dangerous chance in a place where there was nothing but sea and darkness. I could not see the coastline anymore and relied strictly on the compass. I was also traveling at top speed.

An hour and a half into this part of the journey I was beginning to doubt my navigation skills, but my fears went away when I saw the Punta Manabique lighthouse. I curved the boat westward while maintaining the same speed. Another 30 minutes and Barranco's beach was in sight. The journey took almost four hours. By car, it might have taken six to seven hours. I drove my boat up to the small dock and stopped the engine.

No one was on the beach, but I knew it was likely that one of the watchmen had seen me. I secured my boat on the dock, grabbed my bag, and headed on the boardwalk toward the pathway that led to the village.

"Mays, is that you?" a familiar voice said, coming out of the dark.

"Clarence?" I replied.

"My son and I are on duty tonight," he said.

"I'm glad it's someone I know," I said.

"Don't worry, everybody knows you," Clarence said.

"I need your help urgently," I said.

"What's the problem?" he asked.

"I'm looking for a woman approximately 30 years old," I said. "Her name is Carina Gonzalez. She has a son by the name of Ali."

"She came from Honduras a year ago," Clarence replied. "She has been a schoolteacher here for almost a year now. She is an excellent teacher. Her son and my son are good friends."

"Can you take me to them now? I feel they are in grave danger."

"I will," Clarence replied.

The small house was a 15-minute walk from the beach, nestled atop a hill. It was close to the jungle line and about 7 minutes from the nearest neighbor. Clarence knocked on the door several times.

A pretty woman answered. She seemed a little surprised.

"Miss Carina, there is a policeman here to see you," Clarence said.

"Miss Carina, my name is Mays," I said. "I am here to tell you something very important."

As she was about to answer, a boy came to the door.

"This is my son Ali," Carina said.

Ali was about 14 or 15 and shared some features with his mother.

"Ali's father Joe has been missing since the hurricane passed several weeks ago," I said quietly. "The remains of one of his fishing boats were found, but no one has seen him. Now, I am afraid that you and your son might be in danger."

"Joe was here this evening," she replied.

"Really?" I said.

"Yes, he has been here since the hurricane," Carina said, "but he warned me that he expected some trouble when he returns to Blue Lagoon."

"I am afraid the trouble might be coming here, I said, and we have very little time."

"Where is Joe now?" Clarence asked.

"He went to set some lobster nets and should return within the hour," Ali answered.

"Miss Carina, it is important that you and your son are safe tonight, I said, and being here is definitely not safe. I don't have time to explain the details, but you have to leave now."

"I understand," she replied.

"Clarence, take Miss Carina to my sister Krystle then you and the boys watch out for Joe on the shoreline. If you find him, don't return here. It's good to know that Joe is alive. I would like to keep it that way. Go now, please."

Carina, the two boys, and Clarence carried out my suggestion without hesitation. Before leaving I told them to leave the lights and radio on, as if the house was occupied. I assembled and loaded my rifle, checked my loaded Berettas, and prayed for protection. I located a comfortable position where I had a good view of the house and the property. I was ready for action.

I waited quietly in my position; almost 30 minutes went by. Perhaps my hunch was wrong. However, after another 10 minutes I heard the sounds of two jeeps. They approached the house with lights off and entered the property. Four men exited vehicles. I maintained my position. The men walked towards the house with assault rifles in their hands. The first one ferociously kicked the door down. Two of them went in and opened fire, decimating the interior with bullets. If anyone were inside, they would not have survived.

"No one is here!" one of the men cried in Spanish as he exited the house.

"Burn the house!" shouted a familiar voice.

As soon as I recognized the voice, I had second thoughts about shooting. I knew it was Gerald. I did not want to kill him. I would have to make the arrest quickly. I rose from my cover, leaving the rifle behind.

"No one move!" I yelled.

I ran towards the scene with my Beretta in hand. Gerald was surprised to see me. The other three men took a defensive posture. They were armed and had no intention of surrendering.

The one who had kicked down the door had an AR16. Before he could shoot I fired two bullets at him, but he dove for cover. Then I dove to my right while simultaneously firing at the other two men. I rolled into a prone firing position as I landed on the ground. *Two for you, two for him,* I recited in my mind as I emptied the magazine. I reached in my side pocket for the other Beretta. I was under heavy fire and the bullets were passing close by. The three men might have realized that I was out of bullets. I rolled as fast as I could, firing two rounds without aiming. I was under suppressive fire with nowhere to find cover. I plowed my body into the ground, stretched my hands out, and started to return fire.

Suddenly, there was a huge explosion and flames shot everywhere. The bullets ceased coming my way and I was too weak do anything. The three men near the house had gotten the worst of the explosion.

My shirt was bloody, and my right shoulder was heavy and painful. I crawled over to where my rifle was, feeling weak and nauseated. A bullet had pierced my left shoulder and I was losing blood. The more I moved the more it hurt, so I lay still. My sight faded, and a deep peaceful sleep overcame me.

When I opened my eyes, I was at a different place. I was at my sister's house, and James was tending to my shoulder injury.

"You're a lucky man," James said.

"What happened?" I asked.

"That bullet came close to severing your subclavian artery. You also lost a lot of blood. That's what made you so weak. I restored your blood pressure with dextrose, saline, and electrolytes."

"How long have I been here?" I asked.

"Two days," James replied.

"James, is he fully awake?" Krystle asked.

"Yes, and his vital signs have improved," James replied. "He's going to be fine."

"What happened?" I asked.

"Well, Clarence and Joe brought you here. They said you were in a shoot out, and that two gas tanks at the side of the house exploded.

They found three other men fatally burnt from the explosion. Joe said you were out of your jurisdiction and you would be in a lot of trouble if the authorities found out you were here. He also said the three other men were mercenaries from Nicaragua."

"Where is Gerald?" I asked. "He was with those men."

"We did not see him," Clarence replied. "Just you, the three men, and one jeep."

"Gerald fled, thank God," I said. "His father would be hurt if any harm had come to his son."

Moving On

"Mays, what kind of trouble have you gotten yourself into this time?" Krystle asked.

"I don't know, but I hope Joe and Carina are okay."

"They are fine," James replied.

I sat on the side of the bed without any problem. I was getting tired of being in bed. There was a knock at the door.

"It's Joe," a voice said.

Joe entered the room. Seeing him for the first time, he resembled his brother Fabian. Joe looked at me for a moment before he smiled.

"I have your weapons," he said, "and I cleaned the scene."

"Thank you," I said.

He paused, looking at me.

"Tonight I will take you back to Blue Lagoon by boat."

I drank some soup and it was satisfying. I was not ready to leave Barranco but I had to, no later than that night. Joe had not only retrieved my .30-06 Colt rifle and Berettas, but had also recovered two .45 caliber Smith & Wessons and two M16s.

The boat ride back to Blue Lagoon was pleasant and peaceful; I slept most of the way. We arrived just before morning. Joe brought me to the station, and we sat on the porch as he told me everything.

"I was on my way home in my boat, hours before the hurricane, when a large boat approached me," Joe said. "I moved out of its way, but it followed me, and then someone started shooting at me. I had my scuba gear, so I dove into the water just before the larger boat rammed my boat and broke it apart. This happened about three miles off the coast of Sarteneja. I swam to Sarteneja, where I stayed with a friend for two days. I was afraid to return to my place in Blue lagoon. I had to stay low for a while."

He admitted that he had been involved in drug trafficking about five years before with some veterans of the French Foreign Legion and the Nicaraguan revolution, but he left when he had enough money. Those who continued became millionaires, but when the Interpol and the DEA came down on them they began to clean house, and any potential witnesses were in danger.

Joe was very disturbed that Gerald would resort to any means to gain more wealth than he already had.

"He led those men to me," he said.

Now the problem had passed, but he had to be careful. He was planning to relocate Carina and Ali to Blue Lagoon.

"When I was a soldier I made just enough to get by, Joe said, but as a drug trafficker I took the same risk and made much more."

"I might have done the same, given the situation," I replied.

The following week was the first week of September. I went to visit Fabian. His ankle was not broken but badly strained. It was wrapped and he used a crutch as a walking aid. He had managed to supervise and complete all four wells successfully, and they were operating at full capacity.

He did not want to say too much about Gerald, who had left to live with his mother in California.

"Let's go over to Teddy's place," he said.

"Okay, let's go," I said.

Teddy and his wife were on their front porch when we arrived. They were glad to see us. Teddy had some extra building materials left over from the wells and wanted to give them to William. No one objected.

"I heard that the Blue Oasis security escorted William from the club to the border," Teddy said.

Everyone laughed.

"Why is that?" I asked.

"Millicent may have had her prayers finally answered," Fabian said. "William wasted a lot of money at that place."

"He is a very handsome man," Teddy's wife Vicky replied.

"When did this incident happen?" I asked.

"About two weeks ago," Teddy said.

"Yes, I heard the security officers wore gloves and masks and informed customs not to permit him back in the free zone," Fabian said.

"He must have offended one of the girls," Josephine said.

"Since then he has been working and staying home, you can see the improvement," Teddy said.

"Yes, the house is almost finished, and Millicent and the children are happy," Vicky said.

Melanie and Anita walked onto the porch.

"Dad, don't start talking to Mays about the Oasis casino," Anita said. "He will start going there."

"Yes, don't encourage him, dad," Melanie added.

"Next week is Independence Day," Teddy said. "We usually have a picnic on this day from morning to the next morning, and you are invited."

"Thank you very much," I said. "I have to leave now."

The rest of the day, I patrolled the village without incident.

Seven days later was Independence Day, a national holiday. It was a beautiful day, and the cool and gentle breezes circulated the aromas of roasted coffee, spices, and cooked meat throughout the village. The birds were singing again. The people dressed in clean, bright, casual clothing. It was forbidden to work this day, unless you were preparing food, for it was a time to relax and celebrate.

That day I patrolled the town on my horse, and those who saw me greeted me, even the youngest children. A young girl about four or five years old saw me at the store. She was with her mother, a beautiful woman. The little girl said, "Look, mommy! It's Mays, the village policeman!"

I had been here for almost a year. Almost everyone knew me. Most of them were familiar to me but I did not know most of their names. Nevertheless, their public safety was my concern.

That afternoon I was at the station, sitting on the porch. My right shoulder was healing fast, but hurt occasionally. As I looked out on the lagoon, a boat approached. I was nervous at first, but as it came closer I saw Dale, Melanie, Anita, and Ali.

"We came to take you to the picnic at Joe's place," Dale said.

"The food is ready," Melanie said.

"What's on the menu?" I asked.

"Curry goat and fish," Dale replied.

When I arrived at Joe's place, I was surprised to see so many people. There was Ken, Nancy, Millicent and her family, Mitch, Teddy, and many more. All came to celebrate the holiday and enjoy themselves.

The mood was just right. I looked out into the yard, and in one far corner were some hammocks, about five of them under some cool shade provided by three large mango trees. Joe was laying in one of them. I went over and joined him.

"Mays," Joe said.

"Yes man," I replied.

"I want to make you an offer that I wouldn't make to anyone else," he said.

"What kind of offer?"

"You see the other side of this cove?" Joe asked, pointing.

"Yes, I see it. It's a beautiful piece of land. I hear it's for sale for $250,000."

"Yeah, but for you it's $50,000. Fabian and his wife agreed that the price was affordable for you."

"You sure about this?" I asked.

"If I wasn't sure, I would not have sent a boat to bring you here. You went out of your way to save my family. Now I am showing you some gratitude. That's seven acres of prime oceanfront real estate, and an additional seven acres in the rear."

"I don't have $50,000, but I have $45,000. I could pay you the rest in one year."

"That is good," he said. "Next week we talk and finalize the deal. I need you here in Blue Lagoon."

"There they are, lazy rass," said Teddy. Teddy, Fabian, and Mitch walked towards us.

"So, did you guys get him to stay in Blue Lagoon?" Mitch asked. "Your superintendent called me and said he might need you. I told him he hasn't been here a year, give us another two years."

"I have no plans to leave as yet," I replied.

I remained a police officer in Blue Lagoon for three more years and then resigned. During that time I paid Joe for the land and built a comfortable home. Dale and Anita got married, too. They have a large farm and two daughters. Joe and Carina were my neighbors.

We never saw Gerald again after he migrated to the United States. Millicent became a schoolteacher and then a principal. William coaches soccer at the Orange Walk Community College and works with Ken occasionally.

At present I grow papayas, potatoes, and beans on 35 acres of land that I lease. I am a successful farmer. Sometimes I go fishing with Joe, James, Ken, Fabian, Teddy, and Dale.

Last weekend James and I were in San Pedro Bay and saw a fishing boat that drew our attention. I pointed out the captain to James. We strongly agreed that he was Iman. He was without dreadlocks and looked older. He gazed at us for a while, then waved and smiled. We returned the greeting, but then he left abruptly. He was crying as he sailed away.

"He is still crazy Mays," James said.

"I know," I replied. "It's good to see him."

We laughed.

From Blue Lagoon to Barranco, people still call me the village policeman. My arsenal has been put aside, but it is ready. I practise using my weapons often, but secretly. I am always watching and hoping to use my dark talents once more. I am a watchman.

Presently, all is good and peaceful.

The End

Borders and Crossroads

By Fabian Comrie

They say what comes around, goes around, and changes
for better or worse will come.

Rio Verde is a small town 200 miles northeast of Mexico City. It is a typical Mexican village with its stories of fortune and misfortune. Most people here are farmers: farmers of livestock, fruits, vegetables, and ground provisions. Some individuals, nevertheless, may venture into cultivating other lucrative agricultural products that are illicit. The financial benefits of cultivating illicit herbs are enticing and could be substantial, but there is a high risk for trouble sometimes, especially when the operation is smeared in deception. Most of the farmers are legitimate and do not partipate in this activity.

Those who are not full-time farmers have other occupations that are justifiable and equally important to the sustenance of the community.

Oscar and Clemis had been living together in Rio Verde since Oscar was two months old. An informal adoption took place at that time. Oscar's real mother was a student who left him with Clemis as his baby sitter and never returned. They say she ran away with a wealthy businessman from Japan. Clemis never complained or seemed to have any regrets.

Clemis was born in Mexico. Her mother was a model from Brazil and her father was a Mexican farmer. She spoke fluent English, Spanish, and Portuguese. She was also a well-respected schoolteacher in Rio Verde. Before she was a mother, she was supposed to have gotten married to a successful and charismatic business lawyer named Uzel Livingston, but she broke off the engagement because of his involvement with some questionable businesspeople. Being Livingston's spouse at that time would have been too risky for her, but they remained good friends.

An excellent teacher, Clemis taught Oscar to speak English very well. Oscar developed the ability to draw before he could write. Whenever he was writing,he drew nouns he could not spell. In this way, he became an excellent artist.

Birthday Celebration

When Oscar celebrated his 21st birthday, he had a small party at his home. A few of his friends came and they had a good time. They talked about many things. They especially talked and laughed about an incident that involved Oscar, his good friend David, and the police about three years before.

It had been known that some of the poorer farmers cultivated marijuana on the side for recreational use and extra income. The police knew this but overlooked it. When two new police officers were assigned to the village, they decided to raid, extort, and intimidate these farmers. Instead of facing prosecution the farmers gave in, and allowed the officers to confiscate a large portion of their weed. The corrupt police officers then sold the weed to drug dealers after saying they had destroyed it.

Oscar and David discovered where the police officers were hiding the marijuana before selling it. One Saturday evening they decided to raid the stash. They gave some to their friends and kept a substantial amount for themselves. Unfortunately, they were caught. Someone who was keeping an eye on the stash had informed the police.

One Saturday night Oscar and David were parked in the church-yard not far from the police station, smoking and joking. The car windows were halfway closed. The more weed they consumed, the more the smoke and aroma spread.

The police officers found them. One of the officers tapped on the car window. David rolled it down, punched the officer square in the nose, rolled the window back up, but forgot to lock the door. The officers dragged them out, subdued them, and took them straight to jail where they were beaten. Early the next morning, they were released,naked, and bruised from the beating they received. They ran home fast but were seen by some of the villagers.

It was the biggest news in Rio Verde at that time. Some people thought it was humorous, but for Oscar and David it was an unbearable embarrassment.

The news was not pleasing to some of the prominent community leaders. The two police officers were transfered. Even though David and Oscar were the victims, more punishment was in store for them. They had to report to the police station every Saturday for three years.

One of the new policemen was a photographer and an artist, and he taught Oscar a lot about taking and developing pictures. He was also impressed with Oscar's drawing skills. The boys developed a good relationship with the police officers, and after a few months they looked forward to going to the station every Saturday.

"Tonight, you're 21," David said on the night of Oscar's party. "That stuff happened three years ago."

"If that incident didn't happen," Oscar replied, "you probably wouldn't be going to the Police Academy in two months."

"And you wouldn't be so good at photography," said David.

"We're out of beers and sodas, Oscar," Sarah said.

She was about five feet tall, with a medium build and short black hair. She had an assertive personality.

"No more beers for the night," Clemis said. "It may be Oscar's birthday party, but this is my house."

"Yes, Miss Clem," Antonio answered. He was David's younger brother.

"Who needs beer?" said Manny. "We have enough food, and we can play dominoes. Just pretend the punch is beer." He was another school friend and the best soccer player in the village.

The rest of the party went well, and before midnight the food was gone.

"Oscar, your boss wanted to see you tomorrow," Clemis said.

"He just wants to give me my paycheck," Oscar replied. "I'll just see him on Monday."

"Don't save the paychecks," Clemis said. "Always cash them and then save the money. Small businesses usually operate on strict budgets."

"You should listen to your mother," Manny said. "She is my business teacher."

Business as Usual

Oscar had been working as a mechanic and auto body repair technician at Andy's Auto Body Repair for approximately two years. He was a valued technician, but recently had been assembling some artwork for submission to a national contest sponsored by top media and television production companies in Mexico and the United States. Oscar had to submit quality work because there were over 4,000 contestants.

"Mom, I have to take some time off from work," he said, "or else I will never get the work done in time to submit for the contest."

"Do what you must," Clemis replied. "You should have been prepared already."

"I thought I was prepared,but what I have isn't good enough. I am not ready."

Oscar requested time off from work. Andy, the owner and manager, gave him the time off.

That week, Oscar got down to some serious work. He drew many pictures and took numerous photos. At the end of the week he and Clemis selected the best ones for submission.They were satisfied.

After two weeks, Oscar went back to work at the auto repair. He visited the post office every lunch break. After three weeks he began to feel hopeless and fustrated. Finally, after a month, he received a letter from the Competition Committee of Mexican Arts and Culture. The letter was an invitation for an interview the following month. He was required to have a passport. This was the opportunity that Oscar was looking for. He and Clemis were excited at the good news.

Clemis advised Oscar to prepare well for the interview and get the passport early. She also warned him to keep everything confidential.

He would feel good if he won, she said, but he would feel bad if he failed.

Oscar took his mother's advice. He got his passport in time. No one in Rio-Verde knew he was a finalist in the national art contest except his mother and the police officers.

Early, on the day before the interview, he left Rio Verde on a bus to Mexico City. The ride was long. It was night when he arrived. From the bus station he took a taxi to the hotel where they were expecting him. The room was clean and comfortable. He slept well that night.

Oscar arose early that morning for the interview which was at the television station across the street. He dressed sharply in a gray two-piece suit and a light blue shirt. His black suede shoes perfectly matched the suit. He was in good physical shape and looked good. He walked over to the station, entered the lobby via a security checkpoint, and a pretty woman greeted him and escorted him to a waiting room.

"Please wait here, sir," she said, "and someone will be here to take you to the interview."

"Thank you," Oscar said.

Ten minutes later, the moment came.

"Mr. Oscar, this way please," the receptionist said.

She led the way with Oscar a step behind. They took the elevator to the fifth floor and entered a lobby that led to a large office. Two persons introduced themselves as Ed and Monica. Coincidentally, Oscar and Ed were wearing similar colors, and it made Oscar comfortable.

"Good morning," Oscar said in a soft tone.

"Have a seat, please," Monica said, "and congratulations."

"We are congratulating you," Ed said, "because you are one of four finalists selected to represent Mexico at an international art and media exhibition."

"Your drawings are some of the best we have seen," Monica added, "and the techniques you used in these pictures are unusual."

"I use dots, small strokes, and small straight lines," Oscar said.

"That is what makes your art so interesting. Who taught you to draw like that?" Ed asked.

"No one," Oscar replied.

"We will meet in three weeks to work on our presentation project," Monica said. "The four finalists will be going to Las Vegas."

"All the finalists will meet here to see if they can exceed or enhance their artwork for this exhibition," Ed said.

Oscar was happy. He had to stay a day longer in Mexico City to get a visa from the U.S. Embassy. He couldn't sleep that night because he was so excited. When Oscar arrived home, he told his mother the good news and she was happy for him.

"Don't say too much," she said, "until you are certain of everything."

From that day on, Oscar worked furiously at the auto body shop to earn money for the trip to Las Vegas. His expenses were covered, but he wanted to have some money for other things, such as buying something special for his mother and leaving some money for her to live on while he was gone.

Three weeks later, Oscar went back to Mexico City and met the other three finalists. They were exceptionally talented.

Lewis was a graphic artist and a storyteller. He could look at a scene and draw it in detail from memory. He was also versatile computer graphics designer.

Jennifer was a writer, poet, and a newspaper editor. Occasionally, she anchored the News at the local television station in her hometown of Merida, Mexico. She was only 19.

The last finalist was Nicole, a filmmaker who had made two very informative documentaries. Her most recent documentary focused on endangered marine wildlife in the Gulf of California and it had been receiving rave reviews in Mexico.

Oscar felt he was the least accomplished of the finalists. He also realized how much he had to learn.

That week in Mexico City, the four finalists worked together to combine and enhance their work. They made a PowerPoint presentation and a short explanatory film.

Las Vegas

Oscar and the other finalists went home for a week before they left for Las Vegas.

"Mom, What do you want me to bring for you from Las Vegas?" Oscar asked.

"Whatever you feel I deserve," Clemis answered.

"I'll be gone for a week, but it will be different when I return," Oscar said. "I want to attend the University of Mexico and study music and filmmaking."

"Go to Las Vegas, do your best, return safely, and then you can plan for school," Clemis replied.

Oscar always wanted to attend the University of Mexico, but he knew his mother had no money, and he never wanted to leave her alone.

The day came when Oscar had to leave for Mexico City. Although Clemis had mixed feelings, she was very glad that Oscar had an opportunity to showcase his talent. He left Rio Verde early that morning and stayed at the same hotel as he did when he had the interview. The following day, Oscar and the other finalists, along with Ed and Monica, left for Las Vegas.

It was his first flight. He liked it at first, but after two hours he wanted to be on the ground again. Las Vegas was more than what he had expected. The grand hotels, casinos, and slot machines were everywhere. It was a place made for nightlife, entertainment, and family fun.

When they arrived at the hotel, Ed escorted the men to their rooms and Monica escorted the ladies. The hotel was first class and five stars rated. In the evening they met for dinner on the fifth floor.

The hotel restaurant was exquisite. It had a spectacular view of the city and a setting to accommodate any formal occasion. Everyone was together at dinner. They dressed well. Oscar wore the same suit as he did for the interview but a different shirt.

"Tomorrow we have all day to prepare for the exhibition," Ed told them. "I want everyone to meet here at 7:30 a.m. We'll set up, rehearse, and break.

"At 10:30am Saturday, the exhibition starts," he continued. "The collections of work we are showcasing represent Mexican progressive arts and not individual art. However, the media and production companies will have their scouts looking at the individual presentations closely. I am not emphasizing individuality, but these talent scouts will closely examine every one of you. Whoever is selected for an internship or job training has a lot to be grateful for, because this is the chance of a lifetime and the sky is the limit. So represent your country and yourself well."

"I wish you luck guys," Monica added.

The Exhibition

The exhibition was an international event that included representations from all over the world. The next day they prepared and rehearsed as best as possible. Oscar was amazed at how his photos and artwork looked when placed in a proper setting and lighting.

On Saturday, the day of the exibition, everyone was up early. By 10:00 a.m., they stood poised in their assigned positions, waiting for the doors to open. The exhibition hall was enormous.

When the doors opened and the audience started entering, the contestants gradually became comfortable as time went on. The girls drew a lot of attention, especially from men. Their work was good, but they themselves were works of art.

An Asian woman and an African American woman with a Jamaican accent took keen notice of Oscar's and Lewis's work. They kept returning to ask questions. By this time Oscar and Lewis were more relaxed and were interacting with the guests. They made friends with the two women and their conversation lasted a long time.

"I am a music and fine arts major at the University of California, Irvine," the Asian lady said.

"Wow! You must know a lot," Oscar said.

"I know enough to do the work, but I have a lot to learn," the Asian woman replied. "At an event like this, you see art in its rarest and purest form. I have been going to school a long time to learn how to make art like this."

"Interesting," Oscar said.

"My name is Mais," she said. "And your name is?"

"I'm Oscar."

They talked for a very long time, and crowds came and went constantly.

"Those girls are hot," Lewis said.

"I could listen and talk to them forever," Oscar replied.

"They are very knowledgeable, too," Lewis said.

"I agree," Oscar replied, as they watched the two girls leave.

After a few hours, Ed relieved them.

"I want you guys to see the other exhibits," he said. "There is so much to see."

Monica relieved the girls so the finalists could be together. First, they attended the introductory presentation. Some of the media giants and software companies that had representatives present included Microsoft, Fox, CNN, Apple , Disney, and many more. They met some of the other finalists from other parts of the world.

Overall, the show was a wonderful, entertaining, and educational. By 8:00 p.m., the audience began to leave. Ed caught up with them and said he wanted to see everyone before the show was over. An hour later, the exhibition hall was almost empty.

"Guys, let's get together now," Ed said. "I have some good things for you."

Ed gave each of them a theater pass to a popular concert in town and vouchers to a famous casino. Lewis and Oscar wanted to go to the casino, but Jennifer and Nicole wanted to go to the concert. Eventually, everyone went to the concert and they had no regrets. Later they went back to the hotel. Ed left a message for them to pack away the exhibits before 11 a.m. the next day. They were then free to go out, but had to be present for dinner at 6 p.m.

Lewis fell asleep quickly, while Oscar thought about what to buy for his mother. He remembered the hard times they had the previous summer when two months of severe drought devastated the farm. They had no money at that time. He decided to return home with most of the money and give it to Clemis to keep for emergencies. He had $1,000.

The next day they arose early and packed away the work they had on display. Then they went shopping. Oscar bought a watch for his mother and nothing for himself.

At dinner that evening, Ed and Monica congratulated the finalists on a job well done. Ed said he had good news for everyone—tomorrow they would be returning to Mexico. The dinner was good. The three men did not leave any trace of food on their plates. The girls ate less, leaving space for dessert. The men wanted red wine after dinner. They all had ice cream and fruit for dessert.

Then Ed pulled out some envelopes. There were three large ones and a small one. He gave envelopes to each of the finalists, and Oscar received the small one.

"Don't open these envelopes," Monica said. "I will tell you what they contain." Then she read from a letter in her hands.

Jennifer had an invitation from CNN for a 15-month internship. She would most likely receive a job offer when it was over. Nicole had an invitation from the Univision Broadcasting Network in Miami. Lewis was offered a job as a cartoonist at Disney Production Company.

As Monica fell silent, Ed asked that for him and Oscar be excused. While everyone at the table celebrated, they walked away to a window that afforded some privacy and a panoramic view of the city.

"I am not happy that you did not get an invitation," Ed said. "You and the others have amazing potential, but you have a dark spot in your past. The envelope you have is a personal apology from Monica and me. No production or broadcasting company was able to accommodate you as an intern at this time because they found a connection with drugs in your background profile. Even though it happened when you were a juvenile, the incident will not be expunged from your records for another several years. When we spoke with the local police in Rio Verde, they had only good things to say about you. In spite of everything, we wish you the best. Tomorrow we will return to Mexico."

Oscar was disappointed, but he did not express this when he went back to the table. He was happy for his friends, but sad for himself.

Oscar thought he had no one to blame for his disappointments but himself. However, he had not come this far to return home with nothing.

That night he packed away his belongings and spent a long time in the shower. He thought about what to do. The thought of going home empty handed was heavy on his mind. He got dressed in some casual jeans and a black t-shirt. He left out his sports jacket and his tennis shoes to wear later. He lay on the bed and looked over at Lewis, who was watching TV from the other bed.

"What do you think, Lewis?" Oscar asked.

"You're talking about this exhibition?" Lewis asked.

"Yes," Oscar answered.

"It was very good," Lewis said. "I still can't believe it. I will be going to Florida next month, and during my internship I will be making $60,000 for the first year and will get a 25% discount on my housing expenses. It's just like getting paid to attend college."

"I am happy for you, man," Oscar replied.

"Thank you," Lewis said.

"What about you?" Lewis asked.

"I will be doing some projects in Mexico," Oscar said.

"That's great," Lewis replied.

"Let's keep in touch," Lewis said. "I would like to work with you sometime after my internship."

"I would like that," Oscar replied.

The Hour of Decision

They talked for a while and Lewis was getting sleepy. Oscar could not sleep. He lay on the bed trying to relax. He was still uneasy. When the movie was over, he got up and turned off the television. Lewis was asleep.

Quickly and quietly, Oscar put on his shoes, grabbed his two bags, and left the room. He took the elevator to the second floor and then took the stairs from there. Once outside, he looked around to orient himself. He remembered a bus station not too far from the hotel. He started walking. It was about a half mile down the road. When he arrived at the station, he sat in the waiting room. He thought about going to New York, Miami, or San Francisco. Staying in Las Vegas was not an option because he was easy to find there.

He waited for a while then a stranger sat beside him, a tall, slender, white haired man who was missing two of his lower incisors.

"Can I have five dollars, sir?" the man said.

Oscar pulled out two dollars and gave them to him.

"I just came from Los Angeles," the man said. "There are jobs there, but I am not into working hard. Hard work stresses me out and sucks up all my time. I can get ahead with a few good people giving me some spare change. Las Vegas is a tourist town, and the mood here is more relaxed. People are kinder because they are on vacation or going out to be entertained. Los Angeles is about working and hustling."

"I would like to get a job," Oscar said.

"Then go to Orange County and get one," the man said.

Oscar paused before speaking.

"I thought you said Los Angeles was the place."

"Look! Los Angeles, Orange County, Irvine, Cerritos or whatever the shit you want to call it—it's just a different name for the same big city."

Another bus pulled in the station and unloaded the passengers. Oscar went over to the cashier and inquired about the next bus going to Los Angeles.

"That's the last bus for Los Angeles," the cashier said.

"Give me one ticket, please," Oscar said.

"That will be $35, sir."

The passengers were boarding quickly. Oscar waved goodbye to the man he was talking to, but he did not respond. Oscar boarded the bus and sat in one of the front seats where he could see ahead and read the signs. He was afraid and excited, simultaneously. He gazed at the new frontier as the bus headed west for California. After an hour, he fell asleep.

When he awoke he was already in the city of Riverside. He looked at the passenger beside him.

"How long before we get to Orange County?" Oscar asked him.

"The bus stops in Norwalk," the man told him, "and if you get off at Norwalk, you can get a connection to anywhere."

Oscar stayed awake from then on. In Norwalk he got off the bus. He bought a map of the city at a convenience store near the bus station. It was about five a.m. He stayed at the station until daybreak, and then headed west on Firestone Blvd. He walked for almost 20 minutes until he came upon a small taco shop painted red, white, and yellow. There was a carwash next to it. The people there spoke Spanish and it made him feel comfortable. He ordered three chicken tacos and a cup of tea. As he ate, he watched the carwash get ready for business. Some of the workers came over to the taco shop. Most were Latinos.

"How would I be able to get a job at the carwash?" Oscar asked one of the workers.

"Apply at the office at eight o'clock," he said.

"I don't have a permanent address," Oscar said.

"Don't worry. That's all right. Give them a temporary one." Then the man laughed and said to let him know if he didn't get the job.

Oscar went to the office inside the carwash and requested an application. He filled it out as best as he could and turned it in to the clerk.

"Oscar, can I have a word with you?" said the African clerk.

"Yes sir," Oscar replied.

"I appreciate your request for a job," the man said, "but I can't hire anyone right now. I will keep your application for the future, Mr. Oscar."

Oscar left the office and went back to the taco store and sat outside on a bench. It was a hot day and he did not feel like walking about without a purpose. The worker he talked to earlier waved at him.

"Did you get the job?" he asked from a distance.

"No!" Oscar replied.

Then he walked over and sat on the bench with Oscar.

"I only work two days a week here," he said. "I used to work more, but the boss is worried about hiring undocumented workers."

Both men were silent for a moment as they looked out from the taco stand.

"Raul is my name. And you?"

"Oscar is my name."

"When I am not working here, I go to Firestone and Pioneer boulevard and wait for someone to hire me as a day laborer. It's a hassle, but I make more money there than I make here. You don't need an application, just good luck and a good attitude."

"Pioneer and Firestone, is it far?" Oscar asked.

"No, it's just a mile from here," the man said, pointing east.

"I will be there tomorrow morning," Oscar said.

"Wonderful," Raul said. "I have to get to work now." He went back to the carwash.

It was early afternoon and Oscar had to find a place to stay for the night. He headed east on Firestone until he saw a motel. It was not far from Pioneer Blvd. He went inside the lobby and inquired about a room. It was $70 a night, the man said. Oscar had $700 left so he rented a room for one week.

The room was small and smelled like cigarette and beer, but it was clean for the most part. There was a television on the dresser, which he turned on immediately. He took off his shoes and socks and sat on the bed. He spent a few minutes navigating the channels before he stopped on the Spanish news. In less than 20 minutes he fell asleep.

About 6:00 p.m., a loud explosion in a movie, on television, woke him. He left the hotel a short time later, and walked back to the taco shop to get some chicken tacos for dinner. Returning to the motel, he bought a phone card. He called the police station in Rio Verde and left a message for his mother that she was not to worry and that he would be home soon. After, he went to the motel. He had $185 left. The television was his companion, and from the time he turned it on, he never turned it off.

The Intersection

The next day he arose early and went to the intersection of Pioneer and Firestone Blvd. Raul was already there and glad to see Oscar.

"Some of my friends worked like this for several years," Raul said, "saved a lot of money; now they have beautiful properties and homes in Mexico, El Salvador, and Costa Rica."

"Have you saved any money?" Oscar asked.

"Lately I haven't because the work has been slow, but since last week I have been working steady with the same person. Oh! Here he comes. Remember, my friend, never give your real name, never steal, and save as much as you can."

Raul ran across the street to a big black Chevy van. He was overweight, but the way he ran showed he was strong and agile. As he left, he waved at Oscar.

At that moment, a small white Toyota truck pulled up next to Oscar.

"You looking for work?" the driver asked. An Asian man, he looked over his shades through the car window with his chin slightly down.

"Yes, I am looking for work," Oscar replied.

"Let's go, man. Can you drive?"

"Yes, I can."

"Get in," the man said. "Gene is my name."

Gene seemed to be in a hurry and Oscar got in the car without hesitation. They left immediately

"Oscar is my name, Mr. Gene," Oscar said.

"I have to pick up a Ryder truck, clean my old house, and get it ready for inspection soon," Gene said. "You hungry?"

"No sir, I am good," Oscar replied.

They went to get the truck. Oscar had to drive the car while Gene drove the truck. Then they went to a small house in a place called Buena Park. They took all the furniture out of the house and packed it in the truck, then dropped it off at a Salvation Army donation center. The next day they cleaned the house. On the third day they cleaned the yard. The fourth day they took the garbage to the dump and prepared the house for painting.

"Oscar, tomorrow I need some help in order to finish by next Wednesday. The plumber, carpenter, and electrician will be here tomorrow to inspect the house and make sure it's safe. Do you know anyone that can help us?"

"Maybe, but I really don't know anyone," Oscar replied.

In the evening after work, Gene left Oscar at the intersection, and Raul was there.

"Hey, my friend, how is the work going?" Raul asked.

"Man, I have been busy," Oscar replied.

"Really? Beginner's luck. I spent the whole day here and nothing."

"Are you a good painter?"

"Yes, that's what I do half the time," Raul answered.

"We may be able to work tomorrow, then," Oscar said. "My boss is looking for extra help. Be here at 7:30."

"I will be here," Raul said. "Take care."

That night Oscar ate at McDonald's. When he went to the motel, the room was clean and the television was off. He turned the television on, took a long warm shower, and went to sleep. The next day was Saturday. He went to the intersection at 7:30 sharp and Raul was there.

"I have an egg sandwich for you," he said.

Oscar took the sandwich, said thanks, and put it in his backpack.

"Why do you carry a backpack?" Raul asked.

"I have my things in it," Oscar replied.

"Next time leave it at home," Raul said. "People might feel you have a weapon or drugs in it."

They waited for an hour at the intersection before Gene showed up.

"What happened?" Oscar asked. "Why are you so late?"

"Today is Saturday," Gene said. "I never get up before 6:30 a.m. unless I'm going on vacation."

"This is Raul," Oscar said. "He's a painter."

"Okay, you guys are ready. I like that. Let's go, then."

They went to the small house in Buena Park and started painting. All three men worked. Raul was the best painter and Gene implemented some of his ideas. On Wednesday the painting was complete, but they returned on Thursday to clean and redo the areas that needed extra painting.

"This is my first home," Gene said, "and I have renovated it. Next week I will rent it."

"If I had the money, I would buy it now," Raul said.

"I thought you had the money," Oscar said.

"I have the money for one house, not two," Raul said with a smile. "I don't plan to live here all my life. I have five acres of land in Costa Rica."

"If you guys are ready to shut up and get paid, then I'm ready to go home," Gene said.

Gene secured the house, and all three men went to the bank on Firestone Blvd. Gene paid them and Raul was happy. He said it was the highest he had been paid for a paint job. Oscar was happy that he made $400. Raul did not want a ride home. He said the bank was close to his home. Oscar, on the other hand, was far away from the motel. Gene took him there.

"You live in a motel?" Gene asked.

"Yes, but not for long. As soon as I have enough money, I will be going home to Mexico."

Gene laughed. "All you guys talk about returning home, but you never do. What are you doing tomorrow?"

"I will be looking for more work at the intersection," Oscar replied.

"I haven't fired you yet. I still have more work at my house. I have to clean my garage and cut my lawn. The job is yours."

"I'll do it, boss, if you give me a ride in the morning," Oscar replied.

"Deal," Gene said. "See you at 7:30."

Familiar Faces

Gene left and Oscar went to his room. He wanted to talk to his mother, but since she had no phone he decided to write her. He used $350 to pay for one week. It was Friday night, and although he wanted to have a good time he only had $300 left. He recalled seeing a mall down the street near the bank on Firestone Blvd.

He cleaned himself and put on some fresh clothes. He took the bus and went to the mall. He bought some underwear, a pen, a pencil, and some envelopes. He went to a bookstore that sold coffee, tea, and sandwiches. He sat at a table, wrote his mother a letter, and had some tea and a sandwich for dinner. He also drew pictures of Gene's house and the intersection where the workers waited for daily employment. After two hours he felt tired and went to his room at the motel. He watched the Spanish news, but soon after fell asleep.

The next day Gene came and took him to his home in Cerritos.

"This is a nice house," Oscar said.

"It will be nicer when we get the lawn cut and get rid of all that junk in the garage."

"Where do you want to start first, the lawn or the garage?" Oscar asked.

"Let's get the garage today," Gene replied.

The men walked over to the garage and Gene opened the door.

"Wow!" Oscar said. "No wonder the cars are parked outside. This garage is filled with things."

"Don't worry so much. My friend is coming to take most of these things to their garage sale. Whatever he can't sell he'll keep, and for all this I'll get $300."

Half an hour later a truck pulled up. It was Gene's friend, and he had brought some workers to help load the truck. The men worked and packed most of the things away. There were tables, chairs, books, golf clubs, and a television. The work was physically draining, but they finished within a short time. Then Oscar swept and washed the garage floor. The cars were able to fit now.

"I'm finished with the garage now, Mr. Gene," Oscar said, "and I am ready to do the lawn."

"Take a break, man. Just watching you work makes me tired. You move too much and too fast."

"I'll do the backyard," Oscar replied, "and then I will take a break."

"That sounds good," Gene said.

Oscar got the lawnmower and rakes, Gene gave him some trash bags, and they went to work. It was now about 2:30pm and the sun was still at its peak. They managed to get the backyard completed. Oscar felt he could finish the work that day and get paid.

"We got enough work done already," Gene said. He sat on the back porch, and Oscar joined him.

"Care for a glass of water or melon juice?" Gene's wife asked. She was a beautiful Asian woman who seemed 15 years younger than Gene. She poured a glass for both of them. When she was leaving Gene said, "Leave the rest, please."

While resting, Oscar turned to his sketchbook and began drawing from memory, like he was making a comic book. Gene was asleep. Another hour passed, and Oscar bid goodbye to Gene's wife and told her that he would return at 8:30 a.m. Oscar took the bus back to the motel. That night he thought about his mother and his home. He was beginning to regret running away.

The next day, Monday, he took the bus to Gene's house. He was familiar with the area now.

"You're here already?" Gene said. "I was just about to pick you up."

"That's okay," Oscar replied, "I am ready to get started."

Oscar began working in the front yard. It was more detailed work than the backyard due to the landscaping and gardening.

"Today I will ask my daughter to bring pizza on her way home," Gene said.

"I didn't know you had a daughter," Oscar said.

"I have two daughters. Both of them are in college, and the youngest is 22. She's studying medicine at UCLA. The oldest is studying music and fine arts in Irvine. She'll be here soon."

"It will be good to see them," Oscar said.

"You left your drawing book here yesterday. I have to say that you're very good."

"Thank you," Oscar replied.

They returned to work and finished early in the afternoon. Then they took a break, relaxing, in the shaded back yard. It was about 80 degrees, but a mild breeze made it comfortable. Gene's wife made more watermelon juice, and it was good. About mid-afternoon a car pulled into the driveway.

"Dad, I'm home," Gene's daughter said when she saw them in the backyard. Oscar recognized her from the moment he saw her. It was the Asian girl he had met at the exhibition in Las Vegas. He did not want to be identified, so he kept his distance with his back turned.

"Bring the pizza outside," Gene said. "Eat with us."

"It's too hot out here Dad," she said, but she still came and sat beside them. She did not seem to recognize Oscar. She was friendly and smiled at him.

"This is Mais, my daughter," Gene said.

"Hi, my name is Oscar."

"Nice to meet you, Oscar," she replied.

Oscar was surprised to see her react as if she didn't know him. He went on the porch and grabbed his drawing book and told Gene that he was ready to leave. Oscar was satisfied when Gene paid him $250.

"Thank you very much, Mr. Gene. I have to go now."

"Let me give you a ride to the motel," Gene said.

"Dad, I can take him," Mais said. "I'm going to the store, so I'll drop him off."

"It's okay, I'll take him home," Gene said.

"Dad, don't worry," Mais said. "I am not a baby anymore. Save your gas and time."

"I forgot some things at the supermarket that I'd like you to get," Gene's wife said, "and don't take all day, Mais."

"Okay, mother," Mais said.

They got in the car, and before they drove away she said, "You have forgotten me already?"

"No, I still remember you," Oscar replied.

"Then why did you pretend not to know me?"

"I didn't pretend not to know you. I thought that...ah..."

Oscar was at a loss for words.

"That's okay," Mais said. "I didn't want my father to know that we knew each other. He would get curious and worried because you are a bad man."

"Well, what a coincidence," Oscar said.

"Yes, and now I need to know why the world is so small," Mais said.

Oscar told Mais the whole story. She thought it was funny. They went to the grocery store and a few more places before Mais dropped him off at the motel.

"Thank you very much for everything," Oscar said.

"My friend will be here next Saturday. You want to hang with us?" Mais asked.

"Which friend?"

"Man, how can you forget? The prettiest girl at the exhibition— my Jamaican friend Jen."

"Oh yeah. All of us together, really?"

"Yep, it's going to be the three of us, next Saturday," Mais replied.

"Leave your number with me in case anything else comes up," Oscar said.

Oscar and Mais exchanged contact information and said goodbye.

The next day was Sunday. Oscar went to the laundry and the barber nearby. He also mailed the letter to his mother. Sunday evening came and he had a steak burrito and two oranges for dinner. After, he watched television until he fell asleep.

Jose's Auto Body Repair

Tuesday morning and he was at the intersection again. He had paid for two more nights at the motel and had $200 left. If he did not get a job that paid well, he would have to leave for Mexico soon. He waited at the intersection for about a half hour before Raul showed up.

"How are you today, my friend?" Raul asked.

"I'm all right, Raul, and you?"

"I am good."

A red Toyota Tundra playing loud reggaeton music approached them.

"Here comes the devil," Raul said.

"Do you know this man?" Oscar asked.

"No, but something tells me that a man with that flair is trouble from hell," Raul answered.

"Hey," the man in the truck said, "any of you guys know an auto body repairman and mechanic?"

"No man, so sorry," Raul said.

"I can help you, sir," Oscar replied.

"Let's go, and you can show me what you can do," the truck driver said. "If not, I will have to take you back here."

"I'll take that chance, sir," Oscar said.

"Sounds like we have a deal," the truck driver said.

Oscar got in the truck and they left Raul behind. In 20 minutes they arrived at Jose's Auto Body Repair.

"What's your name?" the truck driver asked.

"George, or Geo, is my name," Oscar replied.

"I am Jose and this is my place," the truck driver said.

Jose's Auto Body Repair was located in a spacious warehouse in

Buena Park. It was clean, well organized, and well equipped. The work bay was large and open, and a little office, elevated like a watchtower in one corner, overlooked the bay. The shop also had two restrooms with a shower, a kitchen, and break room with two lazy boy chairs and a large sofa.

Jose gave Oscar a pair of coveralls. His first assignment was to get three cars ready for a paint job. Jose wanted the upholstery taken out and driver's console covered, as well as all areas on the auto that were not to be painted. Within four hours all three cars were ready, and Jose was satisfied.

There were six workers. They worked and communicated well. They were experts in their own right, and they drove new and expensive cars. They acted like business partners instead of regular workers. Jose's work team was efficient and professional.

"Yes, you are a professional," Jose told Oscar. "You are hired. The job pays $12 an hour with no overtime. If you work over eight hours, it's still $12."

"I will take it, sir," Oscar said.

"We start at 8:30am and close at 4:30pm for the record," Jose said, "but off the record we work later, sometimes until 9 pm."

"I don't have a problem with that," Oscar replied.

Oscar prepared three cars for painting. At lunch he introduced himself to the workers, Gilbert, J.R., Arturo, and Carlos. They were skilled auto body technicians.

"Geo, you want to work late tonight?" Jose asked.

"The last bus passes at six, so I have to leave at 5:30," Oscar replied.

"Don't worry, I can give you a ride home," Gilbert said, "and we will be out of here by nine o'clock."

Gilbert was Latino, about 5' 7", 45 years old, clean-shaven, and bald. His attitude was upbeat and he was a good worker. He was Jose's foremost adviser on finances and quality assurance.

J.R. was also about 45, black, six feet tall, and a little on the chubby side. He was talkative and funny, and the overall expert on cars. He had the credentials and the experience. If there was an electrical or mechanical problem that seemed too complicated to rectify, J.R. was the man to see. He was also one of the best jazz bass players in the area and some weekends he moonlighted as a musician.

Arturo was the youngest, at 26; he was a good worker and a playboy. He was tall, handsome, flashy, and charismatic. His cell phone rang constantly with women wanting to speak to him. He drove a new red BMW M3 that Oscar liked very much. The guys called him Mr. Sunset Drive. Whenever he heard that name, it made him smile.

Carlos, on the other hand, was not handsome. He was 30 years old, muscular, loud, and unfriendly. He had a tiger tattooed on his chest, and most of the time his shirt was off.

From the start, Carlos had been resentful of Oscar and overly critical of his work. Oscar managed to stay clear of him.

He worked for the next three days without interacting much with the rest of the workers. Gilbert took him home the first night, but the other nights he took the bus.

"Finally, it's Friday," Arturo said. "We get paid today."

"Today is delivery day, too, man," J.R. said with a smile.

"I have to drop off two cars in T.J. and return two more," Arturo replied. "That's the real winner there."

"Fool, come Monday you will be broke again," Carlos said. "You have too many women to feed here, in Tijuana, and in San Diego."

"You're just jealous because the women know I am the real tiger, and you just have one painted on your chest," Arturo replied.

J.R. laughed and said, "He should have tattooed a pussy cat with a rose."

"Hey guys!" Gilbert said. "Keep it down, please. I'll call you in when the pay is ready."

Later that day, Gilbert began to call them to the office one by one. Oscar was looking forward to his pay like a puppy looking for a treat.

Eventually it was his turn. Oscar ran up the stairs to the office. From there you could see the entire work area below.

"Are you ready for your big paycheck?" Gilbert said.

"Yes, sir," Oscar replied.

It was the first time Oscar had been in the office. It was clean, organized, and more spacious than expected. Gilbert handed Oscar an envelope containing $1,500 in cash. Oscar was surprised.

Jose said, "I like this guy. He's a very good worker, he fits in easily, and he's sharp. Sometimes you have to pay a man not only based on work done, but on future potential. Would you like to work tomorrow?"

"I am very sorry, sir," Oscar replied, "but I have a date tomorrow."

"That's what it's all about, making the money and having a good time," Gilbert said. "Finish up the work today, and we see each other Monday."

While they were talking, Jose took two stacks of cash out of a bag—over $15,000—and gave it to Gilbert, who smiled and said, "That's what hard working is all about."

Carlos, who was paid later, was very vocal about his dissatisfaction.

"It's not fair!" he cried. "My pay is not right! Pay me my f-cking money or I will let the sh-t out of the bag! I work hard for you jackasses! I will not be a mule no more, unless I get more money!"

No one dared to challenge the tall muscleman in his fury.

When Oscar went home to the motel that evening, he went to the office and negotiated for one more week at a 20% discount. Then he put aside $500 in his bag. He wanted to save that money.

The next day was Saturday and he was off from work. Mais was coming by later to take him on a date. It was something he had anticipated and hoped for, but could not count on. He got up early and was walking on Pioneer Blvd. when he saw Raul. They greeted each other and went to a nearby coffee shop for breakfast. They talked about their jobs.

"Oscar, be careful this time," Raul said. "Don't let those men know your name."

"Why is that?" Oscar asked.

"Jose is the type of guy that gives me the chills and a bad feeling," Raul said. "His intentions are easy to read. He is no good. I have been here two years. I am an illegal immigrant, and that is why I am warning you. He and his crew are very nice at first, and then before you get to know what's really going on you're trapped, and it's too late to turn around. Yeah, the money is good until trouble comes. When the trouble comes, it's kill or be killed. You're a good man, but you'll look as bad as them when you're involved and mixed up in their shit."

"I am returning to Mexico soon," Oscar said. "The U.S. streets are not made of gold, just poor people like me and you. When I have two or three gees, I will be ready."

"Look, man," Raul said, "I liked you from the first day we met, and I don't want any harm to come to you."

"I have to take my chances, Raul," Oscar said.

"Well, I hope you succeed, because it's getting harder to make it here. I will not be around to look out for you. Next week I am going Costa Rica to settle. No more hustling. I have enough money and I am contented."

Raul spoke with a conviction that felt credible, but Oscar had doubts.

"I will be careful," Oscar said, "and thanks."

"Please pay for my breakfast," Raul said, "and I will treat you when you visit me in Costa Rica."

They said goodbye to each other, hoping to reunite one day.

Unforgettable Date

Oscar walked back to the motel and rested for a while then he drew a sketch of Raul eating breakfast in the coffee shop. In the afternoon, he received a phone call from Mais who told him to be ready within the hour.

Half an hour later Oscar went to take a shower. Suddenly there was knocking and then the door opened. Jen and Mais entered his room without invitation and went straight for the bathroom. Mais pulled aside the shower curtain. Oscar was naked, but instead of panicking he pretended to be oblivious.

"Oh, an exhibitionist he is, leaving all the doors unlocked," Jen said.

"He thinks he's a model," Mais said. "Look at him showing off."

Oscar dropped the soap, and when he bent over to pick it up the girls decided they had seen enough. Then Jen saw the drawing book on the bed, which kept them interested for a while. Ten minutes later Oscar was fully dressed.

"I want to document your story, Oscar," Mais said, "and make it into a fiction with these same drawings."

"You mean as an undocumented immigrant?" Oscar replied. "My visa hasn't expired."

"Sorry," Mais said. "Didn't mean to be mean."

"So where are we going first?" Jen asked.

"To the movies in Cerritos," Mais replied.

The women felt comfortable with Oscar, and Oscar was also at ease. They went to see 'No Country for Old Men'. It was entertaining. After, they went to a restaurant next to the theater. They sat outside on the terrace. It was summer, but the evening was cooler than usual. There were gas heaters installed on poles. The burners emitted continuous blue flames that made the temperature just right. The three of them ordered ginger tea and cheeseburgers. A three-piece acoustic band was playing Jazz music inside the restaurant.

"Well, Oscar, did you like the movie?" Jen asked.

"No, I did not," he said. "It did not end right."

"I agree, and it's not like there will be a part two," Jen said.

"Why is that?" Oscar asked.

"Well, it's an independent film, and they usually don't have a part two," Jen said.

"Are there restaurants like this in Mexico?" Mais asked.

"There are many places like this in Mexico," Oscar replied.

"When are you going to return to Mexico?" Jen asked.

"Soon," Oscar replied, "maybe in four weeks."

"I want to see you again," Mais said.

"Me too," Oscar said.

"No matter if you're rich or poor," Mais said, "I want us to be good friends."

"Yo tambien," Oscar replied quietly as they looked at each other.

The conversation was entertaining. The women liked and admired him. They took Oscar back to the motel and Mais wrote her contact information inside his drawing book.

"My email and cell phone number are inside your book, so don't lose it, okay?" she said.

"When we visit Mexico, you better show us a good time," Jen said.

The girls laughed as they entered Firestone Blvd. on their way home.

"Mais, I sense you like Oscar too much," Jen said.

"I like him very much and I don't know why," Mais said.

"He seems vulnerable, and pure," Jen said, "but feelings are deceiving."

"He is tough as nails," Mais said. "I feel he could take a beating and keep things together." "That is so sexual," Jen said.

For Oscar, the evening was unforgettable. When he went to the motel lobby to get some ice, the hotel manager called out to him.

"Hey Oscar! You lucky son of a gun!"

"Porque, Amed?" Oscar said.

"Man, you went out with two beautiful women and you didn't invite me!"

"Give me a 50% discount and I will certainly help you out," Oscar said.

"Someone called asking for Geo," Amed said, "a man by the name of Jose."

"Thanks. I will get in touch with him in a while."

That night Oscar called Jose, who asked if he could work on Sunday. The next day Oscar reported for work early.

Jose was there with J.R. and Gilbert. They told Oscar that they had to fire Carlos because he was not working up to standards and was very disrespectful. They were happy that they had a man like Oscar who worked hard. They asked if he could work days and some nights.

"I stay at a motel now, sir," Oscar said, "but I could stay here and work late."

"That's a good idea," J.R. said, "but you can't let anyone know you live here."

"If you have to meet with anyone, tell us first, and it can only be in the daytime," Jose explained firmly, "but I strictly forbid visitors at night. Carlos violated my rules, disrespected my authority, and stole from me many times, so I had to fire him."

"I give you my word, sir," Oscar replied. "I will do my best to get the work done the way you want it."

"I feel Geo is dependable," J.R. said.

"I feel so too," Gilbert replied.

Covert Operation

Oscar worked all day Sunday. On Monday he checked out of the motel. That night he stayed at the garage. There were little things to do. He cleaned the office, the break room, and the two bathrooms. From midnight to six a.m. was his time off. He laid a blanket on the large sofa, used his backpack as a pillow, and there he slept.

In the morning when he arose, Arturo was sitting at the table looking through his drawing book.

"You're an artist," Arturo said.

"Thanks," Oscar replied.

"Geo," Arturo said.

"What, man?"

"If you draw any scenes here, don't let anyone see them," Arturo said mildly. "Your drawings are photographic and very realistic. Jose will not like it, so keep this book where no one can find it. Take what I say seriously."

Oscar began to reflect on what Raul had told him about being careful. Then he got dressed for work. For the rest of the day he worked hard. However, he discovered something that confirmed Raul's suspicions.

Some of the cars did not need repairs and had hidden, sealed compartments that were undetectable by the naked eye. Jose was able to identify these cars and access the secret compartments, which contained large amounts of powder and compressed marijuana. These were fairly new model cars that had recently crossed the border from Mexico. Drug traffickers, posing as customers and tourists, had apparently delivered the cars. He also noticed security cameras in several locations around the shop.

Some of Jose's business was legitimate, and Oscar made sure to work on the cars he was assigned. He kept a low profile and did not even write his mother again. He was now focused on getting home, and the less he revealed about himself, the better. His objective was to work hard, get paid, and return to Mexico.

Friday came and Oscar was disappointed with his pay. Gilbert gave him only $350 in cash.

"Living in the garage is expensive, but better than living on the streets," Jose said. "The wages are comparable or more than what you would receive if you lived in Mexico."

"You're absolutely right, sir," Oscar said.

Oscar pretended to be happy with his pay and kept on working as if he knew nothing. On Saturday, Jose said he would close the shop at midday because he had to meet some friends in Tijuana.

Saturday came.

"I have to pick up a rental car today," Jose said. "I would like you to drive my car and return it here."

"No problem," Oscar replied.

"Have you seen my wallet and cell phone?" Jose asked.

"No, I haven't seen any wallet or cell phone around," Oscar replied.

After everyone had left the shop for the day, Jose and Oscar went to the car rental company, but Jose ran into a problem because the rental service needed his driver's license.

"I have rented many cars here before," Jose said to the agent. "You guys must have a copy of my license on hand."

"Sorry, sir, it is our policy to check the driver's license every time."

"Geo, do you have a driver's license?" Jose asked.

"Yes, I do," Oscar replied.

"Can he rent the car instead of me?"

"Sure," the clerk said, "we can do that."

"Can't find my damn wallet and phone," Jose said quietly to himself.

Oscar carried his blue backpack with him everywhere. It contained his money, passport, driver's license, drawing book, and pencils. The agent said he would have to assign responsibility for the car to the person with the identification.

Oscar handed his license to the agent, along with his passport open to the page with the stamped visa. The agent gave the car keys to another worker and told him to get the car ready. Jose left with the worker.

Oscar hoped that Jose had not seen his real name. He put the receipt in his backpack and went outside. Jose was waiting next to rental.

"Drive the rental," he said. "I will drive my truck."

Oscar followed Jose back to the auto body repair shop.

"Wait here for me," Jose said.

Jose went inside the garage and ten minutes later returned with a large gray backpack that was three times larger than Oscar's blue one.

"I have my passport with me and another cell phone," Jose said, "but no sign of my wallet."

He placed the backpack in the trunk and told Oscar to enter the freeway and drive south towards Tijuana.

"You didn't tell me you had papers, Geo," Jose said.

"No one really asked," Oscar replied. "They just assume that I'm an undocumented worker, or someone who was just released from prison."

"You don't mind going with me to TJ?" Jose said.

"I really want to go. I've never been there."

"Where are you from originally, Geo?" Jose asked.

"Yuma, Arizona," Oscar replied without hesitation.

"No wonder you speak English so good," Jose said. "You were born near the border."

Road to Tijuana

Oscar's only reason for going to Tijuana was to slip away from Jose and return to Rio Verde. They entered the freeway southbound, and Jose fell asleep within minutes.

Oscar was comfortable. As he drove, he thought about home and facing his mother. He felt he had disappointed her. He also felt that he had been working like a donkey and getting ripped off. And he did not know exactly why he was going to Tijuana with Jose, a drug dealer with unknown motives.

About forty minutes later, Jose woke up. He was upset with Oscar's cautious driving.

"I thought we were almost there," Jose said. "You're driving too slow. At this speed, we'll get there tomorrow at midnight!"

Ten minutes later they arrived at a gas station, where Oscar pumped the fuel and Jose paid for it.

"I will drive this time," Jose said.

They left the gas station and entered the freeway. Jose weaved through and around traffic, driving close to 100 miles an hour. Suddenly, out of nowhere, a state trooper approached, flashed his lights, and signaled them to pull over. Jose was frightened.

"Don't tell them we're going to TJ," Jose whispered.

They pulled over on the shoulder and the state trooper pulled up behind them. He did not exit his vehicle but waited with lights flashing. Apparently he suspected something. Five minutes later two more troopers arrived at the scene. One officer approached the driver's side, and the other two approached the rear with their hands on their side arms.

Jose put his hands outside the window and Oscar did the same.

"Driver's license and registration please," the officer on the driver's side said. "Where is your driver's license, sir?"

"I have one here," Jose replied.

"What's your name?" the officer on the right said to Oscar.

"Geo, sir," Oscar replied.

Jose told the officer his name, but the officer said he needed to verify if it was true. Oscar handed the officer his license, passport, and the car's documents. The other two officers took Jose into custody. Ten minutes later the officer returned with Oscar's documents.

"We have to detain Jose," the officer said.

"Why?" Oscar asked.

"His cell phone and wallet were found at a crime scene," the officer replied. "We have to detain him for questioning."

They put Jose in one of the squad cars.

"I need to speak to my lawyer now!" he shouted. Then the officers sped away with him.

"Mr. Oscar, I cannot hold you against your will," the officer said, "but we may need you to give a statement since you were with Jose. Your papers are legitimate. I would like to know why you let him drive."

"Officer, he knows the area very well. I felt it would be best for him to drive."

"Where were you guys going?" the officer inquired.

"We were going to visit our aunt in San Diego," Oscar replied.

"I am going to issue you a warning citation," the officer said. "Don't let this happen again. Be safe and enjoy your stay in California."

The officer entered his squad car and left the scene in seconds. Oscar drove onto the freeway and headed south again. He did not know what to do. Then he decided to return the car. He got off at the next exit to head north.

If Jose's cell phone was found at a crime scene, it could have been planted there, or he could have been the perpetrator. Being close to Jose could mean problems because Oscar could be implicated as an accomplice. He decided to go back to Mexico as soon as he returned the car.

Then he remembered the backpack Jose left in the trunk. He got off at the next exit, where there were two gas stations, several fast food restaurants, and motels. He parked in a semi-secluded area and examined the backpack. It had two locks on it that twisted off easily. Packed at the top were some new t-shirts, but when Oscar looked closer he found a plastic bag filled with large bills. He had never seen so much money before.

He closed the bag immediately, and then made a quick surveillance to see if anyone saw him. He looked in the bag again to make sure what he saw was real. Many thoughts raced through his mind as he brainstormed about what to do. Jose could be released soon or the police may now want him for questioning.

He drove the car to a motel parking lot, locked the doors, and went to rent a room.

"Good afternoon, sir. How can I help you?" The friendly motel clerk said as she smiled.

"I would like a room for the night, non-smoking," Oscar said.

"Sure, we have one room left, sir, non-smoking, for $130," she said.

"I will take it," Oscar said.

Oscar paid cash for the room. He had the backpacks with him. He went to the room, locked the door, turned on the television, and emptied the moneybag. There were about 25 parcels of bills wrapped in thin plastic, mostly $100 bills, all in U.S. currency. There were a few $20 parcels, and each parcel contained approximately 300 bills.

Oscar did not want to count the money. He remembered a movie he saw recently, where the moneybag had a tracking device in it. He did not find a device in the bag, just the money and a few t-shirts.

There was no time to waste. Oscar packed the money back into the backpack and put a stack of $20 bills in his small blue backpack. He stored the backpack in the closet and left the room.

He went to the lobby and asked for the location of the nearest mall. The clerk gave the directions and he found it easily. At the mall he bought some clothes, a small suitcase with wheels, and a large blue backpack. He returned to the hotel and separated the money. He packed half the money in the suitcase and some in the backpack. This time the money was packed within folded clothes. He took Jose's gray backpack and disposed of it in a dumpster. At the motel that evening he called the rental company to see how he could return the car. They told him that he could return the car to any rental office location, but he would have to pay a transfer fee. That evening Oscar checked out of the motel.

"Was the room okay?" the hotel clerk asked.

"The room was fantastic," Oscar replied. "I'm sorry, but I have to go."

"Oh, sorry to hear that," she said.

Oscar left the motel. He knew he would find a car rental office of the same company at the San Diego International Airport.

Oscar was on his way to San Diego again. He drove within the speed limit. It was getting dark. An uneasy feeling came over him. It was the thought of getting arrested for stealing or being assassinated by drug dealers. He constantly checked the rearview mirror to see if anyone was following him.

An hour later he was in San Diego. He saw the signs directing him to the airport. A police car entered the freeway at full speed. The squad car split the traffic swiftly, and in no time was behind him in the far left lane. Oscar was frightened and without delay merged to his right. As he was pulling over to stop, the squad car went by like a rocket. Oscar resumed his course. Within 15 minutes, he was at the rental company near the airport.

He returned the car, paying $100 extra for gas and delivery. He took a taxi from the car rental service to the Mexican border. The fare was $75, and Oscar gave the taxi driver a $10 tip.

On the Run

At the border, Oscar was nervous. After a long walk and going through the gates, he had to face customs and the border guards. He approached one of the shorter lines. The woman in front of him had an open bag on the table that an officer was looking through.

"Next," the officer said.

Oscar was dragging the small suitcase with the wheels and extended handle. His large blue backpack was on his back and the small blue backpack that he always carried was in his hands. The officer looked at him and waved him on to pass. Oscar sighed in relief, but before he had taken two steps, the officer called out, "Sir!"

"Yes sir," Oscar said and turned around.

"Your backpack," the officer said, "the clothes are going to fall out."

"Thank you, sir," Oscar said. He eased the load off his back and stuffed the clothes back into the bag. He headed for the last gate.

At the border there were many taxis waiting for customers. One of the drivers held up his hands and called out to him.

"Sir, I am next!" the chubby taxi driver said as he opened the back trunk. Oscar placed the suitcase and the large backpack in the trunk. He knew he had to move fast, because if Jose was searching for him this would be a crucial spot.

"Where do you want to go, sir?" the taxi driver asked.

"I want to go to Rosarito," Oscar replied.

"It's going to cost $35, sir," he said.

"I am paying too much," Oscar replied.

"No hey problema," the driver said.

In less than 35 minutes they were in Rosarito. Oscar figured he could be followed easily if he took a bus directly to Mexico City. When the taxi dropped him off at a hotel in Rosarito, he was on the move again. He called for another taxi and asked the driver to take him to Ensenada.

Ensenada was approximately 50 miles from Rosarito. The cab driver requested $100 for the trip and Oscar agreed.

"You want the scenic route or the toll road?" the tall, dark brown taxi driver asked.

"Which is best?" Oscar asked.

"I like the toll road," the taxi driver said.

"I want the toll road," Oscar replied.

"The toll road is better at night," the driver said, "but it's expensive, and the old road is better during the day because it is scenic."

"I don't have any pesos," Oscar said, "but if you pay the toll, I will pay you $150 for the trip."

"Yes, it will be a pleasure to take you," the taxi-driver said.

It was about 8:30 p.m. and Oscar was ready to go to Ensenada. He had a substantial amount of money with him and he was nervous. He had to keep his bearings and be extremely cautious. If anyone suspected he had this money, he would be in danger.

One the way to Ensenada, Oscar had a friendly conversation with Pablo, the taxi driver. However, he never disclosed his real name or his final destination. Oscar said his name was Osman.

"Where in Ensenada are you going, Osman?" the driver asked.

"I have a reservation at the Punta Gordo hotel," Oscar replied.

"Nice hotel, not one of the best, but it has the best restaurant."

As they turned a bend, there were blue lights in the near distance. The police had set up a roadblock. The cab slowed and came to a complete stop. Three officers approached the taxi, one with a German shepherd. The police asked for identifications as the dog sniffed the taxi.

"Open the trunk and the back doors!" one of the officers said.

"Pablo, you still working?" another officer said. He seemed to be a higher-ranking officer.

"I have to take this nice gentleman to Ensenada tonight, and make some extra money," Pablo said.

Oscar thought that if he got caught he would just have to accept it. The dog smelled the bags, but the officers were not alerted. They returned the identifications and pointed them on their way.

"What are they looking for?" Oscar asked Pablo.

"Guns and drugs," he answered. "That dog can detect metal, gunpowder, marijuana, and cocaine. We have nothing of the sort, ah ha."

"If I had those things," Oscar said, "I wouldn't be taking a taxi."

"Yeah, drug dealers usually use rentals or regular cars," Pablo added.

Forty minutes later they exited the toll road in the town of Ensenada. The town was alive with pedestrians everywhere.

"Some cruise ships are here for the weekend," Pablo said. "Well, this is it, the Punta Gordo."

Oscar grabbed his three bags and gave him $150.

"Gracias, senor Osman," Pablo said. "Oh blessed hour! Today was a good day for me."

"Taxi! Is that taxi available?" called out a tall man with an American accent.

Si, senor," Pablo replied, "where do you want to go?"

"TJ," the man replied.

"Yes! I will take you, but I travel only by the toll road and the price is a little extra."

"I will pay you $200 if you take me to the border," the man said.

"Ah ha, sir, my price is $250, take it or déjà me solo," Pablo said. "Plus, it is very late."

"I need to go home tonight, Jim," a pretty Latina woman said to the man.

"Okay, I'll take it," the man said.

"Osman, you bring me luck in a strange way," Pablo said. "It's another blessed hour for me. Go with God." He loaded the young couple's baggage.

Oscar did not want to take any chances. When Pablo left the hotel, he hailed another taxi.

"I can't go to Tijuana tonight," the cab driver said.

"I just want to go to another hotel, a five star, the best one," Oscar said.

"That's Mystic Pointe, the best and most expensive," the driver replied. "Why you don't like this hotel, sir?"

"I hear the food is bad," Oscar replied.

"No sir, it's good," the taxi driver said, "but it's no problem, I'll take you to Mystic Pointe. If you don't like there either, I'll take you wheresover, except Tiajuna."

"Sounds like a deal, sir," Oscar replied.

In 15 minutes they arrived at Mystic Pointe resort. Oscar paid the driver $20 when he only asked for $10. The hotel room cost $250 for one night. It was expensive, but it was safe and he had the money. When Oscar went to the room, he checked his bags. The money was present, but he had already spent close to $1,000. If he had taken the bus from Tijuana to Mexico City it would have been less expensive, but probably unsafe.

Oscar opened his wallet and found he had $200 left. From the large backpack he took $300 in $20 bills, and three $100 bills. He had never used the $100 bills before, and wanted to see if they were real or counterfeit. Oscar packed his bags safely into the hotel closet and went to the bar and dining room.

There was an ocean view, the lights were dim, and the new full moon was visible. He went to the glass wall and watched the waves come in and bash against the rocky shores. He sat and thought about what to do with the money. He realized that he needed his mother's help.

"Would you like a drink, sir?" the waiter asked. He was dressed in black pants, black shiny shoes, and a white short-sleeved shirt. He was a short, bald, and black. He spoke fluent Spanish.

"I am very hungry," Oscar said.

"Oh, here is the menu, sir," the waiter said.

The menu was written in English, and the grilled salmon with vegetables caught his eyes. The fresh papaya juice seemed delicious. Oscar signaled the waiter.

"Good choice," he said.

In 15 minutes the waiter brought the food to his table. Oscar liked the smell and began to devour the food. When the waiter returned, he was surprised to see the food gone already.

"Man, you were really hungry," he said.

"You have more fish and juice?" Oscar asked.

"Yes, my friend, I can get you more fish and juice," the waiter said.

The waiter sat at a table not too far from Oscar and watched him eat.

"Sir, if you want something to eat, you can get it, and I will pay for it," Oscar said.

The waiter came and sat at his table and smiled.

"I am not hungry," he said, "I can see from the way you eat that you have a passion for food. You respect and appreciate it. Your plate is clean. Hardly anyone who comes here eats like that. They eat and waste too much food. You eat as if you were poor."

Oscar did not say anything else. He looked out at the view of the Pacific Ocean and moonlit sky. The waiter had sensed that Oscar was an unusual guest—someone from a different socioeconomic background.

"Thank you very much, and have a good evening," Oscar said as he walked away.

Oscar was intimidated. He felt he was easily detectable and too vulnerable, an obvious misfit in this place. He went to his room, locked the door, and turned on the television. Occasionally he dozed off, but he did not sleep fully.

Early in the morning Oscar took a shower, dressed in a different shirt, but wore the same pants. Then he went to the lobby and sat on a sofa, holding onto his bags. When no one was at the reception counter, he went up to the hotel clerk.

"I am ready to check out," Oscar said to the clerk.

"So early? You have until 11 a.m.," the clerk said.

"I have to leave soon and take several buses to Loreto," Oscar said.

"There is a bus from here that goes all the way to Lapaz and crosses the ferry to Mazatlan," the clerk said.

"Really, is that so?" Oscar replied. "Where can I get a ticket?"

"I have tickets here for sale," the clerk replied.

"How much are they?" Oscar asked.

"Two hundred dollars, sir," the clerk answered.

"Why so expensive?" Oscar asked.

"It's a chartered hotel tour bus," the clerk said. "Once it leaves here, it only stops at other hotels. The bus will stop in San Ignacio for the night and everyone sleeps in a hotel."

Oscar handed the clerk two $100 bills from his wallet. The clerk took a marker from the side of the cash register, laid the bills flat on the counter, and marked them firmly. She also inspected the bills under a light. He then put them away in the cash register and gave Oscar the ticket.

"Do you always check for counterfeits?" Oscar asked.

"Yes, especially large bills. It's our policy."

"What if you caught a counterfeit?" Oscar asked.

"We call the police without the perpetrator's knowledge," the clerk said.

"Does that mean they are on their way?" Oscar inquired with a smile.

"Your money is genuine, sir. The bus should arrive at eight. Have a nice trip."

Oscar was worried because he didn't know if the clerk was telling the truth. However, he decided to wait for the bus and get ready for anything.

The bus came on time and had two operators. The two larger bags had to be tagged and placed in the luggage compartment. The passengers were mostly tourists. When Oscar left the hotel, he felt a little less afraid than before. The bus ride was comfortable. It stopped in San Ignacio for lunch and bathroom privileges, but Oscar did not eat. Instead, he sat near the bus so he could guard his luggage inside.

It was another long ride to Loreto. They stopped at a hotel to rest and eat dinner. That night Oscar slept well with the luggage on the floor beside him. The next day the bus drove to La Paz. There they took the ferry to Mazatlan. The bus was scheduled to stay in Mazatlan for two days and then return to Ensenada, but Oscar retrieved his luggage and took a taxi to the train station.

The train was crowded. Oscar sat beside a woman with a backpack similar to his.

"My name is Meriam," the women said.

"I am Oscar."

"Where are you going?" she asked.

"Mexico City," he replied.

"I am going there, too," she said, "to live with my aunt and attend medical school."

"What kind of doctor are you planning on becoming?" Oscar asked.

"General practitioner or obstetrician," she answered.

The two newly acquainted friends conversed all the way to Mexico City, talking about many things. In Mexico City they exchanged contact information then parted company. Oscar took a bus home.

Home at Last

It was Friday night when he arrived. His mother was happy to see him again. He was not sure how to tell her about the money. But if he didn't tell her, she might think he was involved in a robbery, so that same night he told her the story. At first she was afraid, but Oscar convinced her that they would still be in danger even if she turned in the money. The police could not be trusted and the cartels did not forgive.

"We have been in need of money always," Oscar said, "and with this money we will have more options than ever."

They stayed up most of the night and counted the money. It came to $4,170,000. Oscar was eager to spend some of it immediately, but Clemis cautioned him that the money might be traceable. She hid it in a safe place, and advised Oscar to return to work soon and do nothing to draw any suspicion.

"I will have to talk to Livingston about this matter," Clemis said. "He absolutely knows how to manage a situation like this better than I do." Livingston was the millionaire attorney who was a very good friend of Clemis.

"When will we see Livingston?" Oscar asked.

"When he returns from Spain, I will call him," she replied. "He should return in two weeks."

Surprise Visit

One week passed. Oscar went back to his old job. Clemis sent a message to Livingston, the attorney. She was waiting for his reply. Some of Livingston's clients were involved in money laundering and overseas banking. The danger was not over, nor far away.

Clemis had hid the money in a safe place and warned Oscar not to talk about it. Everything was normal again until a familiar person from Los Angeles visited.

Oscar was working in the garden on a Saturday afternoon when the village policeman and Arturo appeared. Since Oscar knew the officer very well, he was not afraid. Arturo introduced himself as a U.S. federal marshal.

"I have been working undercover for two years," he said. "I know you worked for Jose and you were not part of his illegal drug and firearms operations. I am not here to arrest you. However, I am here to warn you that you might be in danger."

Arturo began to explain that evidence placed Jose at the crime scene where Carlos was brutally murdered.

"You mean Carlos the Tiger was murdered?" Oscar asked.

"Yes," Arturo replied, "the week you left, he was killed late that Friday night, and that is why we had an all points bulletin for Jose."

"Did Jose kill him?" Oscar asked.

"Jose might have been set up to look like the perpetrator. So far, some of the evidence points to him. Lots of pure cocaine was found at the garage. I also know that Jose put a hit out on you. I suggest you take all precautions. I have expunged your records at the hotel and car rental places. Be careful and take care of yourself. If I can find you, it will only be a matter of time before Jose's associates locate you or your mother."

Shortly after, Arturo had to leave. Oscar and Clemis shook his hand.

"Arturo, I feel Jose will never stop looking for me," Oscar said.

Arturo and the village policeman had just exited the door. Hearing what Oscar had said, Arturo turned and looked at him.

"Jose is dead," Arturo replied. "He was shot outside a brothel in Tijuana two days ago. But that doesn't mean his orders will not be carried out. This cartel is cleaning house. They never forgive. I can almost guarantee that they will look for you."

Arturo and the policeman left immediately after. They did not inquire about the money. Clemis was more afraid than ever. Two days later the lawyer paid them a visit. He drove a silver Mercedes and parked on the grassy lawn in front of the small house.

"You have to park on the grass every time?" Clemis asked.

"Our car looks good right there," Livingston replied.

"It's too hard to maintain and then have this big car all over it," Clemis said.

"I'll move it right now," Livingston said.

"Don't worry about it. We have a crisis to address. Come inside, please."

That day, lunch was special—stewed chicken made with coconut milk and ginger; steamed rice, fresh avocados, onions, and tomatoes.

"Where is Oscar?" Livingston asked.

"He's in the backyard," Clemis replied, "I will get him." She called for him and Oscar came immediately.

During lunch he explained everything. Livingston thought he was fortunate that the money fell into the best hands.

"Tomorrow, get ready to leave this place," he said. "Take a few clothes and all your important papers, and we will go to the office."

Clemis was certain that Livingston could be trusted. The next day he returned. They got the money and went to Mexico City.

Livingston took them to his office. Two secretaries counted the money electronically.

"Someone is searching for this money," Livingston said. "If a law enforcement agent can find you, anyone can. I strongly suggest that you do not return home to Rio Verde."

"I can't stay here in the city," Clemis said. "You know how much I hate it."

"Don't worry. As soon as we get settled, I will have you stay in one of my homes. An armored vehicle is on the way to get the money. It will be deposited in two separate banks under our names. You have to trust me Clem, until I get it completely clean."

An hour later the armored vehicle came and collected the money. Clemis and Oscar had to sign a few documents. When it was all over, Livingston had a handsome share—$70,000 and the property in Rio Verde. Clemis and Oscar complied with his offer because they had no other choice. That night they stayed in Mexico City. The following day Livingston took them to Playa Del Carmen where they stayed in one of his condominiums.

How they would invest the money and remain under the radar was in the forefront of their minds. It was a lot of money, but it would not last if they spent it foolishly. Late one night Clemis received a call from an excited Livingston.

"Clem, I have an offer that I would want for myself."

"What is it?" she asked.

"A good friend of mine that lives in the United States has two cottages for sale in Mauritius," Livingston said.

"Len, I just can't leave Mexico like this," Clemis said. "I have never heard of Mauritius. I am afraid, too."

"Trust me, there is no rush, but it's best for you and Oscar to leave Mexico for now. I understand the money did not come about by legitimate means, and you're speculating on what moral steps to take. Oscar, who I believe to be truthful, is a lucky man. The money is a gift from heaven. You should not deprive yourselves of this wealth."

"I will talk it over with Oscar," Clemis replied.

"I'll be there on Friday," Livingston said.

A New Day

The next day was Wednesday. Clemis and Oscar talked about leaving Mexico.

"Mom, I don't want to leave Mexico, but it's for our safety," Oscar said. He was ready for any decisions his mother made. All he wanted was the opportunity to attend a university and drive a sports car.

Friday came and Livingston gave them the bank account information. Their U.S. dollars were safely deposited in a Swiss account, and some money was readily available to them if they needed it.

Livingston also gave them airline tickets to Mauritius to see the two cottages. They left the following week. Clemis was pleased that the cottages were situated on a hillside about half a mile from the beach, outside the capital city of Port Louis.

The two-story cottages were made of brick. Both had fireplaces and spectacular views of the sea. They sat together on the same parcel of sloping land.

Oscar and Clemis wanted to purchase the properties immediately. However, Livingston told them to pretend they were not eager and wait. The owner wanted $1.7 million. They were scheduled to stay a week on the island, and then move on to Puerto Rico.

One evening, three days after they had arrived in Mauritius, the owner of the property contacted them, and said he would gladly accept $1.35 million dollars if the money was paid in full. Clem said she would pay $1.3 million because the older cottage needed essential repairs. The owner accepted the offer, and the purchase was completed the following week. The trip to Puerto Rico was canceled, and Clem started renovating the older house.

The renovation cost $75,000 and furniture for both houses cost

$35,000. Oscar used $12,000 to buy two large, flat screen television entertainment systems and four computers, two laptops and two desktops. The houses had just the right interior furnishing. After the renovation of the smaller house was completed, Oscar and Clemis settled in. Clemis also bought a small building near the university for $100,000 and renovated it for $40,000.

The newer cottage was leased to a resort owner. It was used for tourists and businesspeople who preferred a home like atmosphere to the usual hotel. Clemis hired three persons for the up keeping of the property. Housekeepers, cooks, and gardeners were assigned whenever there were guests. The building near the university was renovated into a tea and coffee shop with free wireless internet service. The shop also sold freshly made fruit juices, sandwiches, and pizza. The other side of the building had a photography and painting studio.

Clemis and Oscar never contacted anyone in Rio Verde. Livingston advised them to sever all ties with Mexico. However, Oscar communicated with Mais in Los Angeles. He invited her and her family to Mauritius, and Clemis approved.

Oscar wanted a sports car, but Clem was reluctant. She bought a new Toyota Tundra, and when the business started to improve, she decided to lease a Mercedes C350 for herself and a BMW 328i for Oscar. She told Oscar to let the businesses pay their bills now. They had spent more than half their fortune, but it was well invested.

Within three months, the guest list for the larger cottage was booked two months in advance. The coffee shop was popular with the college students because of its good food and free internet. The shop hours had to be extended and more employees hired. The place was always packed, especially on weekends.

Oscar's studio started out slowly, until he drew a portrait for some students and the word got around. Then he was in demand. He also hired two students to take and edit photos. He started attending college, majoring in cinematography.

Six Months Later

"Oscar?" Clemis said.

"Yes, your Excellency! "Oscar replied.

"Will you be able to accompany me to the market tomorrow before picking up your friends at the airport? And please, address me as your Majesty, not your excellency. I like your majesty better."

"Yes, your Majesty," Oscar answered.

They looked at each other and smiled.

Oscar refers to his mother with a distinguished title at times, insighting a sense of humor. Truly, she has been mananging their business affairs prudently while gradually gaining her nobility as a clever businesswoman. After going to the market, Oscar will receive Mais and her parents at the airport. Oscar has offered to host them for three weeks.

It has been a drastic change for Oscar and Clemis. They have adjusted remarkably. They must, however, continue to maintain a low profile and keep a look out for the unforseen moment when the cartel may appear and demand the money that slipped away from them.

But for now, Oscar and Clemis are looking forward to meeting Mais and her family. The changes have been for better.

CPSIA information can be obtained at www.ICGtesting.com
Printed in the USA
BVOW04*0422130314

347494BV00003B/36/P